PLAYED

A Novel

JEN FREDERICK

PLAYED

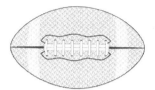

SHE'S BEEN PLAYING IT CLOSE...

Ara Martin and college football star Ty Masters have been best friends since the first day of school when Ty literally ran her over. She fell for him immediately, but having lived under the shadow of her famous father, she knows a relationship with irresistible Ty would only end in heartbreak. For four years, she's kept her feelings hidden. But one drunken encounter weeks before graduation is about to expose Ara's biggest secret and destroy her most treasured relationship.

HE'S BEEN PLAYING FOR KEEPS...

Ty is about to be drafted into the NFL, but his personal life is a mess. He's got an agent he doesn't like, a brother who can't stop offering his opinion, and a beautiful woman he craves but can't have. He can fire his agent and ignore his brother, but he's not sure what to do about Ara. Ty's been able to run down every quarterback he's faced, but his sexy, stubborn best friend keeps slipping through his fingers.

Luckily, he's not one for giving up, and once he gets his hands on her, he's never letting go.

ALSO BY JEN FREDERICK

Sacked (Knox & Ellie)

Jockblocked (Matty & Lucy)

Downed (Ace & Bryant)

Undeclared (Woodlands #1)

Undressed (Woodlands #1.5)

Unspoken (Woodlands #2)

Unraveled (Woodlands #3)

Unrequited (Woodlands #4)

Unwritten (Woodlands #5)

Losing Control (Kerr Chronicles #1)

Taking Control (Kerr Chronicles #2)

Revealed to Him

Last Hit (Hitman #1)

Last Breath (Hitman #2)

Last Hit: Reloaded (Hitman #2.5)

Last Kiss (Hitman #3)

Last Hope (Hitman #4)

To Mel,
My one friend who may love the Green Bay Packers more than me. Love you! Go Pack Go!

1

Ara

"Hey, Ara," a cheerful voice says in my ear.

I jump two feet in the air and slap a hand across my heart. "Holy crap. Can you put some bells on?"

At six feet, five inches and two hundred fifty pounds, there is no explanation for why Ty Masters walks so soundlessly. He's a monster on the football field. Quarterbacks quake at the sound of his pounding strides. Yet he still manages to sneak up on me.

"I could, but what would be the fun in that?" He takes a seat next to me in the booth, forcing me to move over. "Whatcha doing?"

"Having breakfast."

"What a coincidence. I'm hungry myself."

"They don't serve wheatgrass here," I tell him and try to tuck my sketchbook away.

He's not having it. One tug and it's out from under my arm and lying in front of him.

"You should ask to see someone's belongings," I grumble.

"You're not someone. You're Ara." He winks.

I sigh and lay my head on my arm. "What are you even doing up so early?"

1

It's only a little past eight o'clock and Ty's six am football practices ended weeks ago. These days when I see him, it's usually late in the morning. I narrow my eyes at him. Something's going on.

"Early to rise makes you healthy and wise," he quips. "What's my favorite rabbit doing today?" He flips a couple pages and frowns. "No, Blinkie, do *not* eat that carrot. That's from—Oh, crap." He slaps his hand down in frustration. "Why'd you make him eat the carrot from Farmer Brown's garden? Brown hates rabbits. He's going to skin Blinkie and make rabbit stew."

I grab the notebook back and tuck it between me and the side of the café wall. "It's called conflict."

"I don't like it."

"You don't have to read it."

"Ara, someday everyone's going to read it. I'm just making sure it's awesome. Promise me you won't kill the bunny." Behind his glasses, he flaps his ridiculously long eyelashes at me.

I hate how attractive he is. Like, could he have been given bad hair instead of the silky straw-colored stuff that falls perfectly over his forehead? Could his eyes be a muddy brown instead of grass green? Could he have a tummy instead of defined abs, slim waist, broad shoulders? Could his smile have a smidge—just a smidge—less slayage?

I make an exasperated noise in the back of my throat that does nothing to expel the frustration that simmers in my stomach. "First, you know I'm not going to kill the bunny. And second, no one's going to read it. You're not even supposed to be reading it."

He reaches up and tweaks a lock of my hair. "You can't keep anything from me," he teases.

I arch an eyebrow. He'd be surprised.

"When's your dad coming? You should show it to him."

I check my watch. "In an hour, and no, that won't happen and if you want me to talk to you again, you won't mention it to him."

Ty holds his hands up innocently. "My lips are zipped."

"What are you doing here again?"

He grabs my spoon and scoops some of my oatmeal into his mouth. "This is good," he says, without answering.

"Ty."

"Ara."

"Ty."

"Rhyann's breaking up with me this morning." He grins and takes another bite.

"What?" I exclaim. "You two just got back together a week ago."

Rhyann and Ty have been dating on and off since last fall. Admittedly, it's been more off than on, but just last week I saw her coming out of his house early in the morning. Ty volunteered that she'd just passed out at their place, but later on that day during a call that he'd had with his agent (which I heard because Ty put the phone on speaker because he was bored and wanted to play FIFA with his roommate), Ty admitted he was dating someone in response to repeated questions from Dana, said agent. Dana, a guy I think is shadier than an oak tree, told him that being in a serious relationship would help with his draft stock and that Ty was free to "dump her ass" after the draft.

"Did she tell you she was breaking up with you?" To be honest, I'd be surprised if that were the case. She probably just wants to shake him up. Ty's a real catch, what with his NFL prospects and all. In a few months, he's going to sign a big fat multi-million-dollar contract. Everyone wants a piece of him, so for Rhyann to break up with him for good is somewhat impressive on her part.

"Not in so many words, but it's coming."

I don't bother to ask why he's so confident. Ty's been through plenty of breakups. He would know the signs.

"Please move then."

"Why?"

"She's going to throw her water in your face and you're sitting beside me. I don't want to get wet."

"She won't," he says with naïve confidence.

"She will. She's a thrower. Like Crystal, Anna, and Nichole."

3

Not every unhappy girl threw something at Ty, but there were definitely a few. Crystal threw a napkin. Anna dumped a beer pitcher over his head, and Nichole launched a shoe. "Oh, and don't forget Tasha. She threw her phone. It's a miracle someone's eye didn't get taken out."

"I think Tasha tripped. She was always kind of clumsy."

"It had the velocity of a missile. You ducked and it hit me right here." I tap my forehead. "I had a bruise for a week."

"That was bad." He brushes a thumb across the bruise site. It starts to throb in response. "But I made it up to you," he says, completely unaware of how my entire body is straining toward that one little touch.

"How?" It's wild how easy it is for him to light me up. I'm still reliving Bowl night. I'm the only one, though. Ty's never mentioned our drunken hookup three weeks ago, so I assume he doesn't remember. That hurts more than a little. I remember every glorious, wonderful, incredible second of that night.

But I tell myself that the pain I'm feeling now is nothing compared to what I'd suffer if I were in Rhyann's place, having had Ty as a boyfriend only to lose him.

"I watched that post-apoc train movie you still talk about."

"Oh, right. I do love that movie."

A dimple appears on his cheek. I die a little inside. The Masters' half smile is as deadly as a grenade. And can probably do about as much damage.

You're immune, I remind myself.

"I found another set of movies we can watch. It's called the Vengeance Trilogy and—" Ty cuts himself off, his attention caught by a gorgeous redhead striding toward us.

I squint a little at the brightness of Rhyann Kruger's beauty.

"I thought we were meeting for breakfast, Ty?" Rhyann flips her enviable red curls over one shoulder and stares suspiciously at me.

"We are. Ara just happened to be here. Right, Ara?"

"Right, Ty," I say drolly, as if we haven't come to this café on a weekly basis since my freshman year.

I give Ty a nudge. He sighs heavily, takes another bite of my oatmeal, and then directs Rhyann to the booth behind me.

I give Rhyann a thumbs up and turn my attention to my homework. The heat of her glare scorches the top of my head. Ty's girlfriends fall into two categories when it comes to me—they either think I'm going to steal him away or they think that if they become BFFs with me, their relationship with Ty will last longer. I prefer the hate over the fake love. Rhyann has never warmed up to me, and I'm totally fine with that.

But again, I don't blame her. Girlfriends have come and gone in Ty's life. Football and his friends have remained the constants. I knew when I first met him during freshman orientation that I had two choices. I could date him for a short time and be forgotten. Or I could be his friend.

I chose the latter, and four years and countless girlfriends later, Ty and I are best friends. And the girls? Ty barely remembers their names let alone their faces. I made the right choice.

"Why are we here?" Rhyann asks warily.

"To have breakfast?" Ty says.

"At the place you eat with your *friend*." Rhyann says *friend* with the same sort of venomous distaste one reserves for cockroaches and spiders.

"At the place that serves good food. What'll you have?" I hear him push a menu across the table.

I don't think she opens it.

"I don't eat this sort of thing for breakfast. I have a berry beet acai bowl topped with coconut and oats. If you paid even an ounce of attention to me, you'd know this because I have the same thing every morning except Saturdays, and today is not Saturday."

Wow, did it get cold in here or what?

"To be fair, we usually don't eat breakfast together." Ty's voice is smooth and calm, completely unaffected by her chilly retort.

"Whose fault is that?" she snaps.

"Mine, but I do have practice early."

During the football season, Ty would get up every morning

around six and run. After running, he'd down a protein smoothie and go to practice, which, because of how hot it gets down here in the afternoons, has to be in the early morning hours. After practice, he'd have his two classes where he learned about how to manage the money he'll one day have. Then he liked to nap before he had to go back to the training facility to work out and watch film. Being a college football player is like having a full-time job. Almost all of Ty's previous girlfriends didn't understand that. They complained, constantly, about his lack of attention to them. Rhyann is no exception to that rule.

Before Rhyann can respond, Jeanette, the café's sole waitress, strolls over with two glasses of water. "Ready to order?"

"I think we need a minute," Ty says.

"Sure thing. Holler when you're ready."

Once Jeanette is out of earshot, Rhyann starts up again. "I offered to run with you every morning and you turned me down."

"I'm a shit person to spend time with in the morning, you know that. I like to run with my headphones in, and then after I've got to be on the field."

"During the season, I understood all the time commitments you had, but I told myself once they were over, we'd be able to do more things, so it didn't bother me that you missed Thanksgiving or Christmas or even Valentine's Day since it was so close to your Bowl game. But yesterday was my *birthday*. Is there a reason you forgot that?"

Oh, Ty. I sigh into coffee mug. Her birthday, really? I wonder what excuse he'll dream up.

I fell asleep watching WWE.

My brother called and we talked until four in the morning.

I was arguing with my teammate Remy about how many football players we could realistically fit into a Kia Soul.

Swear to God, this was an actual argument that spanned three days between Ty and his roommate. It spread to other members of the team like a kissing disease and wasn't resolved until one of them found an actual Kia Soul and tested it out. For the record, they

6

could fit nine of them in there. Those boys are forced to spend far too much time together.

"No. I don't have a reason I forgot. Sorry."

There's a pregnant pause as both Rhyann and I are shocked into silence by his flat response and lack of excuse. I feel a prick of guilt for eavesdropping on what must now be a mortifying conversation for Rhyann, but it's not like they're whispering. Besides, Ty would've been telling me all about this, word for word, the moment Rhyann left.

"Well," she finally says. "I see how it is. I told myself that once your football season was over, things would be different. We'd be able to spend time together like normal couples do. We'd go to movies, go out to eat, study together, but you always had new excuses. *I have drills. I have the combine. I have the draft. I have tests.*" Her voice cracks slightly. "You had time for everything but me."

"I know," is Ty's dumbass response.

"You know? You know!"

Poor Rhyann. Ty couldn't be more indifferent.

"I told you last winter when you wanted to start dating that I was bad boyfriend material. Football's my priority and everything else comes a distant second."

"Really? What about her?"

Heat scorches my cheeks. Crap.

I know she's pointing at me. I shift to the right, trying to get out of the direct line of fire.

Ty's back rubs against the vinyl as he peers over his shoulder at me. "Who? Ara? Ara's my friend. I don't make time for her, either."

"I saw you two days ago having dinner on campus. And two days before that, you were studying at the Sandwich Shoppe."

"Why does that make you mad? They don't have your acai bowls at either place," Ty stupidly says.

Would it be too obvious if I draped a napkin over my head?

"They don't have my acai bowls? That's your response?" Rhyann's voice grows screechy.

I slump further down in my seat, but it's not far enough,

because seconds later a spray of water hits the back of my head. I fucking *knew* she'd be a thrower.

"Oh, hell. I'm sorry," Ty says, but I think it's more for my benefit than hers.

"Not sorry enough!" she yells. "You're a terrible excuse for a human being and an even worse boyfriend. I don't know why I wasted even a minute on you, let alone four months. Don't call me again. Ever!"

2

Ara

I HAND TY A NAPKIN. SHEEPISHLY, HE PROPS HIS GLASSES ON THE top of his head and dries his face. "That went well."

"Yeah. She didn't seem to care much." He returns the napkin. It's slightly damp and heated from the warmth of his skin. My stupid heart beats a little faster. "How you doing?" He peers down at me.

"I always like a fresh morning glass of water in my face. Perks me the hell up."

"I'm sorry about that," he says ruefully.

"I told you she'd throw something."

He cuffs me lightly on the top of my head before releasing a deep sigh. "I'd stick around to have breakfast with you and your dad, but my agent is coming in." When I make a face, Ty protests, "He's not that bad."

"I didn't say a word."

Ty reaches out and tweaks my cheek. "You don't have to. Call me later?"

"Will do." I watch his broad frame as he heads for the door. I'm not the only one watching. Ty draws female attention everywhere he goes, and why wouldn't he? He's tall and muscular and drop-dead gorgeous and—

Your friend. He's just your friend.

Sighing, I get to my feet to take a bathroom break, but I only manage two steps before someone stops me.

"Hey, Ara."

I can count on one hand the number of people in this world I hate.

Ty's high school girlfriend who told him that she wanted to sleep with his brother to see if they were identical down to their dicks.

My roommate Fleur's sophomore boyfriend who dumped her for a sixteen-year-old local!

My middle school nemesis who didn't tell me that I'd gotten my period the day I wore pink skinny jeans to school.

And this guy in front of me.

"Matt." I force a smile on my face and pretend to be unbothered by the sight of him.

"You look good." He runs his eyes down my frame and then back up to my face. I don't miss how he lingers on my chest. Asshole.

"Oh look, it's Weasel. How's it hanging, Weasel?" A large arm lands around my shoulders.

Relief washes over me as Ty reappears at my side. He must have seen Matt approach me and spun right back around to rescue me. And that's why he's my best friend.

Ty looms forward. "I thought we agreed you wouldn't show your face around Ara anymore?"

Matt, last name Weitzel not Weasel, shoves his hands in his pockets and looks over Ty's shoulder. "It's Weitzel. You know that, but you get off on trying to make me feel low."

Ty stiffens. "Nah, you do that pretty well on your own."

Matt's mouth flattens out and I can tell he's two breaths away from saying something insulting.

"Wow, look at the time. Didn't you have some place you needed to be?" I turn and push at Ty's chest. He goes nowhere, of course. I'd need Thor's hammer to be able to move Ty when he doesn't want to be moved.

"It can wait." He folds his arms across his chest and widens his stance. "I'm not leaving you alone while Weasel is here. He might trip and fall into your chest."

"At least I don't pretend to be her friend while feeling her up," Matt spits back.

"Okay. That's enough," I say.

"When you lie awake at night and wonder why we broke up, your answer is right there, Ara." Matt jerks his chin in Ty's direction. "You're never going to have a real relationship while Meathead is around."

I drop my hand from Ty's chest and face Matt with my own stern expression. "If you think I spend even a minute thinking about you, let alone a minute while I'm in bed, you're more delusional than I thought."

Ty chuckles softly.

"Yeah? Maybe you should spend some time dwelling on it. Otherwise, you're going to be single for the rest of your life."

"Thanks for the advice," I snap.

"Get gone," Ty adds.

Matt tilts his chin upward defiantly. "Or what? You'll hit me? That'd look good in the national press. First round draft prospect Ty Masters arrested for campus assault." He taps his chin. "Have at it, big man."

Ty growls. Literally growls. I feel the reverberations against my back. This is going south really fast.

"Oh hello, Ara, Ty." A tiny blonde appears at Matt's side and winds a small arm around his.

For the first time, I feel almost grateful at the sight of Maribeth Schmidt-Wollums. Matt's stiff frame melts a little.

"Maribeth." I give her a small nod of acknowledgment.

"Maribeth," Ty grunts.

"Did Matt tell you the news?" she coos.

"No. He didn't." I glance toward Matt, who has grown pale. "What's up?"

Maribeth flashes her left hand in my direction. A very familiar sparkling pink diamond nearly blinds me. "We're getting married this summer. Matt proposed on Valentine's Day."

A lump of something hard and sour develops in my throat. I swallow once and then twice, trying to find my voice.

Ty saves me. He leans over and grabs Maribeth's hand. The rock is blinding and familiar. "Nice ring," he says. "Feel like I've seen it somewhere before."

"It was featured in *Southern Living* a few years ago," she gushes. "It's Matt's grandmother's. It's a two—"

"Carat, princess cut diamond in yellow gold," Ty finishes for her.

If possible, Matt grows paler. His lips flap open a couple of times, but no sound comes out.

"How did you know?" Maribeth cocks her head, making her look like a tiny bird.

I place a warning hand on Ty's arm.

"Like I said, feels like I've seen it before," he answers.

I breathe a sigh of relief and so does Matt.

"Congratulations," I tell Maribeth. I actually sound somewhat sincere. Go me.

"I meant...I was going...I planned to tell you before," Matt explains haltingly.

"That wouldn't be necessary. You don't owe me anything." I smile, for my sake more than theirs. "Congrats again. If I don't see you around, best of luck." I point my feet in the direction of the bathroom and walk away, leaving Ty to deal with the two of them.

"Thank you, and best of luck to you, too," I hear Maribeth call after me.

"Remember that it's *happy wife, happy life*, Weasel," Ty adds.

"It's Weitzel," Matt says between gritted teeth.

The rest of the conversation is lost after I enter the washroom. I hurry into an empty stall, slam the door shut and collapse on the toilet. Seeing my ring on Maribeth's hand was a shocker.

Matt and I broke up almost a year ago and I'd heard through the grapevine that he was dating Maribeth. I didn't know it was serious, though. I didn't know I was going to feel like I'd been struck by a pole when I saw the ring I'd sported for the entire summer last year on some other girl's hand.

But, then, I didn't expect to see Matt's dick in another girl's mouth, either, and that happened so...why is this worse?

I drop my head to my hands. I'm over Matt. I hadn't felt right about the engagement from the moment I said yes. The best thing that happened to me was finding him getting a blowjob from his pledge's date at Spring Fling.

Yet...finding out that he's getting married to someone else and so soon feels rotten.

The phone in my pocket buzzes. I pull it out expecting to see my dad wondering where I am.

I'm sorry.

It's from Matt. I delete it and text Ty.

Me: Is it safe?

Ty: Coast is clear. Your dad just walked in.

Me: He didn't see Matt, right?

Dad hates Matt as much as Ty does. And unlike Ty, a restraining hand isn't going to keep Dad from causing a ruckus. It adds to his artist mystique, he says.

Ty: No. Weasel was gone by the time your dad arrived.

Me: Be right out.

I tuck my phone away, unnecessarily wash my hands and stare at myself in the mirror.

"You're over Matt. You've been over him for a long time. You don't care who he marries, who he screws, or if he fails or succeeds."

"You go, girl," says a brunette coming out of one of the stalls. "Whoever he is, he's not worth it."

"Right." I give her a grateful smile.

She winks at me. "You're better off without him, whoever he is."

A pounding on the door cuts off any response. "You okay in there?" Ty's deep voice carries easily through the door.

13

"Is that Matt? Because I'm down for whatever," my newfound friend says.

"No. He's one of the good guys." I open the door. "I'm fine. No need to break down the door," I tell Ty.

He lowers his hand. "Just making sure. You said you'd be right out and then you weren't. I didn't want to leave if you needed me."

"It's all good."

"All right. Call me later?" He makes a telephone sign with his fingers.

"Yes."

"See ya." He salutes me and then jogs off.

"If he's a good guy, then you should use one of those big shoulders to cry on." The girl from the bathroom joins me in the hall to ogle Ty's hot ass.

"He's a good guy because he's my friend," I say.

"Well, there are worse ways to be ruined," the girl says with a saucy smile. "Sunny Pope." She sticks out her hand.

"Ara Martin."

"Nice to meet you, Ara. If you ever need any help in the bathroom again, give me a holler. I'm like a bathroom Batman."

I laugh. "Do you have a sign that I can shoot into the sky?"

"No, but I do have this." She flips a paper towel in my direction. "And if that big boy ever needs companionship and you seriously don't want to provide it, pass this along to him, will ya?"

I look down at the number scrawled across the paper towel and groan.

Not again.

§

"WHAT'S THIS?" Dad asks after we hug out our greeting. He points to the towel that Sunny just handed to me.

"Another girl after Ty," I say and crumple it.

"Oh, to be young and virile." Dad shakes his head. "You young people don't know what to do with the gifts you've been given."

Dad's plenty virile. Apparently that's how I got my current job. He'd slept with the gallery owner, promised her a piece of art, and then wrangled a position for me as an assistant. I wonder how that worked. Did he ask her after he stuck his penis in her or before? I shutter my eyes. Damn. What a terrible image that is.

"Ty does plenty with his gifts," I say. A twinge of something uncomfortable pokes me in my chest, so I change the subject. "What do you plan to do in New York?"

"I have Stephen to see, of course."

Stephen is his agent. "Tell him hello."

"I will. I'll buy you a dress while I'm there. I think Stephen and Tracy are getting married this summer."

"Really? They've been engaged for four years. What's the hurry?" I joke.

"Tracy is tired of being engaged, or so Stephen says. Anyway, it's too bad you can't come with me."

"It's in the middle of the semester. If you'd waited until March, I might've gone with you."

"No spring break?"

I shake my head. "Marissa has a big show she's planning and asked if I could stick around the first weekend."

"Then I'll just go again in March," he says. "We'll stay at The Surrey and empty out my bank account at Barney's."

"I'm in."

Jeanette flutters over with a menu and a mug.

"Coffee?" She tips the pot toward the mug she just deposited in front of him.

"I would love some." Dad flashes a lazy grin, and Jeanette visibly gulps.

I cringe inside, knowing what's coming.

"You have any classes with my daughter here?" Dad asks, dumping five cubes of sugar into his mug.

"Oh, no, I'm not a student." Jeanette flutters a weathered hand against her chest.

"You don't say?" Dad says in what appears like genuine surprise.

"You can't be older than twenty-five. I thought you were one of those returning students."

"Non-trads, Dad."

"Non-grads?" he repeats incorrectly.

"Non-traditional. That's what students are called if they don't matriculate right after high school. Jeanette. My dad, Arthur. Arthur, this is Jeanette. Best waitress in the state." Except for right this minute. I push the carafe upright so that Jeanette, who's busy staring starry-eyed into Dad's smiling face, doesn't pour coffee all over the table. I've a hard limit of wearing one breakfast drink a day and Rhyann's water has met that.

"Sorry," she mutters sheepishly. She whips out her little notebook. "What'll you have?"

Dad looks at me.

"He'll have the eggs Benedict."

"Good choice, honey," he says. "I'll have the eggs Benedict."

Jeanette nods firmly. "Got it."

"Put a little extra love on it, will you?" he calls after her.

The waitress, who doesn't even flirt with Ty, puts an extra swing in her step.

I sigh. "Well, you made her year."

He grins. "That's what I live for."

Isn't that the honest truth?

"So what'd you drive all the way up here for?" I ask.

His handsome face takes on a wounded expression. "A dad can't visit his only daughter without being questioned like a criminal?"

If I were younger, like ten or eleven, I might've fallen for this act. It worked for many years of my life, but I'm older, wiser, have been the veteran of three of Dad's failed marriages. The man is lovable but terribly irresponsible.

"Spill," I say sternly.

He looks around, as if someone is going to save him. "Where's that pretty waitress with our food?"

"It's coming." I wait him out. He drove three hours for a reason, and while I suspect I know what it is, he needs to say it.

Finally, he turns back to me. "I'm getting a divorce."

"I figured." I try saying it flatly, but I guess I'm not successful because he winces.

"Now, honey," he starts, but Jeanette finally appears with our breakfast. He immediately digs in as if it's the first meal he's had after a week of fasting.

"Thanks, Jeanette," I say.

"No problem. I'm here all morning." She winks.

Dad grins.

I want to slide under the table.

"I'm good," he finally says. Jeanette gets the hint. She tops off my dad's coffee and then saunters away.

Dad, ever appreciative of the womanly form, can't take his eyes off of Jeanette's ass.

I clear my throat and he tears his gaze away and meets my eyes with sheepishness.

"Habit," he says by way of explanation.

"That might be the reason for your divorce."

This is too much for him. He sets down his fork. "Ara, you know I'm a loyal man. I didn't cheat on your mother and I didn't cheat on Holly. Or Marissa," he adds as an afterthought. "I hope that's not too awkward for you."

Just a little, Dad. But I don't tell him. It's not his fault that Marissa's sort of flaky and has given over the running of her gallery to Van Riley, a vengeful asshole.

"You do have a mistress, though." I remind him.

"My art is not a mistress. It's a calling. Speaking of which"—he fumbles for his phone—"I started work on this new piece last night. I'm calling it 'departure' with a small d. What do you think?"

I take the phone and zoom in on the image. Whatever his flaws and faults, Dad is a brilliant artist. The metal sculpture isn't yet polished, and the shape is still vague, but the melancholic beauty sings even through the screen.

"It's gorgeous." I hand him back the phone.

"I think it's the best thing I've done all year. As heartbreaking as it is for me to lose Holly, it's been inspiring." Yeah, he sounds real torn up. "I've already sold this piece to a collector in Singapore for a substantial sum. In fact, that's why I have to go up to New York this weekend. He wants to meet me. I deposited a little something in your account, by the way. Buy something pretty for yourself."

"I don't need anything."

"I know, but you're my only daughter and I like to spoil you."

And it makes him feel better. I'm the one woman who's remained constant in his life, but then I'm the only woman he's never had a romantic relationship with. If that's not a life lesson, I don't know what is.

"Oh, and Ara, before I forget, you need to call your mother."

"Really?" Suddenly, my appetite is gone.

"It's been almost three months," he chides gently. "And whatever your issues are, she's still the woman who carried you in her body for nine months and gave you life. That's a wonderful, precious gift."

"All right." I give in because if I don't, Dad'll start writing odes to Mom's fecund gloriousness. I would rather hear Maribeth's wedding plans. I don't know why he's always so gracious toward Mom given that she walked out on us when I was eight. Her last words before walking out the door were literally, "I give up."

What kind of mom does that anyway? She cut off all contact while she went on some long jaunt around the world. Dad sat up nearly every night waiting for a phone call. He grew thin; his beard grew long. His work became dark, twisted, and more in demand than ever.

When she returned, tanned, prettier than I remembered, Dad was thrilled. They never got back together, thankfully, but he's never held any real grudge. I asked him why once and he'd said that even though the flame of passion died, the embers of friendship remained.

Life lesson number two. Friends last forever and hurt a helluva lot less.

3

Ty

DANA MULLEN, MY AGENT, IS ALREADY SITTING IN THE CLUB when I arrive. Several members stand up and greet me. I make nice with all of them, but it takes nearly thirty minutes to wind through the well-wishers. Even as I take my seat, I can feel their eyes boring into the back of my head. They want to be in the know. They want to be the first to report whatever news will be given to me by Dana.

I heard from a solid source that Masters is going number five. His agent was at the club talking about it.

"You're late," Dana says.

A month ago, he would've been falling over his own dick in an effort to be nice to me. If I'd been late, even by several hours, Dana would've said that he'd gotten the appointment time wrong. Now that my signature is on the agent contract, he's had a reversal in attitude.

I don't love it, but this is my bed and I'll lie in it.

"Sorry," I say, although I'm really not. I wasn't going to leave Ara until her asshole ex was long gone. I'm surprised he had the balls to show up at the Row House—he knows it's a place Ara hangs out at. She and I and a bunch of our friends have been going there to eat and study since our freshman year.

I suspect he wanted to see her. Not only wanted to see her, but wanted to shove his girlfriend and the big rock in Ara's face. Fucking prick. I'd like to have shoved my fist into his face, but he's right. If I hit him, or anyone, for that matter, it'd be front-page news on every national sports site.

"It's fine because I'm your agent, but remember there are always eyes watching you. And I'm not talking about the liver-dicked members of this godforsaken club."

The Mansion is the ritziest place in town. The wealthy locals have memberships here to play golf, make business deals, and gossip. Watching people meet is a spectator sport here. I prefer to prove myself on the field, so none of this attention is comfortable for me. My back itches and the chair feels two sizes too small.

"If you like the membership so little, why are we here?"

"I didn't realize there was a better place to meet. Remember, it's all about the optics." He brushes a hand over his arm. "The one drawback of podunk college towns like this one is the shit food and the low-rent lodging. Jesus, what I'd give for a decent mattress. Kid, you will love it in these big markets. The clubs, the women, the food." He shakes his head. "You don't know what you're missing."

I decide against reminding Dana that I come from a small town in Illinois. To him, everything but the coast is considered flyover country.

I grab the menu. Getting water thrown in my face and dealing with Ara's ex has worked up my appetite.

"I ordered for you," Dana says.

I pause, breathe through my nose, and gather my patience. "Thanks."

"Speaking of food, how's the diet going?" Dana's oblivious, either intentionally or not, to my irritation.

"Good."

"Weight?"

"I texted you that last night."

He quirks both eyebrows up. "You didn't weigh yourself this morning?"

"No. My weight's the same last night as it's been for the last twenty days. I doubt it's going to be different today." It's hard to keep an even tone, but I remind myself that Dana wants the same thing I want—for me to get picked in one of the top five draft slots come April.

"Well, don't miss tonight," he cautions, like I'm five and am gorging myself every day.

I run my tongue across the inside of my lip before answering. "I won't."

"And the knee?"

"It's perfect." And that's no lie. "I haven't had pain in weeks and no treatments. I probably just tore a ligament and needed a little time to heal."

The waiter arrives with our food. Unsurprisingly, my meal's chicken breast and broccoli. I've had so many chicken breasts, I may start laying eggs.

Without argument, I dig in because I understand Dana's reasoning. There'll be plenty of days to veg out in front of the sofa drinking beer and eating pizza after my career is over.

"The important thing here is that we seed the right rumors. I think you should do a pre-combine mini-camp event to stave off any rumors that your knee is bad."

"My knee's not bad."

"Sure, that's what you say."

"That's how it is." I lay down my fork and glare at Dana.

He smiles broadly. "People are watching us."

I glance around and see he's right. Dammit. I pick up my fork and resume eating. The bland chicken tastes like cardboard. I grab my glass of water and drain it while snippets of nearby conversations float my way.

"...Masters looks tense today."

"Bet he's worried about his draft placement. His brother was number three."

"No way he beats that."

The sides of the fork bite into my palm.

21

"I'm glad you're confident, but I'm not the one you have to convince. A pre-combine mini is the perfect way to show the scouts and execs that you're worth every penny of a multi-million-dollar contract. Plus, you'll have a leg up on all those guys at the combine. It won't matter how you perform there. In the location we choose, with our own timers, with the optimum field conditions, we'll do all the combine tests. The four/forty run, three-cone drill, vertical jump, et cetera. All of it."

The idea has appeal. "I'd still go to the combine, right?"

The combine is a weeklong event where the NFL teams invite about three hundred players. There, every orifice of your body and every crevice of your life is measured and weighed. The defensive linemen and linebackers are scheduled to start on the third day.

"Of course, but there'd be no pressure on you."

"You scared I'm not going to blow my competition out of the water?" I have zero doubt that I'm going to be the best in my class, by a long shot. If I don't get drafted high it's because the team picking wants a quarterback or right guard or running back, not because there's a better defensive end in the pool this year.

Last year might've been a different story. Last year I would've competed against my brother who plays the same position. And that sort of competition kills my mom, hurts my dad. So while he entered the draft, I waited another year. Everyone thinks I wanted the Championship and that I played my fifth year to achieve it. Everyone's wrong.

It was a risk. I could've played like shit. I could've injured myself. But it all worked out perfectly. Knox, my brother, got drafted third. I won a National Championship. My family was over the moon, which makes me happy.

Dana pops the perfect balloon. "You're not competing against the blowhards in the draft, son. You're competing against your brother. Every stat has to be better or you're not going to get drafted as high."

"I know." I take a deep cleansing breath to dislodge the rock that's settled in my gut. I love my brother. Love him to bits, but that love doesn't mean I don't want to smash every record he set.

"Now tell me everything else."

I want to rub a hand down my face, but given the eyes watching me, I know that gesture will be taken wrong.

Masters looked nervous at lunch. Think something was wrong with him.

"A girl I was dating broke up with me."

"Dammit," Dana curses, but he does it while smiling. He's great at putting on a show. "Why the hell can't you keep one dumb bitch satisfied?"

Ara's ex is now only the second person I'd like to punch today. I restrain myself and force one side of my mouth up in what I hope is a credible smile. "Because I'm not interested in her and she figured it out because she's not a dumb bitch."

"Find a dumb bitch, then, and fuck her into submission, okay?"

I summon up all reasons why I chose Dana Mullen as an agent before answering. "I'm not into dumb women, and even dumb ones can figure out that my focus is on training and getting ready for the draft."

"Christ, kid, you can't multi-task?"

I stare stonily back at him.

"Listen up. These execs want to pretend that you're all perfect homebodies wanting nothing more to do than pork your high school girlfriend until she pops out three kids. The more reason you have to stay at home and keep your dick tucked away, the better. So either gull some dumb broad who's happy riding your big dick for two months or find yourself a smart bitch who'll play along. Either one is good for me."

My hand curls into a fist. I pull it onto my lap before the gossips notice.

Masters punched out his agent at lunch.

Dana leans forward, a hand on the table, his voice pitched low so only I can hear him. "I know you signed with me for one reason only and that was so that I could get you drafted number one. And

I'm going to deliver on that, by any means necessary. Sometimes it's going to mean doing some non-conventional thing—"

Bells ding in my head, but I shut them down quick.

"—Sometimes it means doing things that might not seem right on the surface, but you gotta trust me. We're on the same team. Go Team Ty."

He holds out a fist. I stare at it sullenly.

Masters left his agent hanging.

I force my own fist up and bump his.

Nah, they were fist bumping. Some deal was going down. A good one.

I force another breath past the rock and smile. "Go Team Ty."

"Now let's talk about interviews," Dana says.

Inwardly I groan, but I keep the fake smile on my face the rest of our meeting.

§

AFTER THE MEETING WITH DANA, I meander over to the training facility. It's quiet now that the season is over. Most of the coaches are off on recruiting trips. The locker feels like a ghost town. I half expect tumbleweed to blow through. Ace, my former QB, walks out of the admin office.

Close enough, I think.

"What's up?" he asks. "Usually we don't see you around here until the afternoon."

"I thought I'd get a few reps in this morning. Anyone else around?" I don't like interviews, eating chicken breasts, and maintaining a fake relationship. All that seems stupid. What's going to sell me as a player is how I work on the field. I'd rather spend my time in the gym and on the practice field.

"Remy was here at six but left about an hour ago."

That's no surprise. The draft is stacked with running backs this year and Remy's anxious about where he's going to fall. That makes two of us, but my chances are better than his so I don't feel like I've got the right to complain. Around Remy—hell, around everyone but Ara, I keep my mouth closed.

"Travarius?" I ask.

Ace falls in step beside me, a folder in his left paw.

"Nope. Too early. At this time of day, Remy's the only one awake. The rest of you lazy sacks of shit don't roll in 'til around noon."

"Sounds about right."

"How's the knee?" Ace asks.

I glance down at his folder and then up at his face. "Is this an official question from JR Anderson aspiring sports reporter or a casual one from Ace, my QB?"

"Friend."

"It's fine." Then I wonder. "Have you heard anything?"

"Nope. No one from this department is going to talk and even if they did, so what? A few injections is normal. What player hasn't had them?"

My brother, I think. But I don't bother bringing up that comparison.

Ace taps the folder against his hand. "These are a bunch of interview queries, though. I'll send them to your agent."

I grab at the folder. "Nah, I got these."

"You handling all your PR yourself? That's what you pay the agent the big bucks for."

"I like to know who's calling." Dana wants me to do every interview, while I'd like to have my test results speak for themselves. It's like he has no confidence in my abilities.

"These days? It's everyone." He starts to leave but then circles back. "Just a word of caution. I think these reporters smell something."

There's a mild uptick in my heart rate. "Why? Are there questions in there?"

"No. It's just...some of these reporters aren't only from sports outlets."

"What kind of interview requests did Knox get?" Ace used to play with my brother before he transferred.

"I have no clue," he admits. "I didn't work in the PR department. Probably nothing to worry about, but no harm in being alert, right?"

"Right," I affirm with confidence I'm not really feeling, and my right knee starts to throb. Fuck. "These interviews are all the same. I could do them in my sleep. *I'm excited about the combine. I'm looking forward to the draft. I don't care what team drafts me so long as I get the opportunity to play on Sundays. I'd love to play with my brother in New York.*

The last one is a lie, but it's the one I have to sell the hardest.

"Yeah. You got this." He slaps the folder against my chest. "Don't spend too much time looking through these. Like I said, that's what you're paying your agent to do."

"It can't be that many." The folder's thin.

"A couple hundred," Ace says cheerfully.

I blanch. "A couple hundred?" I peek inside and realize that it's a spreadsheet and not an individual printout. "Holy shit. I thought I'd have to do one."

"What's your agent going to say?"

"Dana?" I grimace. "He's of the opinion, the more press, the better."

"Doesn't seem like you agree."

"The more you open your mouth, the greater the chance you say something dumb. Better to keep my mouth shut than talk and be crucified." This is the sort of thing that Knox loves to do. He's friendly and outgoing. "My stats can speak for themselves."

"It's your career," Ace says as the door closes. It's clear he thinks I'm making a mistake. I probably am, but I just want to play. I hate all the pretty boy media shit you're forced to do these days.

It's not enough to have game. You've got to be a brand. Everyone's measuring you by how many endorsements you have. How many followers on the 'gram. How many jerseys you're selling. All of it goes into where you fall in the draft.

But if the current state of the league has taught players anything, it's that you can commit nearly any sin short of murder and as long as you excel on the field, all's forgiven.

Not that I intend to sin. I've got everything planned and if I can just stay focused, then the outside distractions aren't going to be a problem.

Not the annoying agent.

Not the angry ex.

The only thing the matters is how I play, and I play football damn good.

4

Ty

A GOOD WORKOUT HELPS ME SWEAT AWAY THE TENSION, AND BY the time I arrive home, my morning moodiness is gone. Halfway in the door, my phone buzzes.

Did you see the news?

The text's from my brother.

Me: No

Knox: Joshua London got picked up last night for a DUI.

Oh shit. Josh London is a beast. Three hundred pounds but lightning fast. Teams are salivating over him.

I type with one hand.

Me: Is it out

Knox: No, but soon. Some "anon" agent is spilling tea on SM that he's a problem in the locker room and this won't be the last of the bad news about him

I hate those anonymous sources. They can say all the crap they want about a player and the player has no way of punching back. Any denial makes it look like you're hiding something.

Me: Sux tb him

Knox: No kidding. How'd the workout go? Weight?

Sigh. Even from Knox. Tiredly, I type out my response.

253

Knox sends me the thumbs up.

I get five more texts. All of them about London. Poor dude. Granted, asshole shouldn't drink and drive, but this is going to cost him several million dollars. Hope he enjoyed his night at the bar.

Remy voices my exact thoughts when I walk into our kitchen. "You hear about London? Fool boy just had his most expensive night out ever. If I don't hear that it involved bathing in Ace champagne while Victoria's Secret models took turns sucking him off, I'm gonna be real disappointed."

"Knox texted me. Is it out yet?"

"I haven't seen it on the news. I guess his coach must've called in a favor." Remy leans against the counter and reads the incoming tweets on his phone.

"It's going to get out there."

"I keep searching his name. Nothing's trending yet."

I walk over to the fridge and pull out a bunch of ingredients for a smoothie. "Used to be that you'd be excited if you trended. These days it means you're dead or you did something wrong."

"Truth, brother. Truth. How's the knee?"

I stifle my annoyance and pack the blender to the top. "Fine."

"Hurts, huh?"

"I think it's phantom pain," I tell him. "My knee's been fine since the Bowl game."

"Funny how a championship is the best upper."

"Good for our draft stock, too."

We exchange a muted high-five.

"You're not putting enough sweetener in there. It's gonna taste like grass," Remy observes.

"I'm not even supposed to have sweetener," I grumble, but I squirt an extra serving of agave syrup into the blender.

Wyatt Majors, another lineman, ambles through. From the state of his hair, he just woke up.

I motion to the blender. "Want one?"

He grimaces. "How many vegetables have you stuck in there?"

"A few."

"He shoved in a whole bag of baby spinach," Remy volunteers.

"Pass. Since I'm not training for shit anymore, I'm going to eat like a normal person."

After graduation, Wyatt's going to work at a construction company now that football is over. He strolls over to the cabinet and breaks open a bag of chips. My mouth waters.

"Asshole," Remy mutters under his breath.

We sniff the air like goddamned junkies and then force our attention back on the blender.

"This stuff tastes better than it looks," Remy says.

The green sludge swirls in the plastic container.

"Looks like cow puke," Wyatt yells over his shoulder.

Man, our friend is an asshole. I turn the blender on high to drown out the sound of the crunch of the chips.

"How about the plastic wrap over Wyatt's toilet?" Remy hollers into my ear.

"Alwyn shares a room with him. We going to drag him down, too?" I yell back.

Remy strokes his chin.

"I hear you plotting something against me," Wyatt shouts over the blender.

I shut it off. "No need to scream, bro. We're standing right here."

Wyatt gives me the finger and shoves another handful of chips into his mouth.

I lick my lips. "That junk food is going to kill you."

"Dude, you couldn't be more jealous if I was standing here with Miss America," my friend taunts.

"Who is Miss America these days? Anyone hot? They all look pretty plastic-y to me," I muse.

"She's a Latina and she's smoking," Remy informs us. "You guys oughta watch those pageants. Hot chicks parading around in skin-tight dresses and bikinis. Only thing better is if they doused the girls with oil and had a little wrestling event."

"You need to take that remote away from Nichole," Wyatt says.

I pour the blended concoction into two glasses and hand Remy one. "He can't. She's already pissed at him because he bought that egg speaker." The egg-shaped Bluetooth speaker set Remy back a cool three grand.

"Is that what was shaking the house last night?" Wyatt rolls his eyes.

"Boy, you have no idea how fine this girl is. She puts out four thousand watts of power and is coated with rose gold. She's so beautiful it brings a tear to my eye." Remy sniffles and wipes away a non-existent tear.

"And you wonder why Nichole's mad," I say.

"I gotta see this," Wyatt says.

Remy eyes Wyatt's chip-coated fingers with mild disgust. "You're not getting in the door until you wash your hands." As Wyatt shoves more chips in his mouth, Remy turns to me. "Heard your girl threw a pitcher of Bloody Marys in your face last night."

"It was a glass of water and it was this morning. Where'd you hear that?" I gulp down my drink.

"Nichole heard it from somebody. You oughta be careful. One of your exes is gonna plant a story about you," Remy cautions.

"They've all broken up with me," I protest.

Remy looks up from his phone. Wyatt stops eating. Together they stare at me in disbelief.

"What?" I ask, feeling a mite defensive. "It's true."

"It's true like the pool turning green after someone pisses in it is true," Wyatt says.

"Hey, now, all of them knew I was here to play ball." I scowl into the bottom of my empty glass. I never lied to a single girl.

Remy nods. "True. Lots of girls talk a good game, but once they're with you, it's always complaints about how you're missing things when they know you have to prepare. But"—he puts his phone down—"truth is that the bigwigs upstairs like to hear that you've settled down. Nothing gets them harder for a player than knowing you got a family and a mouth to feed. That way they know you aren't spending all your nights at the club or partying on some boat. Even if you didn't have a woman, you should lie and say you do."

Every year at the combine, along with all the physical stuff, you're required to take exams that test your general intelligence, and then you interview with the general managers or presidents of operations. These folks are spending millions of dollars on you. They want every aspect of your life laid bare.

Remy's repeating the same thing Dana told me, so no doubt Remy's agent has given him the same lecture. The front office guys would like nothing more than to hear you're in a committed relationship to a girl you've known since you were five and that you plan to have three kids right away.

These things scream stable family man who is going to be a credit to the organization instead of reckless rookie who plans to spend his new millions on flashy cars, flashy women and bottles of Ace at the club.

"What are you planning on saying?" I ask Remy, because we spent an hour the other night looking for Nichole's ring after she screamed that she wouldn't fuck him if he was the last dick on earth.

"We're on again. She's all in. I think she can smell the money."

"Frankly, I thought Rhyann would stick around for that," I admit. Rhyann came on to me after Thanksgiving. She was pretty, polished, and came off fairly sophisticated. I figured she knew the score, but missing her birthday was apparently the last straw.

"Oh shit, it's out," Remy says suddenly.

I hustle over to his side. He's swiping through the Josh London hashtag. The mentions aren't pretty.

Dumbass. Call yourself an uber.

What do you expect from a kid who spends his free time getting his head bashed in.

Player you played yourself out of a few million dollars.

But it's not the random fans on the internet that worry us. It's the sports reporters who chime in.

NFL source calls London a "time bomb." Not worth the first round risk.

"Damn," Remy whistles. "Out of the first round over a DUI?"

"That's one source." I lay my hand over Remy's and force the phone down to the counter. "No point in reading any more of that. You're going to give yourself an ulcer."

"I can't wait until the draft is over," he confesses and flips the phone over because he's an addict and can't stop reading the bad news. "You should get yourself a girl."

"In four weeks? Should I put up an ad on the SU connections site? 'Wanted, girl who doesn't care if I ignore her for four weeks but will pretend to be madly in love with me so NFL execs will give me good grades at the combine.'"

"What about Ara?" Wyatt pipes up.

I stiffen. Her juicy ass and long legs flash in front of my eyes. "What about her?"

"She'd pretend for you. She's your best friend. Plus, she's smart and all so that would make them happy."

"She'd laugh her face off if I even suggested it." Plus, I wouldn't be able to handle it. My dick would explode from want.

"Never know until you ask."

My response to Wyatt is lost when the doorbell rings.

"You get it," Remy begs us. "And if it's Nichole, I'm not home."

With that, he runs upstairs.

"Coward," Wyatt yells after him.

"Yup," comes the cheerful response. Nichole has that boy by the balls.

"You heard the man—get the door." I grab the blender and make a big show of cleaning up.

Wyatt huffs his exasperation but goes to see who's visiting. It's not one of our teammates. They'd walk in. Ara, too. So it's gotta be a girl.

A high-pitched voice reaches me. A high-pitched familiar voice. Oh, hell. I wipe my hands on the towel and go out to rescue Wyatt.

5

Ara

JUST BEFORE DINNER, I GET A TEXT FROM MY ROOMMATE, FLEUR Emerson.

Her: Heard Ty got in a huge fight with his girlfriend.

Oh, he's gonna love this. Not. I try to downplay it, because Ty hates being the topic of social media and, for the most part, he's been able to avoid it.

Me: She threw water at him this morning and he wiped it off. Not much of a fight.

Her: This morning? It happened 5 min ago. Shouting at his house. It's all over campus.

Oh no. I pull up the campus app where everyone posts anonymously sourced shit. It's a rancid place full of hateful people, but if you want to know what people at SU are gossiping about, Whistle is the place to go.

Masters got faced at his own house.
Nah. Jessica Rabbit got eaten.
I'd give my entire student loan check to smash her ass. What's his problem?
I'd give my ovary to smash Masters.
She's a dumb bitch anyway.

Wonder if this'll hurt his draft stock.
Isn't she his sixth girlfriend in the last month?
Those aren't girlfriends, they're cum depositories.

I close the app after that last one. Like I said, rancid place, hateful people.

I throw on a sweatshirt over my jogging shirt, shove my feet into a pair of sneakers, and jog the five blocks over to Ty's house.

When I arrive, I find him sitting on one of the lawn chairs set up on the front porch. His long legs are stretched out in front of him and his head is tipped back. A bag of ice rests on his forehead.

I drop into the empty chair beside him. "Was it a frying pan? That seems cliché."

"The remote. That sucker is harder than it looks." He sticks one of his legs under mine so that my calves dangle across his shins. I guess he thinks I need an ottoman. My legs *are* way shorter than his.

I reach over and lift the bag of ice. There's a slight gash above his eye and a mottled redness surrounding it. I wince. "Looks bad."

"Worst injury I ever suffered," he jokes. "I may have to drop out of the draft."

"If it scars, at least make up a good story, like 'I was wounded fighting off four thugs who were trying to rob a poor old lady. I managed to save her, but the last attacker got in one good kick, leaving this mark.'" I lightly poke one side of the rapidly forming bruise, and Ty makes some indistinct sound. I ignore it and press on the other side. It looks tender and sore.

"Let's up the number to ten and say I'm saving a litter of puppies. Remember how upset your classmates were when you killed off the horse last semester?"

"Crazy how animals are more sympathetic than grannies." Last year I took a creative writing class and one assignment was to write a short story that delivered pathos. I wrote about a girl who went riding with her pony across a frozen pond. They came upon a weak ice patch and the girl fell into the cold water. The pony sacrificed his life for hers.

The class crucified me. To his credit, Ty thought my idea was terrible and didn't hesitate to tell me so in long, ranting terms. If only I'd listened to him. But, at the time, I thought, what does he know. He's a finance major, not a creative thinker.

Oh, how wrong I was, and Ty never gives me a moment of peace about it.

"Say 'I told you so' one more time and you'll have a matching scar above your other eye." I drop the bag of ice back onto his forehead.

He groans. "Ouch. I'm a wounded man. Be careful with me."

"Why'd she come back? I thought she was done with you in the morning." Absently, I finger comb his hair, enjoying the silky feel of it against my skin. When he leans into my touch, my entire body sings.

God, this guy. He's so gorgeous. And being with him is so...easy. Our friendship is probably the most important relationship in my life, and I like to think it's that way for him, too. He's never come out and said *Ara, you're the bestest BFF ever and I couldn't live without you.*

But some things don't need to be said. I know Ty values what we have as much as I do.

"She had a sweatshirt of mine and was doing me a favor by returning it, or so she said."

I smile wryly. "How long was she hoarding that so she could use it as an excuse to see you again?"

"I don't know. I don't remember giving her anything to wear. I mean..." He trails off.

I wait for him to finish and when he doesn't, I tug on his hair. "You mean what?"

He slumps a little lower in the chair. "We never slept together."

I bolt upright, knocking the bag off his head. "*What?*"

"You okay there, Screechy McScreecherson?"

"You never slept with her?"

He gives a quick glance toward the front door and then the sidewalk. "Can you say it louder? I don't think the guys at the end of the street heard you."

Guilty, I lower my voice. "I thought, well, why'd you date her in the first place?"

He reaches down and picks up the bag of ice. It's nearly melted, but he resettles it on his forehead before leaning back again. "Who knows. Knox and Ellie are pretty happy. I thought maybe it was time to find someone."

"But you never slept with her?" This is mind-blowing to me. Ty's such a physical creature. He loves physical contact. When we watch a movie, he's got his head on my lap. When we walk, he often slings an arm around my shoulder. He has no problem being affectionate with his teammates. The asses Ty has slapped number in the hundreds. I've always assumed he's slept with every single one of his girlfriends and then some.

Then again...his brother was a virgin who saved himself for marriage. Could Ty be? No. No way.

I open my mouth and then shut it. Then open it again. Then shut it. If Ty's a virgin, that's his business, not mine.

But he's my best friend. Best friends share things like that.

Granted, I've never told him about losing my V-card, so why would I expect him to divulge that information to me?

"I can hear your gears grinding," he says with a chuckle.

I glance at his beautiful face. "Were you not attracted to Rhyann? Is that even possible? She's so beautiful she'd turn straight girls bi."

The eyebrow not covered by the plastic bag shoots up. "Is this your coy way of seeing if I'll give you permission to pursue Rhyann? If so, be my guest, but I want to be able to videotape any and all of your sexy times."

I dig my heel into his shin to punish him. "No, I don't want to pursue your ex-girlfriend, thank you very much." I shake my head. "I still can't believe it, though."

"What's so hard to believe? I've been busy. It's probably why she wanted to break up in the first place."

"That and you forgot her birthday."

"Indeed." He does not sound broken up about this in any way. "She's better off with someone else. The thing is, I don't get why she's mad at me. She accused me of cheating on her."

"Did you tell her that she was only ever the mistress, never the wife?"

He jiggles my leg. "What's that supposed to mean?"

I shrug. "It means that you, like my dad, have a first love and it's not a girl or woman. For you, it's football. For Dad, it's his art. No mere female could ever compare."

Do I sound bitter? I hope not. I'm resigned.

"How is your dad, anyway?"

"Good. He says hi. As I suspected, he and Holly have broken up, but, good news. He's been inspired to create a new iron piece that will sell for a gazillion dollars."

Ty looks amused. "Your dad is the only man I know that gets richer with every divorce instead of poorer."

"This isn't a good trait." I kick Ty again.

He pretends like it hurts. "Okay, then. Should we talk about something else?"

I guess I do sound a little bitter. "Yes, like, how are you going to deal with the Rhyann thing? It's all over Whisper."

Ty groans and slides the ice bag down until it covers both his eyes. "Fuck. I don't even know why she was so angry. I figured she'd gotten it all out of her system at the Row House."

"She probably went home, stewed about it, thought up a dozen more things to say and wanted you to know them all."

"That sounds about right." He sighs deeply.

The rise and fall of his chest grabs my eye. Ty's body is like a work of art. I'm observing it purely from an aesthetics point of view. Purely. Not sexually. Not as in, I'd like to rip his well-worn, fitted T-shirt in two and expose his slabs of hard muscle. Nothing like that.

I sigh, too.

"I thought she was a cool chick," he says. "She told me she understood that I was busy and didn't need to be babysat."

"She wanted in your pants. She would've said anything."

My eyes drift down to said pants. He's wearing athletic shorts that do very little to disguise exactly what Rhyann was so attracted to in the first place. My body tightens and I force another heavy breath out. I know from firsthand experience the glory of the package beneath those shorts. The night of the Bowl game, I had my hands all over him.

Worse, his hands were on me. I cast him a speculative glance. Does he remember a thing from that night? He must not because he's never said a word. His attitude toward me has never changed. He's never treated me with anything but sincere fraternal affection.

So, no, he doesn't remember that his hot mouth was plastered against mine. That his long fingers stroked their way from ankle to thigh. That his firm body rubbed against mine in ways that still wake me up sweating in the middle of the night.

"I guess." He shifts as if he can feel my gaze. I avert my eyes and he thankfully changes the subject. He pushes to his feet, catching the bag as it slides off his face. "Let's go eat," he suggests. "There's a plain, skinless chicken breast inside that has your name on it."

"Wow, that's so enticing. I'm crushed that I have to say no."

"Come on," he wheedles. "Besides, I need you to tell me what they're saying on Whistle. You can read the bad posts to me while I cook. I'll even use butter for you."

"Oh, well, for a pat of butter, I'll definitely stay for dinner."

He grabs my hand and drags me inside. "How bad is it out there?"

He's not talking about the weather or the campus. He's referring to the social media. These days, stars like Ty can't even fart without some online asshat wondering if he's eating too many beans, and if so, is that going to reduce his speed at the combine? Or worse, does it mean that he's not dedicated enough to the sport to avoid doing stupid things?

42

"It'll be fine. You know how people get. It'll all blow over by the end of the day. Besides, most everyone is talking about that kid who got the DUI charge."

Ty makes a face. "That stupid asshole."

But his tone is more sympathetic than judgmental. I stroke a hand down his back, telling myself that it's a friendly soothing gesture rather than my desire to lay hands on his body again. His anxiety level is creeping up.

"You really think Rhyann's right about me being a bad boyfriend?" Ty asks as we reach the kitchen.

"Yes," I answer immediately. "You're a terrible boyfriend." I drop my hand. It's wrong of me to be touching him like this.

"Damn."

His response to his umpteenth breakup seems so uncharacteristic for Ty, particularly since he never slept with this woman.

"I can't tell if you're upset about getting dumped again or whether you're upset you got dumped by Rhyann." I rummage for a pan and set it on the stove.

"Dana says I should be dating someone. Remy, too." He reaches into the fridge and grabs the chicken. "What do you think? Should I find a girl before the combine?"

Absolutely not. I like it when you're not dating anyone. I don't enjoy images of other girls touching you, loving you swimming around in my head. It's easier for me when you're single. But then it's hard, because I think about all the what ifs and possibilities that really should never, ever see the light of day.

I don't voice a single one of those thoughts. "I don't know. If you want to be in a relationship, then you need to work harder at it. Like football."

"Way too much effort." He seasons the meat and flops it onto the waiting pan.

I grow exasperated. "Are you really thinking about going out with someone because of the draft?"

He scratches his nose and then looks down, pretending to be engrossed by the cooking food. "Maybe not just for the draft. But it does make sense to find someone here at college, right? That way we know she likes me for something other than the size of my wallet."

I offer a dry laugh. "You think girls are dating you because of your sparkling personality? They already see you as a meal ticket, Ty."

"That's grim. Could you at least pretty up the truth and tell me that the girls are dying for me because of my ripped body?"

"No." I stare at his averted profile, glad that he can't see I'm completely lying. "We're too young to think about marriage."

"You were going to get married," he points out. "And you didn't break up with him until you found out he was cheating."

"Please don't follow my terrible relationship example." I think back to the image of Matt and Maribeth holding hands. "You don't have time to foster a long-term relationship. You've got your rookie year coming up. All you're going to be doing is thinking about the game."

He doesn't answer right away. In the kitchen window, his reflection is blurred and faint, like a poor photocopy of a photocopy. And then it hits me.

Ty's brother got married the previous Christmas. There was some convoluted reason due to his girlfriend's academic cheating and getting banned from being around the team, which Knox used to wife that poor girl up. But it's not Knox getting married that eats at Ty, it's that Knox got drafted number three last year. Knox left college early. Entered the draft early. Already has one great rookie season under his belt. And Ty's feeling the pressure.

"You do not need a girlfriend to get drafted high," I reassure him.

He doesn't immediately agree, which means someone has half convinced him that he does. I give up trying to encourage him. He'll have to figure it out himself. Ty's one of the most stubborn and maddening people I know.

Too bad I love him so much.

In a totally platonic, fraternal way, of course.

6

Ara

AFTER OUR BLAND DINNER, TY GOES TO THE GYM TO SWEAT OFF his anxiety while I go home to face my own.

My dad sent me a text from the airplane that reminded me to call my mom. He added two lines of hearts and a phone. I wonder what Arthur Von de Menthe's adoring public would say about his abuse of emojis. There'd probably be an article in the *New Yorker* about how he's turning pop culture on its head.

Dully, I search through my contacts and find Mom's phone. Maybe she's busy and can't answer. A voicemail shows that I attempted contact. I cross my fingers.

"Hello, Aramintha."

Even Dad, who came up with my ridiculous name, never calls me anything but Ara.

"Hi Mom." I flip open my sketchbook. At least I can occupy myself with something enjoyable during this talk.

"You sound so excited to speak to me," she says drolly. There's a shuffling of paper in the background. It's the sound of a thousand insurance policies being sold. Yup, my mom sells insurance, a profession light years away from my arty dad.

"How's business?" I ask.

"It's very good. Young people are reckless and don't foresee the need for good risk aversion products, but the same can't be said about the older generations."

Mom has a real disdain for anyone under the age of thirty. I think she might've been born old.

"I'm good. Thanks for asking. Just working on my senior paper." Just doodling in my sketchbook. Farmer Brown bears a suspicious resemblance to my mother. I erase the sharp chin and make it more rounded.

"I suppose it's a paper on art."

"Yup. I'm writing on the intersectionality of politics and Picasso."

"Such a waste." The rustling on her end is a little faster, as if she's shaking them imagining that it's my shoulders instead. "Are you still working at the gallery?"

"Yes."

"Do you plan to work there after you graduate?"

"No."

"And what will you do?"

"I've applied places," I say defensively. To date, I've only had a few interviews and the one place that did offer me a position did so only after learning that the famous sculptor Arthur von de Menthe was my dad.

"Why you went into art, I'll never know. Your father won't be around to support you forever."

"I know that. I like art and I know a lot about it."

"Because of the way your father raised you."

"Well, he had to, didn't he," I snap. "You weren't around."

There's a brief hesitation, followed by more paper rattling. "Post-partum depression is a very real illness, Aramintha. You shouldn't diminish it."

"You left when I was eight!"

"Are you a doctor, Aramintha?"

"What?"

"Are you?" she presses.

"You know I'm not."

"Then you shouldn't be diagnosing anyone, should you?"

I clench my teeth and remain silent abiding by the adage that if I don't have anything to say, I should shut the hell up.

Mom continues. "As I was saying, if you had gotten a business degree, you could come work for me since apparently you can't get a job on your own."

I text Fleur.

Come into my room and tell me we have to go study right away. I'm about to commit matricide.

"I told your father a hundred times not to encourage your art obsession. At least you aren't trying to be an actual artist. Not that you have the talent of your father, of course."

I redraw the pointy chin on Farmer Brown.

My door flies open.

"Ara! It's time to go study!" Fleur shouts. Her eyes are sparkling mischievously. "Oh no! I didn't realize you were on the phone!"

"I gotta go, Mom. Good talking to you. Thanks for the words of encouragement."

She squawks something, but I hang up before I can make sense of it.

I throw myself backwards on my bed.

"That bad, huh?"

"I'm going to need a glass of wine to calm down," I tell my roommate.

"Sorry, honey." Fleur always is slightly bewildered by the antagonism between me and my mom. Fleur and her mom have an awesome relationship. They talk on the phone once a week. They text daily. My ass can't relate.

"Do you know that my parents used to be best friends?"

"Really? What happened?"

I roll off the bed and gather my research materials. "I happened. Mom got knocked up and Dad wanted to get married. They did, but Dad's first love is his art. Mom didn't like coming in second.

She divorced him because of his emotional neglect. Now they barely talk."

"That sucks."

"Yeah." I don't want to dwell on it. "We better go or there won't be a table at the Commons left."

Fleur runs to grab her bag and we hustle over to the Commons, a large gathering place that has self-serve food and booze. It gets crowded after five, but sometimes you can find a spot around the time that students are hitting the bars.

We're in luck because a group is leaving right when we arrive. I hurry over and spread my research material over the gray specked tabletop while Fleur goes and gets us a tiny bottle of wine to share.

When I started the paper, I was excited about the project, but lately it's become a chore instead of a pleasure. The hundreds of pages of research I've amassed and must distill into one coherent paper are piled up dauntingly.

I reshuffle a few pages and flip open my computer.

"How many pages are you on?" I look up to see Fleur bearing the wine and a single piece of pie.

"Where's your dessert?" I ask, reaching for the plate.

She twists out of my reach. "Ha ha. Get your own if you want one." She plops onto the chair next to me and proceeds to shovel half the pie in her mouth.

Damn. I abandon my laptop and make a begging motion with my hands. "You have to share. I had dinner with Ty and he's still on his veggies-and-chicken-only diet."

"You poor girl." She offers me a forkful of delectable pastry and fruit.

"Thank you," I mumble, mouth too full to answer properly.

"So where are you, seriously?" she asks, setting the plate aside.

"I'm on page four. Tell me again why I decided to do an independent study?"

"Because you would only have class on Tuesday and Thursday, leaving you more time to party, party, party," she recites.

I crawl back up on my chair. "And how much partying have we done?"

"After the National Championship game, we drank for two days straight."

"I felt terrible afterward." I sniff my shoulder. "I swear that if I'm in the right position, I can still smell the Jäger from the bombs we did. It's baked into my skin forever." Not to mention the pathetic lack of control I have over my lust when I'm drinking.

"It was a rough week of recovery, for sure." She polishes off another bite and then flips her wheat-blonde hair over one shoulder. "So let's go out this weekend and get in another party."

"I should write at least four more pages." I thumb listlessly through my research. "I can't believe this thing has to be thirty pages. Who can write thirty pages on anything?"

"Professors."

"But I'm not a professor. I'm a lowly undergrad." I lay my head on the table. "Why didn't you stop my foolishness? This is your job as my best friend."

"First, your best friend is Ty Masters, as he has informed me on nearly every occasion that I have ever seen him. Second, I did question your sanity, but you were all *I'll only have to attend classes two days a week* and *Thirty pages? That's like a page a day for a month. I could do that in my sleep.* And *Classes are for suckers. I'm a senior. This is what seniors do.* And so, in the face of all that logic, I just shut up."

I don't even bother to raise my head to give her the finger. After a few moments, a big bite of pie appears before my eyes. Since I'm easy, I open my mouth, inhale the pie and then sit up like a big girl.

"Thirty pages and you already have four written. And you have, what, ten weeks left?"

I nod, my mouth full of pastry.

"Easy," she continues. "That's like three hundred words a day. You could write that in your sleep."

"I've never written anything longer than ten pages and that was double-spaced with extra-wide margins and a bigger font," I whine. "These four pages are all I've written since January."

"Well, now stress and deadlines will spur you forward." Fleur's not very sympathetic, but that's why I love her. You need a friend who kicks you in the pants.

"You're right." I straighten my papers again. "You're right. I can do this."

She reaches out and taps a blue bejeweled fingernail on a corner of my sketchpad that shows discoloration from the water bath it received this morning. "Rhyann really did throw water in his face. I thought that might be an exaggeration when I heard it."

"Nope. One hundred percent true."

"She looked like a thrower."

"I know, right? That's what I told Ty."

"You were there when they broke up?"

I'm about to launch into a full explanation of what went down when a gorgeous brunette appears at our table. She's wearing a pair of the hottest black skinny jeans, torn at the thigh on the right and the knee on the left. Her top is a striped menswear-inspired thing with a corset waist cinched tight. I look down at my battered Southern U T-shirt and surreptitiously try to brush off the crumbs that are clinging to the fabric right above the T and H.

"Hi."

"Hi," Fleur and I say in unison, while glancing at each other as if to ask, *do you know her?*

The brunette focuses on me. "You're Ara Martin, right?"

"Yes. Have we met before?"

"No. I don't think so. I'm Kathleen Leighton." She holds out her hand.

I look at it, then at my best friend, and then Kathleen's hand again before shaking it. Is this a business meeting?

She takes a seat. "I saw you at the Row House this morning with Ty Masters," she explains.

Fleur lets out an audible groan. This isn't the first time that some girl has tried to get to Ty through me, as evidenced by the Bathroom Batgirl, but before I can tell Kathleen that I don't run Masters' Tinder account, she barrels ahead. "I'm sure you've heard this all before, but I'm a big believer in seizing opportunities when they appear. I couldn't help but overhear some of the, ah, conversation that Ty had with his ex-girlfriend."

"Couldn't help, my ass," Fleur mumbles.

The new girl ignores my roommate and fixes a blinding white smile on me. "I'd love an introduction."

"To Ty?" I ask stupidly.

"That's right."

"What for?" I blame the brightness of her smile for numbing a few of my brain cells.

The lips curve even wider. She has a Kylie Jenner mouth—wide and very sexy. Why are there so many gorgeous girls on this campus?

"Because he's gorgeous, skilled, and available."

"If you really overheard, then you'd know he's a terrible boyfriend."

She waves an airy hand. "Maybe to others, but I could manage someone like him."

Manage him? Like he's a restaurant or business?

"I'm quite good at keeping busy," she continues, "I don't need someone to pay attention to me twenty-four-seven."

"You say that now, but the tenth time he cancels on you, it'll be a different story," I tell her, gathering my wits. "I'm sharing this with you so as to avoid a tragic end where you go to prison for trying to kill him."

"Are you saving him for yourself?" She cocks an eyebrow in a quizzical manner.

"Yes," Fleur pipes up.

"No," I say at the same time.

I send my friend a glare. "No, I'm not. We're friends." I turn to Kathleen. "If you really believe in the direct method, then go talk to Ty."

"Oh, I plan to, but I saw you here and knew I should introduce myself since we'll probably be seeing a lot of each other because you're obviously a very close friend of Ty's."

My jaw drops down. I can't help but be impressed by her ballsy self-confidence. I sit up straighter. "Well, you've got ovaries of steel, but Ty makes his own decisions."

"Of course, but it doesn't hurt for his good friend to put in a word for me. You're wondering what's in it for you," she says, misreading me entirely. "I'll tell you. I can help Ty achieve his great potential. And as his friend, I know that's what you want."

It's hard to argue with that.

"Every girl would like to get her claws in Ty, but just because you date him doesn't mean you'll end up with a ring on your finger. Ty's interest in Rhyann died right after she met his brother," Fleur informs the new girl.

I scowl at Fleur for bringing up something so personal about Ty to a total stranger. When I try kicking her under the table, I miss and end up striking the center pole. "Ow!"

The two ignore me.

"His twin, you mean?" Kathleen prompts.

She's really done her research.

Fleur nods confidently. "If you can't tell them apart, then you're doomed."

Kathleen is unfazed. "I could tell them apart once I got to know them."

"Ha!" Fleur exclaims. "Not even their mother can always tell them apart. I don't know anyone who can except Knox's wife and Ara here." She points to me triumphantly. I want to sink into the floor.

Kathleen's smile and confidence don't waver. She drops a card onto my papers. "I'll be talking to Ty later, but if you run into him first and you want to help him out, tell him to call me."

She gives the two of us a finger wave and sashays off, leaving her white card lying in the middle of our table. Fleur and I both stare at it.

"What just happened?" I ask slowly.

"I think you got hit on by proxy."

"I shouldn't be impressed, but I am."

"She must be pre-law." Fleur plucks the card off the table and examines it. "Who has cards in college?"

I take it from her. "Ambitious people." The cardstock is heavy. "Smart people." Her name followed by all her contact information is printed in black embossed lettering. "People who already have jobs."

I let it fall to the tabletop.

Fleur grabs my hand, her grip surprisingly strong. "Now's the time," she says urgently.

I quirk a questioning eyebrow. "The time for what?"

"To be honest about your feelings toward Ty. Once he graduates, the opportunity will be gone. He'll be in some big city getting hit on by a different girl every night and you'll be dealing with overly pretentious art collectors who don't know a Picasso from a Pasternak."

"Pasternak's not a collector favorite. Lots of people wouldn't know who he is."

"You're avoiding the subject."

With a sigh, I tug my hand out of hers. "I'm trying to, but you aren't allowing it. Ty and I are friends. We'll be friends for a long time. That's worth more than anything."

The real truth is that Ty is a terrible boyfriend. And I don't blame these girls for breaking up with him. He never pays attention to them. Never answers their calls. Never replies to their texts. Calls them only when he wants something.

He has one true love. It's football. I don't think he's capable of multi-tasking. Until the game is over for him, he's just going to go through an endless cycle of short relationships. Do I want to be his forever friend or one of the hundred girls he dates for three months and then forgets? I mean, I get that playing pro football is something only a tiny fraction of a fraction of people get to do. But I don't want to be with someone where I place second in his heart. I'd grow to hate him like my mom grew to hate my dad.

"If you say so," Fleur murmurs, but her heart's not in it. She pushes her plate to the side and pulls out her project planner. "If it were me, I'd have Ty handcuffed to me by the end of the week."

I don't doubt it. Fleur student teaches a class of rowdy five-year-olds. Ty went once to give a talk to the kids and said he'd rather spend a month being a tackle dummy than go through the terror of answering questions from twenty inquisitive children. But Fleur eats up the noisy rabble-rousers. It gives her energy. Handling one grown football player would be nothing for her.

It would take everything I had and then some to throw my lot in with Ty. We'd have maybe five minutes of happiness followed by years of recrimination and that is if he even remembered me down the road.

I push the morbid thoughts aside and reapply myself to my paper, punching out a full page of words. Section One is almost coming to a close, I note with satisfaction.

"There you are."

I nearly groan out loud in dismay to see Van Riley appear at my table.

Fleur wrinkles her nose. "What do you want?"

Which is what I'd like to say, but he's technically my boss so I paste a pretty smile on my face and say, "I'm here. Did you need something?"

"Come in early tomorrow," he orders.

"Tomorrow's Sunday."

"Aren't you bright? Seven am." He walks off without another word.

"What an asshole," Fleur gripes.

"Assholes are ashamed to be compared to him," I mutter, but enter an alarm in my phone. I've always felt a tad guilty about Van Riley, which is why I let him abuse me. It took him three years to get hired at Marissa Baron's gallery. It took me three minutes. And Van has never let me forget it.

7

Ty

AFTER ARA LEAVES, I KICK REMY'S ASS IN FIFA FOR A COUPLE hours.

"Ara turn you down or something?" he whines after I score another goal on him.

"Nope." I position my player on the left side of the pitch. "Never asked her."

"Why not?"

"Because she'd take my balls and toss them on the street, like what I'm doing to you now." Plus, it'd ruin our friendship. Besides, you don't play games with people, especially ones you care about.

Remy mutters a curse and jogs his gassed-out star player to meet mine. I power kick the ball down field to avoid Messi. Remy chases after me and pokes the ball out of bounds, giving me a free corner kick.

"Goddammit!" he yells, throwing his controller on the cushion. "I'm going to get a drink. You?"

"Pass." I'm not drinking until after the draft. As I'm lining up to do my free kick, my phone buzzes. I grab it.

Wanna skype?

Y. 5 min.

"Remy, it's your lucky day. I'm done. Gotta call my bro." I toss my controller on the coffee table. "Practice, will ya? I'm getting bored," I call over my shoulder.

A booming "Fuck you!" follows me up the stairs to my room.

Grinning, I flick on my laptop and ring up Knox.

When he appears on the screen, I nearly fall over in surprise. "When'd you get your hair cut?"

He rubs a hand over the back of his undercut. "Weird, isn't it? I got it done yesterday. You?"

I catch myself almost doing the same action and stuff my hands under my thighs. "Day before."

Looking at Knox is like looking in the mirror. We're exactly the same, down to the small mole we both have at the base of the neck. I'd been growing my hair out since the Championship game, but decided that I should have it cut for the combine. And now here is Knox, who lives a thousand miles away in New York City, getting the same exact cut. Sometimes even I am weirded out by the twin connection.

Knox laughs. "Wait until I tell Ellie. She's gonna freak."

That makes two of us. "Did you have something you needed?"

"I felt a disturbance in the force." He grins.

We're twins. A thousand miles of distance and we still know exactly how the other feels. In some ways, it's comforting. I'm never really alone. In other ways, it's a hassle. It'd be nice to have a moment of privacy, but since that's not the case with us, there's no point in lying about it.

"Rhyann broke up with me."

"Good. She wasn't right for you," he says blithely.

"She broke up with me because I forgot her birthday."

"Nah, you forgot her birthday because she wasn't the right one."

Knox believes in destiny. He said he felt the earth move when he first laid eyes on Ellie and knew immediately that she was his soulmate. He uses that word, too. *Soulmate.*

That's where we differ. I believe in making your own future.

Knox believes in fate, and when he met Rhyann and she couldn't tell us apart, he immediately dismissed her as *not for me.*

"Well, whatever the reason, I'm currently single. Dana thinks that's going to hurt my draft stock."

Knox falls silent at the mention of my agent. My brother is not a fan of Dana's, disliking the way Dana hounded me right after the Championship game. Knox felt like I should sign with his agent, but I wanted to go my own path.

"I don't know. I did get questions at the combine about Ellie, and they all seemed pretty happy to find out we were married. That said, as long as you can deliver on the field, it doesn't matter what you do off of it. I can't imagine someone passing you up for another player because you don't have a girl."

I scrub a hand down my face. "This is bullshit, you know. I'm not going to date some random chick just to up my draft stock."

"Speaking of the bullshit—" His face slides off the edge of the camera lens as he digs for something. He returns with a piece of paper. "I'm gonna send this to you, but here's a list of questions that me and a couple of my teammates remember being asked at the combine. Want to practice?"

I grimace, but nod. "Go ahead."

"Okay, first up, 'Do you want to be a cat or a dog?'"

I'm prepared for this one, because it's one of the more well-known stupid questions we get.

"Depends on what type of cat or dog. Are we talking domestic or wild? Is it small lap dog versus kitten, or hunting dog versus a Maine coon?"

Knox gives me the thumbs up. It's always good to ask for clarification to see if the questioner will give you a hint as to what answer he's looking for. "Let's go with domestic animals, regardless of size."

"It'd depend on the situation. If I need to climb, I'd want to be a cat. If I need to find something, then a dog."

"I like that." He nods approvingly. "Looks like you prepared for that one. Okay, let me see if I can find one you aren't ready for..." He trails off as he scans the paper. "It's Friday night. You're at an away game and a fan finds her way into your bedroom. Do you have sex with her or do you send her away?"

"Is that really a question on the list?"

He peers at me over the paper. "Are you refusing to answer?"

"No." I scowl. "I'm tired and I've got to sleep."

"Are you a pussy?"

"I already answered the cat versus dog bullshit."

Knox busts out laughing. "All right. But there're going to be questions like that. I had an exec ask me if Ellie was going to travel around with the team. Apparently, some of the new wives do that."

"What'd you tell them?"

"That she'd be at home."

"Was that the right answer?"

"Don't know. I was drafted before the team that asked got a crack at me. You're going to be fine. Don't worry."

"I'm not worrying."

"Sure."

We both know I am. Everyone is. An athlete that says he isn't nervous before the combine is one that's going to fall on his face. Nerves keep your edges sharp.

Knox fills me in on his plans to take Ellie to France before draft day, but assures me he'll be back in time to go Eakins Oval with me. Everyone assumes I'm getting an invite to the draft which is only extended to twenty-five or so players.

Even if I do get the FedEx-ed letter that is sent out, I'm not sure I want to attend. There's always a small percentage that turn down the invitation. I've never enjoyed the celebrity part of the game, but Knox says I shouldn't miss it. We'll see. After discussing what to get Mom for Mother's Day as well as her upcoming June birthday, we say our goodbyes.

I climb into bed and shoot Ara a text.

Me: What's better? Cat or dog?

Her: Why not both?

Me: Choose one.

Her: Don't want to.

Me: U really want to have both a cat and dog?

Her: Yes. And to eat ice cream for breakfast. Why? Is that bad?

I start chuckling.

Me: No. We're adults now. We get to choose how we adult.

Her: I'll bring you a pint of Cherry Garcia tomorrow.

My mouth salivates at the thought of ice cream. When was the last time I had something good like that?

Me: Don't tempt me.

Her: Party pooper. Day after draft, we're eating everything. French fries, double cheeseburgers with fried onion rings, chocolate shakes with the real whipped cream.

Me: Stop.

Her: I have sexy pics. Will send.

An image of Ara's smooth, bare skin flashes in front of me. My tongue tingles, as if it just tasted something sweet. My fingers curl into my palms, recalling something soft and knee-weakeningly wet on them. Forcefully, I push those sensations out of my head. Ara's a friend, not an object of lust. I shake myself like a dog and reply.

Me: I'm blocking you.

She sends me a picture of a Shake Shack burger. The girl is evil.

Me: I'm done with you.

Her: You'll never be done with me. Mwahahaha

She attaches a gif of Gru laughing maniacally.

Her: Off to bed. Will send you more food porn in the morning.

Me: I'm really blocking you.

Her: I know you can't live without me. Kisses!

I shove the phone under my pillow. She's probably right. I'll miss my friends when I graduate, but not Ara because we'll always stay in touch. I can't imagine life without her.

§

I WAKE up to the smell of pancakes and bacon grease. My stomach rumbles in anticipation.

"You don't get any of that," I tell it. It rumbles again mockingly.

Damn it, Ara. She knows better than to tempt me. I'm going to have to replace her saltshaker with sugar or something to get back at her.

I haul my ass out of bed, get my running clothes on, and wander downstairs.

Instead of Ara, though, it's Remy's girlfriend frying up food at the stove. Guess Ara is saved. Remy's at the counter shoveling carbs in his mouth while his girlfriend flips over another piece of fat. I grow faint with want.

"It's whole wheat made with agave syrup and oats. The meat's turkey bacon. Grab a plate." She waves a spatula in my direction.

I don't have to be told twice. I rush over to the counter and fill up a plate. "You're an angel, Nichole." I kiss her cheek.

"I know I am."

I give Remy a thumbs up, which he returns. His mouth is too full to answer and soon mine will be too. With a grin, I dig in.

"I hear you're taking applications for a new girlfriend," she mentions as she flips another cake from the pan to the plate.

"Yes. Is this a proposal? Because if so, I accept. I knew you'd wise up and realize the better man is me."

"Fuck you, Masters. You can't take my girl," Remy protests, spitting bits of cake and syrup out.

"I'm not taking anyone. It's Nichole who's leaving you. And I'm sorry, man, but it's every dude for himself." I pat my lap. "Come over here, sweet thing. Let me give you some morning love."

Remy turns to his girlfriend for help. "Baby, stick up for your man."

"What's your offer?" she asks me instead. "Remy's promised to buy me a Beemer out of his signing bonus."

"What a cheap bastard. A Beemer? That's the cheap B car. I'm springing for Bentleys for everyone."

She pretends to think it over. "I don't know. That sounds intriguing."

My roommate jumps out of his chair, grabs his girlfriend, and throws her over his shoulder. "I'll show you intriguing."

She beats her small fists against Remy's back. "Put me down! You're messing with my hair."

"You shouldn't have threatened me." He slaps her ass. "Better get the stove, Masters," he cautions before disappearing up the stairs.

"Ask Ara," Nichole yells.

"Ask her what?"

But Remy's carried Nichole too far away for me to hear her response.

I pull out my phone and send Ara a text.

Me: Am I supposed to ask you something?

Her: Like how amazing I am?

Me: Besides that. Nichole said I should ask you.

Her: What?

Me: Dunno. That's why I'm asking you.

Her: No clue. Go ask her to clarify.

Me: Can't. Remy hauled her away for being mouthy.

*Her: *cue 100 eyerolls**

Me: Want to come over? I've got turkey bacon and ww pancakes.

Her: I'd rather stab my throat with a fork. Besides, am waiting for Jerkface to show up. Supposed to meet him at 7.

Me: It's 7:20.

Her: I know.

Me: It's Sunday.

Her: I know this too.

Me: Why are you meeting him on Sunday?

But I know why. Ara feels guilty because, according to Van Asshole, she took the job that was supposed to go to him. She tried to quit after she found out, but instead the gallery owner hired Van Asshole, too. Ever since then, Ara's bent over backwards to make up for what she calls her 'privileged background.' And Van Asshole takes full advantage.

Her: Bc I'm still in my sucking up phase.

Me: You've been in your sucking up phase for almost six months now.

Her: Again, I know this.

Me: Let me know if i can talk some sense into him.
Her: With your fists?
Me: I'm not ruling it out.
Her: Shit. He's here. Talk to you later.

I drop the phone on the counter and pick up my fork. I'm not a fan of that Riley guy. He's been abusing Ara for months. She said it's easier this way, less drama. But it shouldn't be either scenario. She sucks Riley's metaphorical dick for the better part of two semesters or she endures endless sniping and criticism? Fuck both those options.

Ara got that job because she knows a helluva lot about art, not just because her dad is one of the foremost modern sculptors. She would've gotten the job regardless of who her father is. Not that I can convince Ara of that. If she were an athlete, she could prove herself on the field. Apparently in an art gallery you can't do that.

The one thing I've always loved about sports is that you're measured by your skill and performance, not by how good of a public speaker you are or how many people you know. It's the stats you rack up on the field that count.

It's why I hate the drama of the non-physical shit at the combine. I'm fine with grading us based on how fast we run the four/forty or how far we jump. But whether I've got a girlfriend? Whether I answer the cat versus dog question right? Whether the president of operations think I smell okay? I hate all of that.

I hate it for me and I hate it for Ara. Since I can't punch out the NFL execs, though, maybe I could pound Riley's face into the dirt.

I sigh. Yeah, probably not.

But if Ara asked, I definitely would.

8

Ara

VAN SNEERS AT MY YOGA PANTS AND T-SHIRT. "THIS IS AN ART gallery not a gym. Wear something appropriate next time."

"I thought I was here to copy." I give myself a once over. I showered this morning and felt good about even doing that.

"It's still a place of business and thus, you should wear business-appropriate attire." He sniffs and readjusts the sleeve of his perfectly pressed black button down.

I swear I took a shower. "Okay. Next time I come in on a Sunday morning, I'll dress up. For now, I'm here." I spread my arms out. "What do you want me to do?"

"Copy this." He shoves a handout at me.

"How many?" I ask. They look to be prints of Thompson Moore's gagtastic work.

The brochure is a five-color glossy touting the upcoming showing of a local multimedia artist specializing in grass art, which is exactly what it sounds like—the application of grass on canvas.

Thompson Moore, whose name makes me think of the paint line, is selling moderately well to a certain set that finds his rural paintings appealing. I find them boring and try-hard, and despite his niche audience, I don't find him worthy of a showing. I suggested to Marissa that Moore's work might not be the best use of her space. Van bit my head off for being non-supportive and Marissa cried.

Dad, on the other hand, nearly laughed his ass off when I told him of Marissa's new signing.

"Five hundred. And then bind them. Or is that beneath you?"

Despite the fact I was hired a year before Van Asshole and despite the fact that we are both in the same grade, he became my de facto supervisor when Marissa extended him the full-time assistant's job after graduation. That invitation came after Marissa learned that Dad was marrying Holly.

"Five hundred folded brochures coming right up." I'm in no mood to argue. My heart's a little sore over the idea of Ty dating someone new already.

I almost fell apart when I heard he was getting back together with Rhyann after the Bowl game. They had been broken up since Christmas and I thought it was over for them or I'd like to think I'd have never kissed him Bowl night.

It doesn't matter. He doesn't remember what happened. If he did, he would've said something to me.

Right?

Ty's been a stand-up guy to the girls he's dated. He was never into one-night stands despite the many, many, many offers. He tried to be upfront with the girls, telling them that football was his focus. I have to believe if he remembered our hookup, he wouldn't have jumped at Rhyann's invitation to return to her side.

Or he hated the experience with me so much that he had to erase that from his mind by immediately having sex with someone else.

That thought causes actual physical pain. I hold a hand to my stomach.

"Are you actually going to make copies, or is that kind of manual labor too menial for von de Menthe's daughter?" Van Asshole snipes.

I look up from the copier to see him standing at the door,

hands on his hips, disgust on his face. He really hates me, from the moment that we first met. I got the job because of who my father is and he doesn't let me forget it for a minute. On the plus side, Van Asshole is consistent, if nothing else. Since he got the job in August, he's done nothing but look at me with jealous loathing.

"I'm copying." I set the papers into the machine and punch the start key. To irritate Van and make myself feel better, I smile as bright and wide as I can.

Predictably, Van Asshole is instantly suspicious. "Why are you so cheerful?"

"Got laid last night," I lie for the sheer pleasure of watching him grow even more perturbed.

"You're disgusting," he mutters.

"If you stick around, I'm going to assume you want details."

He whirls, slamming the door to the copy room behind him. I allow myself a small grin.

The copying takes longer than I anticipate. Van Asshole checks on me twice, but only stays long enough to grab the few bound copies I've managed to make. While he's tapping his toe impatiently at the door, I hum as if I'm reliving the graphic details of my wild night.

"Don't say it," Van warns.

"Say what?" I ask innocently.

"Whatever is going on in your filthy mind. It's sexual harassment to talk about your lurid sex activities."

"I wasn't offering any details. It sounds like your imagination is working overtime, though."

"Ugh." He grimaces. "Can you do this faster? We need them before the turn of the century."

"I am only one person, Van," I say stiffly. I wonder how much bail money I would need if I assaulted Van with the stapler. Might be worth it.

"Marissa wants me to go to the store and get some tablecloths, so I'm going to have to trust you to do this job."

"It's copying and binding," I say with exaggerated patience. "I'm not five."

He plucks a speck of dust off his sleeve. "Make sure everything is in order. The last time you did it, some of the handouts were messed up. I had to cover for you and Marissa was so upset."

"I don't remember doing the last handouts," I say. We both know full well that he did them and not me. Besides, technically we're both assistants. I want to shout that he's not my boss, but both of us know that Marissa would back him over me any day.

I'd leave, but I need this job on my résumé and I need a good recommendation from Marissa so I don't have to work under Van Asshole for the rest of my life.

My tongue is sore from biting on it though.

"I'm sure you did," he lies through his perfect teeth.

Inwardly, I seethe. Outwardly, I give him a terse nod. "Like I said, I'll get it done."

"Fine. Marissa will be in at three."

I allow myself the childish pleasure of sticking my tongue out behind his back before turning back to the copier.

About ten minutes and a few hundred copies later, I hear, "Knock. Knock."

"Come in," I yell.

Ty saunters in sporting a Southern U football T-shirt stretched across his broad chest. His hands are stuffed into the pockets of his loose-fitting joggers and on his feet are a pair of athletic slides. Despite the casual attire, he's so attractive I forget to breathe.

Van and I share this office, but even so, it's a tiny space—barely big enough to accommodate a copy machine slash printer, a rickety table, and stock shelves full of catering supplies. Marissa hosts a lot of parties here.

With Ty, the small room seems to shrink until there's barely any place I can move without bumping into him. Carefully, I edge around the table toward the copier and gesture for my friend to take a seat.

"What're you here for?"

Instead of sitting down, he leans over my shoulder. "Figured I'd come and see if you needed any help. Do you?"

"Sure. How good are you at binding shit?"

"I've got my master's certificate in binding things." He playfully flexes for me.

"That'll come in handy," I say sarcastically, mostly to cover up the way that my mouth grows dry at how every part of his body is so perfect.

His T-shirt is so worn that it clings to his abs in a way that should be outlawed. With his arm lifted and his biceps flexed, I can see the chiseled perfection of his stomach and chest.

I push the rock-hard biceps out of my way because friends are not supposed to be ogling friends like this. I point to the chair and the binding machine. "We're doing five hundred of these babies, so don't wear yourself out on the first batch."

Ty gives me a jaunty salute and then drops into the chair. When he starts to fiddle with the knobs, I rush over.

"Don't do that." I bat his hands away. "Van will have a fit. I once moved his armrest to the side and didn't reposition it the right way and he had a litter of kittens, yelling about how I shouldn't be touching his stuff."

Ty's face grows dark. "Van Riley is a punk drunk on his own tiny amount of power."

"I know." I sigh and rub a weary hand across my forehead. "But when I graduate, I'll be done with him forever. At my next job, I promise you can play with the chair to your heart's content."

He mumbles about wanting to play with something else.

"What?"

"Nothing." He blows his hair out of his face. "I FaceTimed with Knox last night."

"Yeah? What's he have to say?" I stack the first article onto the feeder, dial fifty copies and let the machine do its work.

"He got a haircut the other day."

Ty sounds disgruntled and the sour expression on his face makes me laugh. "Let me guess. He has the same exact cut."

"Yes." He slams his palm on the desk. "How is that possible?"

"I think the better question is, why are you surprised?" Ty and Knox have a unique, almost eerie, connection. When Knox was going through a bad time with his girlfriend, Ty knew immediately. When Ty tore a ligament in his leg in the second to last game of the season but didn't tell anyone other than me, Knox was on the phone with him that night. They seem to know when the other is hurting or happy. Whether this is normal or extraordinary, I wouldn't know. Ty's the only twin I've ever encountered.

"I guess I shouldn't be by now." He tips his head over the back of the chair at an angle that makes my neck ache just to watch. "Knox wanted me to go to the same school as him. Did I tell you this?"

He had, a while back, but it's obvious he wants to talk so I make a noncommittal noise in the back of my throat. Wordlessly, I hand him a stack of papers. He sticks the first set into the binding machine.

"He wanted me to go to Western with him. Talked about all the Championships we could win together. He'd play the right side and I'd play the left. It's rare for a team to have one good pass rusher, let alone two, so our defense would dominate."

"But you came here instead," I say for him.

"Yep. Mom and Dad weren't thrilled because they worried we'd play against each other. Knox was pissed off because he felt that we shouldn't separate, but I..." He trails off.

"You wanted to have your own identity," I supply.

"That sounds stupid when you say it out loud," he grumbles.

I pluck the second stack of collated papers off the copy machine and dump them on the desk. "Which is why I said it." I run a hand up the back of his undercut. "Knox probably got his hair cut this way because Ellie saw the same Snapchat post of Oliver Graham as I did. That's why I thought you should do it."

"Yeah?" He leans into my palm.

The soft hair tickles my nerve endings and sends a tingling

sensation from my hand to the middle of my legs. I drop my hand abruptly. His head falls back.

"Hey," he protests.

I point to the papers. "Get to work."

My tone is sharper than I intended, but Ty is unbothered. He merely pulls out his phone, plays some old-school hip-hop, and gets to work. For the next thirty minutes, I copy and collate while he runs the binding machine. Or rather, I copy and brood while he binds.

I don't know why I'm acting like this. Ty and I have been friends for four years. After our first encounter when he asked me out as a joke, we agreed that we'd be the best of friends and that's what we've been. For four years, I've leaned on him and he's leaned on me and all those awkward physical reactions that pop up with people you're attracted to have been easily pushed aside. Most of the time.

I guess my melancholy and recently discovered clinginess are due to the fact that we're parting in a little over two months. He'll be in whatever city, playing ball, being bombarded with more salacious invitations than he can handle, and I'll be in some gallery, putting together buy brochures for the artist du jour.

"That's a heavy sigh," he remarks.

I twirl around to find him standing right behind me. At some point while I was brooding, he'd crept closer. Now there's barely enough space between us to fit one of the assignments. If I breathe, my tits will brush against his chest. So I don't breathe. But I can't help but notice the citrus scent of his shampoo, the mango orange one I bought him two weeks ago. Even though it's only nearing lunchtime, stubble has started to form on his chin. The urge to touch it is nearly irresistible.

I swallow, and the lump in my throat scratches every inch as it goes down to sit like a ball of lead in my gut.

"Something wrong?" Ty asks, dipping his head close to mine. His bright, gorgeous green eyes peer into mine. I can see myself in his pupil as he examines me.

I run my tongue across my lip to wet its dry surface. His eyes follow the trail. A gleam is there, one that my dirty mind reads as desire. *Stop fantasizing*, I scold myself. I lean back against the copier, trying to create some distance, but there isn't any to be found.

There's only his hard body a puff away from mine. I take a shallow breath.

"Ara?"

Is his voice husky or am I imagining it?

"Yeah?" I croak.

"You okay?"

I gather the two wits I have left and twist around to face the copy machine. Only now my ass is nestled up against his groin. Is that a—I close my eyes. *Get a grip on yourself, girl!*

"Of course I am," I say out loud.

"Your face was red." He leans forward, his arm reaching out.

"What are—"

His hand bypasses me and grabs a stack of papers off the copier. I slump against the machine, partly in relief and partly in regret. He wasn't there to feel me up, to tell me that our friendship wasn't enough or that he was tired of being my barely older brother on campus. He was reaching for more papers to bind.

I feel him shuffle back to the desk and I wait until the heat in my cheeks dwindles and my heart is pumping at a normal rate before turning around.

I drag the collar of my sweatshirt up over my mouth and stare at my muddled reflection in the window that overlooks the back alley. My ponytail is askew. My baby hairs have gotten loose and are curling around my face. I have a zit on the side of my cheek that won't seem to go away. I blame that on stress.

Fleur's warning rings in my ears. If I don't make a move on Ty now, it'll be too late...

I give myself a mental slap.

No. I'm not making a move on my friend. That's stupid. He'd run away screaming or fall over and laugh himself into a hernia. Neither response would be amusing to me. We're friends. Really good friends and that will last longer than any relationship, as evidenced by my long-running single status and his long-running inability to keep a relationship status.

"How's the paper going?" His question pulls me out of my stupid reverie.

"Decent. I wrote two pages last night."

"Sounds good. How about our bunny?"

My heart lurches again. It sounds like he's saying baby. *What about our baby?*

"I told you to pretend that you've never seen it."

"You have any new pages?" he asks, ignoring my previous statement.

"If I did, you can't read them."

"Why? I liked it."

"You like it because we're friends."

"Ah, no. You don't hesitate to tell me when I've had a bad game."

"That's because you have a huge ego. Mine, as it relates to this project, is weak and fragile."

"Hmmm. Okay."

I cast a look over my shoulder. His head is down. I can only see his profile—the sharp jawline, the proud nose, the long eyelashes. I sigh silently and turn back to the copier. It beeps to let me know that it's out of paper. I bend down to change it. Behind me, Ty coughs.

"There's a bottle of water in my backpack," I tell him.

"Got it." He sounds funny, but it's probably because he's choking.

"This room is so dry," I say.

"Uh huh."

I shove the paper drawer closed and restart the machine. It whirs happily as it swallows a page and spits it out again.

"Who's Kathleen Leighton?" he says suddenly.

I spin around and see Kathleen's business card between his long fingers.

"Ahhhhh," I stall. What do I tell him? I can say it's no one or I can tell him the truth. I guess I need to know whether he needs it. "Your agent still on your case about finding a girlfriend before the combine?"

The corner of his lip twitches. I'll take that as a yes. Then a speculative expression creeps into his eyes.

"Oh no." I'd back away but I'm already snugged up against the copy machine.

"Why not?" He stands up.

"Because."

He takes a step forward. "You know me better than anyone except my family. We wouldn't have to make up a complicated backstory. We say that we've been friends since your freshman year and recently discovered our feelings. Scouts, coaches, GMs will eat that shit up. Plus, I trust you."

"No."

"Why not?" he cajoles. "Come on. You'd be perfect."

His feet are almost touching mine.

"All these fake dating situations end up the same way. Someone catches feelings and then gets hurt. Worse, our friendship would suffer."

"You're too smart to fall in love with me." He smiles confidently, reaching a hand out to touch my cheek.

I duck out of the way and scowl. Of course, he thinks he's immune.

"I'm talking about you," I say sourly. "I don't want you to fall for me because then I'll have to break your heart and all our friends will get upset. They'll have to choose sides and since everyone loves me, you'll be all alone." Out of desperation, I grab the card from his fingers and hold it in front of his nose. "This girl wants you. Call her."

I let it go. Predictably, he catches it. I turn and press the start button on the copier.

"What's this?" he asks. His voice isn't right at my ear, so I presume he's backed off. Thank God.

"If you're serious about getting a new girl, this one wants to audition."

"Explain."

"She approached me and Fleur when we were studying at the student union. Said that she saw Rhyann break up with you and figured she could handle you."

"She sounds one apple short of a full barrel."

I choke on a muffled laugh. "Fleur and I figure her for pre-law major. She knows what she wants and is going to acquire you."

Ty's still silent. I peek over my shoulder to see him staring at the card like he's entranced.

"If you need a girl, then here's one who's ready, willing, and able. She already knows you're a terrible boyfriend and says that she can handle you because she's got a busy schedule." The pitch for Ty to date someone else makes me slightly sick to my stomach. But we both know he can't date me. And if he's so intrigued by her dumb business card, he might as well pursue her.

"She said all that?" He raises disbelieving eyes to meet mine.

"All of it. Ask Fleur if you don't believe me. She was there the whole time."

"No, I believe you. It's just...weird. Right? That's weird."

"It is, but...."

"But what?" he prompts.

"But this is the kind of thing I think you can expect. Didn't you tell me that Knox ran into a girl who snuck into the locker room by riding in a dirty laundry bin?"

He makes a face and nods.

"Sounds like having a girlfriend is good protection, and if it helps you in the draft, then maybe it's for the best."

"I still think this is bananas." But he tucks the card in his pocket.

My heart sinks. Suddenly, I don't want Ty around. "I can finish the rest by myself."

He eyes the pile of unbound brochures skeptically. "Really."

"Yes." I give him a push. "Besides, Marissa and Van will be back and if they see you helping me, I'll get in trouble."

"Those two need a boot up their ass," he grumbles. "I don't know why you haven't quit yet."

"Because this looks good on my résumé."

"You only need to put down that Artie's your dad."

This time I push Ty as hard as I can. "Okay, and you can drop Dana and sign with your brother's agent."

"Low blow, Martin." But he's not seriously offended and, more importantly, he leaves.

I sag in relief the moment he's gone. Really. Relief is totally what I'm feeling. Not regret.

9

Ara

"I CANNOT BELIEVE YOU GAVE HIM HER CARD."

Fleur hasn't stopped glaring at me in disgust since I came home.

I drop onto the sofa and say, "Why should I be the one to stand between destiny and true love?"

She throws a pillow at me. "Seriously, you make me so annoyed sometimes."

I shove the pillow behind my head. "And you need to give up on this pipe dream that Ty and I are going to end up together."

"You're Ty's destiny and you know it."

"Because I can tell the two of them apart? That's not the basis of a real relationship!" I scoff. "I want to be with someone who loves me for me, not because I have one good party trick."

"You have more than that," she hisses back. "You're best friends. You spend all your free time together. You know each other inside and out. *And* you have that one really good party trick."

"If that's the criteria for a relationship, you and I should get married," I point out.

"We're not sexually attracted to each other."

"That's Ty and my problem."

"Right. Like you wouldn't attack Ty if he crooked his finger at you? Ha!"

"I guess I should've said it's Ty's problem."

This shuts her up for a moment. She slumps onto the cushion next to me. I pat her head, thinking back to the night of the Bowl game when he was very attracted to me, judging by the size of his boner and the way his lips devoured mine, his hands fused to my body.

But it must've been the alcohol fueling his desire because he hasn't touched me since. Hell, he doesn't remember touching me at all.

"I'm sorry. I didn't mean to make you feel bad." Her hand lands on my shoulder.

"You didn't make me feel bad." Fleur's not the one with the memory loss. "But you need to give up on this Ty and me thing. It's not going to happen."

"Fine, be a dream killer," she says but changes the subject. "Should we eat?"

"Yeah. Mexican?"

"Give me five. I gotta pee." Fleur hops up and races to the bathroom.

While she's gone, I take the time to straighten my messy pony-tail and swipe new gloss across my lips. I wish I could forget about Bowl night. It's not doing me any good. Plus, because my imagina-tion seems to have broken free of any sensible boundaries, I'm bringing the mood down around me. I force the dangerous thoughts deep into the safe house in the back of my head. No good comes from entertaining fantasies about Ty.

Fleur joins me at the door, wearing a cropped hoodie paired with black yoga pants, same as me.

"I think the thing I'm going to miss the most is wearing yoga pants twenty-four-seven," she says.

"Me, too."

"I'm starting to feel homesick over all of our friends."

"Ah ha!" I point a finger at her.

"What?"

"Sorry. I was thinking about how we're all being nostalgic because graduation is coming so soon." Realization slaps me awake. Fleur's infected like me. I knew my stirred-up feelings toward Ty weren't genuine. We're all feeling a bit melancholic. Yeah, that's it.

"You could keep working at Marissa's. Then we could keep hanging out together," Fleur says for the hundredth time as we leave the apartment.

"She's already given the permanent job to Van." Which is why he acts like my boss, even though I have worked for Marissa longer.

"Only because you told her you were looking at other places. Even your dad wants you to stay. One word from him and Van Riley would be out the door, waiting by the curb like a trash can."

Which is exactly why I'm not staying. I'd gotten the job from Marissa because she thought I was a package deal. Hire me, get a gallery showing with my father. And Dad was ready to make good on that expectation until I told him no. I want to get a job on my own merit. Besides, I can't pimp out my dad for a job.

"I'll find something else," I say, but my words lack confidence. I haven't had a decent interview for months.

"I know you will. I'm so done with school. I don't even know if I can last until Spring Break."

"Spring Break is two weeks away."

"My point exactly. I'm counting the hours until I'm on that flight to the Bahamas." She raises both arms in the air. "Sun, beach, hot boys, get ready because Fleur the Hurricane is coming!"

"I think you should change your Spring Break name. Hurricanes and resorts don't mix."

"Fleur the Happy Holiday Helper is coming," she yells.

"Not to be *that* person, but it sounds like you're opening up a happy ending parlor."

Fleur drops her arms. "You know what? I'm glad you're not coming to the Bahamas with us."

She scowls but lets me link arms with her. I will miss Fleur. And Ty. And all of our other friends. That's why I'm so antsy around Ty. Not for any other reason.

If I tell myself this enough times, it'll be true.

It has to be true.

10

Ara

"WELL, I'M OFF. I'M SUPPOSED TO MEET GREG IN TEN MINUTES," Fleur says, wiping her mouth. She slides out of the booth and throws a ten on the table.

Ty, who conveniently showed up outside our apartment right at dinnertime, picks up the cash and shoves it back at her. "It's on me."

Fleur tucks the bill away without another word. "Thanks, Ty," she chirps and leans down to place a peck on his cheek.

"No problem."

"You coming home tonight?" I ask.

"Probably not," she says. "Greg's roommate is pulling an all-nighter with his study group so we've got the place to ourselves."

"Kinky," Ty murmurs. "Don't do anything that would put you in the hospital."

She laughs. "I'll take that under advisement."

"That's your advice?" I tease after Fleur leaves. "Not to get hurt?"

"Seems like a solid recommendation to me. Tell me how our bunny is doing. You didn't answer me earlier," Ty says between bites of his chicken breast. The bird isn't on the menu here, but Ty's a local celebrity so they stumbled over themselves to agree to his special order.

Frankly, I think it's a crime to eat bland chicken at the best Mexican eatery in town, but then again, I'm not the one striving for a multi-million-dollar signing bonus.

"The bunny is cowering under a bush, waiting for the farmer to leave."

He grimaces. "When do I get to see the new stuff?"

"I'm going with never." The only reason Ty even knows Blinkie the Bunny exists is because he's a nosy jerk who likes to rifle through people's desks when they go to the bathroom.

"Ah, come on." His lower lip juts out slightly in an endearing pout.

I squint to make his features look a little less perfect. "You shouldn't even know it exists."

"But I do." He adjusts his glasses cheekily. The boy is totally unrepentant about reading my notebook.

"Because you invaded my privacy," I point out, jabbing my fork in his direction.

He leans back, out of fork range, and crosses his arms. His biceps muscles flex. Does he do that on purpose? Taunt me with his perfect arms? "How was I supposed to know that your red notebook labeled 'history notes' had such secrets?"

"You're not even taking history," I remind him. "There was no need to look at my history notes in the first place."

"Ara, Ara," he says. "We have no secrets. I was thinking that you could add me to your book. I could slay the farmer. Save our bunny."

I can feel my cheeks heat up. "The hero is not you."

"He should be. All heroes are tall and handsome with a rocking bod." He waves a hand in front of his face. "That's me." This kid has no shortage of ego. "I hope when you draw me in, I'm doing some cool horse riding tricks."

"Seriously?"

"Yes, seriously. Those things are dope. I want to mount a house from a run. Maybe storm up some steps. Remember when Aragorn rode into the hall in *Return of the King*? I definitely want to do that. Also, I want to smite people with my sword. Are you taking this down?"

"No. No, I am not taking this down." But I am smiling. I can't help it. His ridiculous recitation makes me laugh.

He grins in response. "That's okay. I'll remind you later."

"Ara!" a cheery and somewhat familiar voice calls.

I turn and nearly choke on my fajita. It's the shark. Kathleen. Did she follow me here? Nah, that'd be too...weird? Stalkerish? Although, we are talking about Ty Masters here. Once a girl crept into his hotel room at an away game and left her underwear on his bedspread. Used underwear. It was as gross as it sounds.

"Uh, hi, Kathleen." I give a tepid wave back and then shoot a glance in Ty's direction. His face shows no sign of recognition, meaning he's not drawing an immediate connection between the card I gave him earlier and this girl.

Which is good, but then I immediately chastise myself for caring. If Ty wants to date this woman, it's his business. I'll support him.

Kathleen sways over to our table, looking gorgeous with her brunette hair side-parted and artfully framed around her pale, small face. Would it kill him to attract women who are marginally less beautiful?

I paste on a bright smile. "Are you stalking me? Because I'm gonna be straight with you—you're not my type. If I was going to date girls, it'd be my roommate Fleur. I like the sweet, cute kind."

"Really?" Ty interjects. "Fleur? I would've pegged you as going for someone more glamorous."

"Fleur can look glamorous," I object.

"She's got a baby face. She's cute, like a doll, but not your type. You need someone more—"

"Annnnyway," I interrupt with exaggerated impatience. "What's up?" I ask Kathleen, who remains standing at the side of the table with her pageant-perfect smile still affixed to her face.

"It's strange how we've run into each other twice in the same amount of days." She holds out her hand to Ty. "I'm Kathleen. We haven't met before."

He shakes it briefly and proceeds to refold his arms. "Ty." He doesn't give his last name. Fuck, I love this guy. Platonically, I mean.

Kathleen is not at all flustered by Ty's lack of response. Not that she should be. He's like this with everyone but a rare few. Probably another reason why Rhyann broke up with him.

"I met your friend the other day. Well, met is really the wrong word. Accosted is more accurate. I've been dying to meet you, and when I saw Ara here, I thought it was a perfect opportunity to introduce myself."

He arches an eyebrow in my direction—a wordless *what the fuck* request for aid. What to do? I shouldn't sabotage him, right? That'd be wrong.

"The card," I tell him, hiding my regret. As a friend, I should help him.

"Card?" His eyes narrow as he remembers. He pats his chest and then leans forward and pulls the damn thing from the back pocket of his jeans. "Business card. Right."

I stare at him bug-eyed. He was carrying that thing around? All day?

Kathleen beams. "That's right. You've had it with you all this time, have you."

It's not a question but a statement of fact. One that sounds like she's the one who spent the afternoon in Ty's pocket.

"I, ah, I showed it to a friend." Ty stumbles over his words, pauses, and then hits the restart button, full of his usual Masters swagger. "You wanted to meet?"

Kathleen gestures to a chair. "May I sit?"

Ty opens his mouth, but I speak first. "Sure." I mean, if he's going to carry the damn thing around he must want to meet her. I kick the chair out rather ungraciously.

He frowns but stands up to hold the chair for her. His mama

taught him well. I try to keep the scowl off my face. If this is what my friend wants, I should support it, even if it kills me.

Kathleen beams at him as she takes a seat. "You dated a former sorority sister of mine. Jennie Martin? Blonde, petite, very pretty."

Ty gives me another questioning look. Jennie was junior year, spring semester. She lasted until Spring Break and then was super pissed when he wouldn't go to the Caymans with her.

"The Caymans girl," I explain.

He nods slowly. "Jennie. I remember her."

But it's clear to both me and Kathleen that he doesn't remember much at all. This short-term memory loss doesn't bother Kathleen, who keeps smiling. Don't her cheeks grow tired? I don't know that I can physically keep smiling longer than thirty seconds.

"Jennie's a sweetheart and always said how you were the best boyfriend she ever had."

I hide a smirk. Jennie screamed at Ty that he showed less emotion than a pumpkin. Fleur and I called him the Great Pumpkin for a whole month. Ty's lips twitch slightly, signaling the return of his memory—or at least parts of it.

"She was a nice girl," Ty says graciously.

"But not one that fit you well, right?" Kathleen says.

"I wouldn't say that," he demurs. He's not one to make complaints about exes, especially not to a stranger.

"Do you know why I gave Ara my card?"

"Can't say that I do." His face is blank.

I give the girl credit. He's showing no interest, but she's undeterred, which I'd admire any other time, but this is my man that she's trying to capture. *No, Ara,* I scold myself, *Ty is not your man.*

But I want him to be, a tiny voice says. The image of Ty sliding down Kathleen's body makes me want to hurl. Why did I invite her to sit? I might as well have laid myself bare on the table and invited people to whip me. It would've been less painful.

"I think we'd be a good match." She shifts, somehow closing the distance between him and her. "I've watched you play for four years. I've read most of your interviews. You're focused and driven, which is something that's so rare to find in men these days. The last handful of guys I dated had more interest in getting stoned than studying the stock market. And I have family money so I'm not interested in yours. What I am interested in is you. I believe in being straightforward. When I saw Ara the other day, I jumped on the chance to get an introduction. I'm not the type of person who needs coddling or will be angry that you can't go on vacation or that you're focused on your sport. I admire that about you. That's damn sexy." She holds out her phone. "Want to give me your number? That way you don't have to be the one to call."

Ty scratches his cheek. Worryingly, I wonder if he's as impressed as I am. Kathleen knows what she wants and she's going after it. He likes confident people. I want to scream, *bitch, he's mine.*

"I don't answer the phone, to be honest. And I'm shit at responding to texts," he replies.

Kathleen doesn't care. "Like I told your friend. I'm a busy woman and don't need a lot of attention. You'll see."

The two stare at each other, but I see a wavering in Ty's expression. It sends a bolt of anxiety through me and perhaps that's why I recklessly blurt out his digits.

"Ara?" Again, said with the same *what the fuck* air as before.

I stare back in horror at what I've done. Kathleen grins happily. I've got to get out of here, before I stupidly start planning their wedding.

"Anyway, we have to get going." I stand up in such haste that the table rocks. Ty gets to his feet immediately, still bewildered. "Ty has a meeting and I do, too."

I grab his hand and pull him with me. Kathleen waves, clearly pleased with the outcome. Once we're a safe distance away, he lays into me.

Stopping short, he swings me around by the shoulder. "What in the hell, Ara? You gave my phone number out to some random woman?"

"I just...I don't know." I scratch my head. I can't really tell him that I was worried I'd be so overwhelmed with jealousy that I overcorrected badly. "I was just shocked by how pragmatic she is. Maybe that's what you need. You were asking me to pretend with you this morning. Well, here's someone who doesn't want to pretend, who says she's down with you being the absentee boyfriend, who looks good on camera. Your engagement would probably be a featured Instagram story."

Because the sad truth is that I can't pretend with Ty. It's taken all of my energy to continue acting like we're just friends since Bowl night. If I had to act like his girlfriend, knowing that it was all for show, I'd lose it. I'd be found sitting in the tree in front of the Admin building, wearing a blanket torn from Ty's bed with his jersey wrapped around my head, reciting his stats.

"Are you nuts?" Yes, Ty, I am not in complete control of myself. He rants on. "A woman I don't know propositions me out of the blue and wants to be my girlfriend after seeing my current girlfriend epically dump me in public for being inattentive and disinterested?" He shakes his head. "That raises red flags immediately. Big, huge red flags, Ara."

"You're carrying her card around," I wail.

"I showed it to Remy. I don't know why I stuck it back into my pocket. But you're right. It's an option I should keep open. You turned me down after all." He sticks both hands in his pockets and starts walking.

"What?" I scurry behind him. "Are you saying that if I hadn't turned you down, you wouldn't call her?"

"Why would I need to?"

Fake date him and he'll see how much he loves you.

The idea is so tempting, but I know that anything more than a friendship is a mirage. We've had four years of friendship and he's not shown any interest in me as a woman since our very first meeting.

I force out a laughing response. "Everyone is turning you down these days. Rhyann. Me. I guess you could make do with Kathleen."

I can't believe I manage to get those words out.

"Doubtful." Ty doesn't notice my struggle. And why should he? In his mind, I'm Ara, his best friend, not Ara, sex goddess.

"She has your number."

"Thanks to you."

I snap then, partly mad at myself for pushing Kathleen and partly mad at Ty for not wanting me like I want him.

"You've been eating chicken breast instead of steak, and broccoli instead of fries for the last two months. You work out eight hours a day, watch tape, practice your interview questions, all for a better position in the draft. This girl could be the difference between being drafted first or tenth."

"You sound like my agent," he mutters, still looking straight ahead.

"So you'll call her?"

"Why are you hassling me about this? Do you really want me to date someone?"

I look down so he can't see the flash of pain across my face. I don't even know why I'm supporting this, because the idea of him and Kathleen as a couple makes my stomach cramp.

It should be me, cries that silly internal voice.

A groan lodges in my throat. Damn Fleur for putting ideas in my head. Or, rather, for reigniting old ideas that I thought I'd snuffed out.

"I just want what's best for you," I tell him.

He slows down and slings an arm around my shoulders. "I know. But let me figure that out. 'Kay?"

I nod and we walk toward my apartment, but the silence is strained between us. His arm feels heavy and the rock in my chest makes each step an effort.

I feel like the distance between us is growing already, despite being by each other's side most of our waking days.

Graduation is coming up. We're all moving away from each other. The past friendship we've enjoyed won't ever be the same. I'm pushing him away, I know I am. But I have to.

It's the only way to prepare my heart for when I truly lose him.

11

Ty

"THAT BITCH!" ARA YELLS OVER THE PHONE. "I'M GOING TO HER apartment and burning all her books."

"I'm not sure she has any," I reply with a smile. I'm not happy with what I'm reading on my ex's Instagram account, but I am pleased that Ara sounds normal.

In the past couple of days, she's been weirdly distant. And her trying to hook me up with the shark makes no sense unless...unless Ara remembers that I mauled her on Bowl night and she's trying to gently place me back into my friend slot.

I take off my glasses and pinch the bridge of my nose. Ara and everyone else thinks I stopped drinking because of my training, but I really laid off the booze because the last time I partied, I think I attacked my friend. I'm not really sure. I have flashes of memory from that night—of bare limbs, taut nipples, and scorching slickness.

I broached the topic the following morning, telling her that I was sorry I was so drunk and if I'd done anything to offend her, she should let me know.

I have no idea what you're talking about Ty, was her uncharacteristically cold response. And that was that. Subject closed. I could tell by the expression on her face that I shouldn't ever bring it up again.

And I haven't. I wish I could remember everything, but, then again, isn't it better that I don't? Remembering that I had my mouth on her body, her tit in my mouth, my fingers inside of her but never, ever being able to relive it again would probably give me bluer balls than a Smurf has.

"Where does she get off saying that you're unreliable and can't be trusted? She's the one who broke up with you. Three times!" Ara's ranting. I take comfort in that. We're the same. No matter what I did in the past, she still considers me her best friend.

"Taking her back might be the character flaw that kills my draft prospects," I tease.

"Don't even joke about this," Ara huffs. "I'm making a dummy account right now and am going to blast her for all I'm worth."

"Sure. No one is going to believe an account that's a day old and anonymous isn't related to me."

Ara stops talking, but her silent fuming is probably making the cell phone towers quake in fear.

My phone beeps and the screen says my agent is calling.

"I gotta go. My agent's on the phone."

"I swear to God, that girl's gonna die. She better be ordering a big fat steak with cheesecake for dessert because it's going to be the last meal she eats." With that, Ara hangs up.

I can just see her hurling the phone on the bed. It makes me smile for the first time since I got the twenty or so alerts that I was being smeared all over social media. The worst stuff is on the anonymous community board where I'm being accused of every-thing from forcing Rhyann to abort my baby to cheating on her with an underage townie.

I answer reluctantly and brace myself for a lecture.

"What's going on, Masters?" Dana demands.

"Hello to you, too."

"I got a scout asking why your online profile is so messy these days. I had to assure him that you were not, in fact, under investigation for any statutory rape charges."

I blanch. I hadn't realized those underground rumors were out there. Still, now's not the time to show any fear. "All that stuff is bullshit, Dana. You know that. My nose is cleaner than an operating room."

"Then go buy that girl a piece of jewelry and a pair of expensive shoes and tell her to shut the fuck up."

"Gifts aren't going to get her to delete this stuff. I'd be surprised if she even answered the door if I appeared in front of her." Rhyann has her own money, anyway. Or, her family has money.

"If she's not bribable, then we threaten her. Give me her number and I'll tell her that if she doesn't take this post down and apologize, we're going to make her into the next college porn star."

Alarm spikes. "No. We're not doing that. This'll die down soon enough."

"Uh-huh, because you've been drafted before so you know all."

I drag my tongue along the inside of my lip and think of all the ways I can crush Dana between my two hands. After several seconds of strained violence, I say, "We're not going there."

Dana launches into a lengthy rant about how I've hired him to protect my interests but I'm tying his hands. I place Dana on speaker and leave the phone on the bed. Walking over to the window, I pull down the slats of the shade. From here, if I really crane my neck, I can make out Ara's apartment complex.

If she made even the first sign that she wanted me, I'd be over there in a heartbeat. But she's turned me down cold. I can get the hint. Her friendship is too precious for me to fuck it up with sex. I can get that anywhere. I won't find someone as loyal, kind, funny as Ara. Or as hot, my dick reminds me.

I bang my head against the blinds.

"You there, Masters?"

"Yes," I call out.

"If you don't like my plans, tell me how you're going to fix this."

I spot a blonde ponytail bouncing down the sidewalk and an idea springs to mind. "Let me call you back."

ॐ

"YOU LOOK GREAT, BRYANT." I give my coach's daughter a kiss on the cheek. "Thanks for meeting me here."

"Thanks, sweetie. You are looking amazing yourself." She pats me on the arm and takes a seat. "What's up?"

I push a sweet tea in her direction. "This good?"

"Of course. You're so thoughtful." Bryant's the type of girl who'd say that even if she hated sweet tea, but after five years of her hanging around the football team and having dinners with her family, I know what she likes. Sweet tea and sweet cakes.

Just on cue, the waitress stops by with the lemon meringue pie I'd ordered along with the protein shake I'm planning to have.

"This is for me, too?" Bryant taps her chest. "Why, Ty Masters, I feel like you're buttering me up for something and I'm here for it." She gives me a wink and dives into her dessert.

"I'm here to butter you up," I acknowledge and push the card across the table. "You know her?"

The coach's daughter pats her mouth with a napkin before picking up the card. "Kathleen Leighton. Is she a professor?"

"No. College student. Senior."

She taps the corner of the card against her cheek. "Sounds familiar. Let me look her up."

I wait, drinking my spinach and carrot concoction, as Bryant taps diligently on her phone screen.

A little furrow appears in her forehead. "Hmm. Not in any house. What's her major?"

"I don't know." I think of her blunt proposal. "Business, maybe?"

"Can you tell me a little more about how you came to get this card?"

"Sure. She saw Rhyann dump me last weekend and gave this to

90

Ara afterward, saying that she wanted to fill the empty girlfriend position."

Bryant coughs in apparent surprise. She sets her glass down and pats the corners of her mouth. "Give a girl a warning before you say outrageous things."

"It's the truth."

"You have an empty girlfriend position?" she asks, although she has to know by now about the scene at the café as well as Rhyann's ugly social media slurs. Bryant's all knowing—at least when it comes to the football team.

"And a rapidly diminishing reputation. I just got off the phone with my agent who wanted to go nuclear on Rhyann. Which I'm not going to do," I quickly add when Bryant's expression grows concerned. "But maybe if I have a current girlfriend, people will chalk Rhyann's shit up to jealousy."

"Maybe," Bryant muses.

"Plus, being in a committed relationship will help elevate my draft stock." Ara must believe this as well since she gave out my phone number like it was candy on Halloween. Easy and without a second thought.

"You're considering this girl instead of all the other ones you know?" Bryant asks as she delicately forks a tiny morsel of pie into her mouth.

"Well, you're taken."

"I wasn't referring to me."

I give her a confused look.

She doesn't roll her eyes, but close enough. "I see you aren't ready for that concept so I'll move along. I can certainly find out more information for you."

"Honest opinion, Bryant. You've been around football as much as anyone. You think having a partner is going to help me in the draft?"

She sets her fork down. "My dad had several calls this morning as to whether there was any investigation going on about Rhyann's accusations, I'm sorry to say. He assured them that there wasn't a more upstanding student athlete than yourself, but..." She trails off.

"But rumors have a way of taking on a life of their own," I finish grimly.

"Unfortunately. I don't know if you being single is going to hurt you, but having a partner wouldn't hurt you, so long as she wasn't scandalous. Which"—she holds up the card—"I doubt this woman is."

"Right."

"But there are other options."

"Like what?"

"Well, I think you'll figure out what those are when you're good and ready."

"There you are. I thought you were coming over to the house." Ace appears at our table, bending over to kiss his girlfriend's cheek.

"I was, but Ty lured me here with cake."

My former QB pulls a chair over and straddles it. "Where's my pie?"

"Is your name Bryant?" I ask.

"It can be for a piece of lemon meringue."

"I'll get it for you, baby," Bryant offers.

"Nah, you rest your pretty feet. Ty here will get it for us."

I rise before I get buried in sugar. "On that note, I'm gonna leave."

"Got an appointment?" Ace asks.

"I do now."

I slap him on the back. Bryant places a hand on my arm before I can walk off.

I glance down at her. "Yeah?"

"I want to clarify what I said before. A partner could help your draft stock but hurt other areas of your life, so you want to be careful."

"And are you going to tell me what I should be careful of or is that one of those cryptic areas where I'll know it when I'm ready?"

"The latter, sweetie."

"Don't call him that," Ace objects. "You know I don't like that."

"It's just a southern thing, darling."

"I'm a Yankee. Please respect my fragile ego."

Bryant laughs and I take my leave before their light flirtation turns uncomfortable for me. Since the two of them got together, they can barely sit in the same room for five seconds without crawling all over each other.

As I walk home, I ponder Bryant's words. Other options that I'll figure out when I'm ready? Like my life's a game and I have to level up before I can access a better cache of weapons?

What the hell? None of that makes a damn lick of sense. I rub a hand over my forehead. I just want to play ball. Why's everyone making it so hard?

I pull out my phone.

Me: Where are you?

Ara replies immediately. *Going to study.*

Translation: she'll be at the Commons.

Me: Meet you there

Suddenly, I feel a shit ton better. She may not want me as a man, but she loves me as her friend. And that's enough for me.

Has to be or I'll lose her.

And I'm not into losing.

12

Ty

I stop by the campus café closest to my house and pick up a muffin for Ara. The carbs tempt me, but I grab a banana instead.

Ara's dark head is easy to pick out at the Commons. I make my way over to her, waving to a few people who I don't know but call out to me anyway.

"What are we doing about Rhyann?" Ara asks as soon as I reach her.

"Nothing. The less attention we pay her, the better."

Ara clicks her tongue. "She needs to suffer."

"She is. She's lonely and without me, remember?" I make a joke, but my attention's diverted. To Ara's left, a bearded guy whose hair is standing up in the front tracks her movements. I catch his eyes and frown. After about a second, he averts his eyes.

"Who's the asshole who's staring at you?"

"Huh?" she mumbles, half the muffin already in her mouth.

As unobtrusively as possible, I tilt my head in the boy's direction. "The guy with a bottle of product in his hair at three o'clock."

She swivels in the opposite direction.

"Your three o'clock. Not mine."

"Oh."

She spins the right way and I regret pointing him out because their gazes lock. He smiles at her and then she smiles back. I scowl at both of them until the kid lowers his gaze to his books.

"What about him? He's cute," she says, returning her attention to me.

"He looks like a doorknob with eyes."

"Come on. He's got a cute face."

"I don't think his balls have dropped yet."

"He looks familiar." She twists to stare at him again, which is a mistake because the boy waves and then gets to his feet.

"Good job. He thinks you want to talk to him."

"I think I know him."

"Hey, Ara," the over-gelled punk says excitedly.

"Hi!" She gives a little wave but doesn't say his name.

I cross my arms and stretch my legs out, forming a small but important barrier between the Doorknob and Ara. Ara hasn't dated at all since her loser fiancé cheated on her. Plus, she's naïve when it comes to guys. I could've told her that Weasel would've stuck his penis down any available opening at the first opportunity, but she seemed enamored with him so I kept my mouth shut.

After seeing her cry for about two weeks, I regret my silence and I won't do it again.

"You studying for the test? Me, too. I can't believe we're having a midterm our senior year," Doorknob says.

"God, I know. That's unbelievable." Ara clearly doesn't know what class he's talking about. She bites her lip in thought.

The asshat's eyes fall to her mouth and he gasps quietly. Dude, she's thinking about the fucking test and not your dick.

Comprehension sets in for Ara while Doorknob is fantasizing about her mouth. "Ohhhhh, the Comparative Art exam. Yes, I know. It's maddening that we're getting a midterm. It should be just one final."

There's no way that Ara's worried about a test in art. She could probably write the thing.

"We could study together. If you're having trouble, that is," Doorknob offers.

"Actually, I'm good." Ara turns him down, but gently.

She needs to be more obvious. By the way he's still standing here, the boy thinks he has a chance. I clear my throat so he gets the message that he should leave.

"If you need a break after it, my house is having a little party," he blurts out before I can say anything. "You should come."

"Maybe?" She looks to me. "Do we have something going on Friday night?"

We do now. "Yeah, we have plans."

"We do?" She turns back to the frat boy. "What time is the party?"

He beams at her. "Nine-ish? But you're welcome to come and pregame."

Pregame? Is he in high school?

"Should I bring anything?"

"Just your beautiful self. I'll be mad if you don't show." He gives her a warm, appreciative gaze and I nearly puke in my mouth. "I need to get back to the books."

"Okay. See you Friday, then."

Doorknob nearly stumbles over his feet getting back to his chair. Once he's seated, he can't stop staring. I nudge Ara's chair with my foot until her back is mostly to him.

"Are you really going to a frat party Friday night?" I ask, not bothering to lower my voice.

"Why not? I don't have anything else going on." She kicks my foot away from her chair leg.

"You could come and hang out with me and Remy. Nichole's coming over and cooking dinner for us."

"Another round of chicken breasts? No thanks, and stop glaring at Calvin."

I raise a brow. "You remember his name now."

She grins sheepishly. "It just came to me. Look, come with us, then. I'm sure they'd love to have you."

"Who's us?" Is she referring to her and that pretty boy as an "us"? Since when does she have a "we" that doesn't include me?

"We as in Fleur and me." Her brows crash together. "What's wrong with you? Do you know something about Calvin that I should be aware of?"

The temptation to make up a story nearly chokes me, but my better angels gain the upper hand. "No. I just don't like him."

"If you think of a reason why, let me know. Otherwise, I'm going to go and drink someone else's booze Friday."

That doesn't sit right with me. Ara and Fleur sitting in the corner with plastic cups filled with piss-warm beer. Predatory guys ready to drop a roofie in their unsuspecting glasses.

"I'm coming with," I announce.

"Suit yourself." She gets up. "I gotta go. I'm supposed to run some errands for Van Asshole."

"Call me before you go on Friday," I bellow after her.

She waves. Doorknob waves back, thinking it's for him. Fool.

I hang around for a minute and watch her leave. Lately, looking at her back bothers me. Ever since the National Championship game, I've been feeling off. I keep telling myself that it's worry over the combine and the draft, but I think it's more than that.

Although that's part of it. I know I'm going to go in the first round, knock on wood. I'm projected to be in the top five, maybe even the top two. I'm doubtful that this Rhyann thing is going to have much impact, particularly when I've done nothing but be a bad boyfriend. I don't think that counts against me. I was a shitty partner because I was focused on the game.

I should be thrilled. A big check is in my future. Even if I got injured on the first play, knock on wood, that guaranteed signing bonus would set me up for life.

But just below the surface of my skin, discontent lurks like an itch I can't scratch. I can't pinpoint the source.

Maybe it is just the agent, combine, draft thing. Maybe it's a low-grade worry over the social media storm. Maybe that's all it is. But the football things don't explain why watching Doorknob flirt with Ara made me tense and angry or why I don't like seeing her walk away anymore.

I try not to think about how much I want her because I've heard enough lectures from Mom about how you shouldn't be friends with a girl just on the off chance she gets lonely enough to want your penis.

And my friendship with Ara has never been about that. I've not been cooling my heels in any damn friendzone. I enjoy spending time with her, in part because most of the other aspects of my life are such a sausage fest.

At least, I *was* content with being friends. Something happened Bowl night. Maybe it was just a fevered dream—one that I'm having far too often. Because Ara's becoming the itch I can't scratch. The source of a mysterious sensation of dissatisfaction.

I've always loved Ara the person. She's the first one I think of when I wake up and the last one I contact before I go to sleep. She never falls lower than two on my text list. That won't change because we're graduating.

What's different now is that I feel like I had a taste of something beautiful, and now I can't even get to the well again. But I'm trying damn hard to respect the boundaries of friendship because I can't really imagine my life without Ara in it.

❦

AT HOME I find Remy doing pushups in the living room.

"Is the weight room closed?" I joke, tossing my keys and backpack on the table.

He jerks his head to his laptop. "I just saw a video of Rose doing a set of squats at six hundred."

Lamar Rose is one of the top five rated running backs in the draft, and behind the five are about three more that are only a hair slower or less powerful. The draft is gonna be thick with running backs, which isn't good for Remy.

I flick a finger over the trackpad and press play. It's not just a video of Rose doing squats. It's him running the 40 in full pads, him doing lateral cone exercises, him being fast off the snap.

I look over my shoulder at Remy, who's sweating like a horse after a two-mile race. "You got this, bro," I encourage him. He grunts in response.

I scroll down Remy's Twitter feed. It's full of combine and draft speculation. I halt on one tweet and read it out loud.

Fred Dixon being snubbed by the combine. Didn't get an invite. Rumor is he refuses to submit to med exam.

I sit down in surprise. "Dixon didn't get an invite to the combine? Dude is a monster. He had eight sacks last year before his injury."

"Injury being the key word," Remy says, allowing himself a small rest. "Sounds like he's been slacking off rehab."

"Damn."

"Good for you, though. Less competition. Speaking of competition, DJ Colvin announced his engagement."

"No fucking way." I scroll farther down and then stop when I see it. It's a link to his girlfriend's Instagram account. The picture is of her hand and a big-ass diamond ring. "You think he paid cash for that or a loan?"

"Loan. Definitely loan."

"Damn." The comments are full of well-wishers, several of whom I recognize. "Fuck." My vocabulary is reduced to one-syllable expletives.

"What is it?"

"Bernard Joseph congratulated him. Or I guess, technically, her, since it's her 'gram." Joseph is an outspoken wideout playing for the team that has the number five pick in the draft.

Remy stops at this news. "So Colvin must be in talks with the Sharks. What about you?"

"Don't know." The same team had expressed interest in me, but I don't have any social media accounts where I can interact with the players. It seemed safer that way. Too many guys get into trouble with shit they're posting online, but I also guess it means that I lose out on some connections as well.

"Your agent hasn't said anything?"

"No."

"It's because of your ex," he concludes. "You gotta rein her in."

"What are your suggestions? Because I doubt anything short of taking her back is going to change her position. At this point, I'd rather take a python into my bed than allow Rhyann there."

"What's your agent say?"

"Smear campaign."

"What else?"

"That's it."

"You need a new agent."

"Like yours?"

Remy finishes his pushups and sits back on his haunches. "Hey, guy got me Jay-Z tickets and a two-hundred-grand marketing guarantee. What's not to like?"

The scrum for high-ticket players like Remy and me is rough, kind of like the line of scrimmage in football. Even though there are rules, anything goes. On the night after the Championship game, agents were everywhere, offering things like cars, marketing campaigns, special access to models and actresses. I don't know how much of those promises were fluff or real.

The marketing advance is the most substantial of the promises, since it's essentially a guarantee of commercial endorsement money that you hope to earn later. It's not really extra money because it only shifts when you're getting the cash—either before you sign the endorsement deal or after.

A good agent is supposed to be someone who looks out for you, long term. And the more money you make, the more money he makes. It's supposed to be a win-win. But the feel I get from a lot of these agents is that they're going to drain you dry until you're a worthless husk. Then they're moving on.

"He's hooking me up with a financial advisor, too, so I don't blow all that guaranteed money," Remy adds.

The roster of people wanting their hooks in players like us are endless. It's enough to make you want to bury your head in the sand.

"You're getting a finance degree," I point out. "Can't you manage your own money?"

"Nah, that's just so I can be sure I won't be ripped off. I don't have a dad like yours I can trust."

Dad is handling Knox's money and is willing to handle mine as well. As of now, I haven't made a decision regarding that. It makes sense, though, to leave everything with him.

There's a short lull in the conversation, and then I admit, "I asked Ara to pretend to be my girlfriend until after the draft."

He perks up. "What'd she say?"

"Hell, no."

"Not surprised. She doesn't like playing games."

"No shit."

"Guess you shouldn't have broken up with Rhyann, then," Remy says with a sigh.

"I didn't break up with Rhyann. She dumped me," I remind him.

He gives me an incredulous look. "Bro. You wanted her to dump you. After she mixed up you and Knox, you became the worst boyfriend on the island of bad boyfriends. Everyone knew it was coming."

"I didn't break up with her because she mixed me and my brother up. You know I don't believe in that mystical shit."

Remy gets up.

"I don't," I yell at his back.

He keeps walking.

I dig Kathleen Leighton's card out of my pocket and pick up my phone. Desperate times and all that shit.

13

Ara

"Hey, isn't that Ty Masters?" Calvin cranes his head to see around me. "You two are real close, aren't you?"

I don't even have to turn to know it is Ty. I can read the crowd. Already people are murmuring to themselves. Some are picking up their phones and trying to surreptitiously photograph him. By the end of the night, a brave few will have asked him directly for a selfie. I take another bite of my steak. I love red meat. I don't know how Ty is living without it right now.

"We've known each other for a while," I admit.

"When did you meet?"

"My freshman year."

He peeks around me again. "Guess he's dating again. That was quick."

My head whips around so fast I almost break my neck just in time to see Ty take a seat across from Kathleen. The buttery, rich flavor of the filet I just shoved in my mouth turns into a brick of paste.

Resolutely, I force another bite in my mouth so I can pretend that the sight of Ty with yet another beautiful woman doesn't twist my insides into knots.

"So how'd the two of you meet? You a big fan? A friend intro-duce you?" Calvin asks.

"We ran into each other my freshman year." Literally. I change the subject. "How'd you think the test went?"

My dinner companion wrinkles his nose. "Not great, but then, does it really matter? It's our last semester. I'll be in my job before the grades even come out."

"Oh, where are you working?"

"I've got a few things lined up. Nothing solid yet, but I'm working on it." He winks at me. "Good thing about being in a fraternity is all the connections you make. One of my older broth-ers, who graduated last year, is helping me out with some gigs after I'm done here."

"That's great." I swirl some mashed potatoes around on my plate.

"How about you?"

"I'm waiting to hear from a gallery in Dallas."

"Dallas, huh? That's pretty far away. Your dad hook you up?"

Inwardly I groan. He knows my dad? No wonder this dude asked me out in the last weeks before graduation.

I play innocent. "My dad? What do you mean?"

Calvin's confidence falters. "Ah, isn't your dad Arthur von de Menthe?"

I chew on my meat for a moment, wondering how exactly to respond. Very few people know that Arthur von de Menthe is my father, mostly because my last name is Martin, which is also Dad's legal last name. The fancy Dutch-sounding one is his pseudonym.

"How do you know that?"

"Oh, isn't it common knowledge?" Calvin draws back in slight surprise. "I mean, he's come to campus before and people have seen you together. I didn't realize it was a secret. Is it a problem?"

"No. Not really. I was just surprised. Not many people know that Artie is my dad."

"Artie? Is that what you call him?"

I nod.

"Is that how you know Ty? Some connection between your dad and the Masters family?"

"No." This line of questioning is really strange, particularly for Calvin. "What line of job did you say you were getting into?"

He smiles and says, "Just some odd gigs set up by a friend."

"What was your major?"

"English with a Communications minor. The Comparative Art class is my Fine Arts credit."

"Huh." Briefly, I wonder what 'odd gigs' go with an English and Communications major, but since my interest in Calvin is waning, I don't ask.

"It looks like the post by Ty's ex is a case of the green monster," Calvin comments.

"No question. Ty's a good guy. She made all that stuff up to hurt him."

"Do you think it will?"

"No. Because none of it's true." Ty is convinced it will blow over, so I am, too. I still want to do something to get Rhyann back, like putting shellfish in her muffler to make it stink for days.

"What is the story there?" Calvin asks curiously. "I heard that his ex threw a pie in his face."

"There was no pie."

"You were there?" His eyebrows shoot up and his face becomes bright with interest.

This is weird. Calvin has shown more interest in Ty than he does in me. English plus Communications? Is he a...reporter? I toss my napkin on the table and grab my purse. "I'm going to the bathroom. I'll be back."

❧

UNLIKE THE OTHER day at the Row House, there's no helpful woman in the bathroom who I can share my dating woes with. On the plus side, there's no woman handing me her phone number on a paper towel to give to Ty.

Ordinarily, I'd text Ty for help, but he's with *that* woman. Fleur is over at her boyfriend's. Remy and Nichole are having dinner. I hate bothering either of them.

"Sorry, Fleur, but you're my roommate. This falls under the roomie contract, clause one."

Me: Date is going downhill. Need a rescue.

There's no response. Not even the three little dots to signal she's thinking of replying and just hasn't managed to type it all out. I stare at the screen and will Fleur to answer. She doesn't.

I text Remy.

Me: Help. Bad date. Can u pretend u love me?

This time, I get an immediate reply.

Remy: Where's Ty

It's just not the one I want.

Me: He's out with the card girl. Kathleen.

Remy: Oh right forgot. did you text him, maybe he's in same boat

He's not. He was smiling at her when I popped into the bathroom.

Me: Remy, you're my only hope.

Remy: Quoting Star Wars lines won't cut it. i'm busy here. nic and me are enjoying some alone time. get it?

Me: You're a terrible friend.

You: Ill still wear black on Wed w u

I burst out laughing at the *Mean Girls* reference. He sends me the shrugging emoji to signal the end of our conversation. I slap new lip gloss on and give myself a short pep talk.

"He's awkward and nervous and trying to ask you questions about your life. That's a helluva lot better than trying to talk about himself the entire dinner. Get it together, girl. You are not now or ever going to date Ty Masters. He's your friend. You made your peace with that years ago."

The girl in the mirror smirks at me, so I leave.

And run right into Ty. I know it's him because my nose hits his breastbone and his shoulders blot out all the light.

I back away, rubbing my nose.

"Where did you come from?"

"There." He jerks his head toward the door that says Gents.

"Oh."

He doesn't respond, and a sense of discomfort slithers down my spine. I look to the right and then the left and then down at our feet. He's wearing the black boots with the orange lining—not that the lining can be seen, but I know that it exists because I was there when he bought them.

"Are you dating that guy now?"

I jump a little at the harsh tone in his voice. "Who? Calvin? No." He caught me in a moment of weakness, but I don't say that out loud. "Fleur was going over to her boyfriend's and the apartment seemed empty. When Calvin called—"

"He called? How'd he get your number?" Ty looks down his nose at me.

My back stiffens. "Our class has a study group list. Mine is on it."

"That's safe," Ty drawls in a sarcastic tone that means the exact opposite. "He looks like a pansy-ass."

"A pansy-ass?"

"You know. A flower. Weak."

I chafe at Ty's criticism of my date. "He could be a hardy weed."

He throws a dismissive hand in front of his face. "Either way, I don't like him. Is this because I wouldn't eat steak with you?"

"No." I scowl. "I'm not doing things just because it would spite you."

"You sure? Because after you broke up with Matt, we ate and drank at all his favorite places for an entire month."

So I'm petty. Sue me. "I am not here because you are on a rubber chicken diet. Not everything in my life revolves around you."

He barrels on as though I hadn't said a word. "Are you that lonely that you'll go out with just anyone? That's not pathetic or anything."

My jaw falls open. Seriously? "Well, what about you?" I retort.

"You're like her next acquisition. She's got her Birkin bag, and next to that there's you."

Ty folds his arms across his chest, a move designed to intimidate. "Kathleen's a power player. She knows what she wants and goes and gets it. Besides, you're the one who gave me the fucking card. If you didn't think I should go out with her, why bring it up in the first place? Why give her my phone number?"

"You can't think for yourself now? You didn't have to pick up the phone if she called. You know what? Enjoy your stupid date and leave me alone." I stomp off, fuming.

"He's a flower," Ty yells after me. "I have boots that have more heft than him."

I give him the finger and keep walking.

"Everything okay?" Calvin asks when I return to the table.

"Yes, everything's perfect. I can't wait until we graduate. I'm so done with all of this."

"But then we have to get jobs."

"Don't remind me," I say sourly.

We finish the rest of the meal in silence.

14

Ara

TY AND I TREAT EACH OTHER WITH STRAINED POLITENESS AFTER
our dates. It's a relief when Spring Break arrives. Fleur, Leon, and a
bunch of others head to the Bahamas. I fly to see my dad in New
York. Ty stays at campus.

The distance, I think, will be good for all of us. It's not. I'm
miserable the whole time. Stephen and Tracy are knee deep in
wedding plans and Dad spends most of his time meeting with a new
client over a commission.

I take long walks along the Hudson and try to convince myself
that it doesn't matter that Ty is going to end up with a woman
other than me. That's how it's always been.

When I return to campus, I'm feeling particularly low, which is
why I said yes to Matt's invitation to his fraternity's house party. He
was all tearful about his broken engagement. The fight with Maribeth had something to do with her not approving of a trip Matt
wanted to take with his dickhead friends. I pretended to care and
did such a good job of it, Matt begged me to stop by tonight and
help him drink his sorrows away. Stupid things are done by stupid
people. I'm the stupid one here, if anyone's wondering.

"Is Ty going to glare at us all night?" Fleur hisses in my ear. I slump further down in the sofa cushion, trying to avoid Ty's narrowed eyes. He's not wearing his glasses tonight, so his disapproval is extra clear.

"I don't know, but I think I need to move out of the line of sight. Even if I were a cat I'd be dead, because at this point there'd be no lives left to be reincarnated."

"Right?"

"It's because of his size," I add. "If he were smaller, he'd look constipated, but because he's big, it's menacing."

"Whatever." She waves a drunk, dismissive hand in front of us and then points to my ex. "So what the hell is up with you and him? You two getting back together?"

I look over at my ex, whose khaki pants are sagging under his butt and grimace. "No way."

"Then why are we here?"

"Free booze?"

"We're seniors. We don't go places for free booze anymore."

I hold up the cheap plastic cup. "The evidence would disprove that. We're easy marks."

"You're an easy mark. I'm a good friend."

"This is true." My life is blessed with good friends. When Fleur found out I said yes to this party, she immediately got on the phone and told everyone we were going out, including Ty.

"Speaking of easy marks, I didn't even give Doorknob Boy the kick in the ass like he deserved."

"I thought you told him he was no better than a prostitute, trying to sell himself for a story," Fleur asks.

"That's true." I feel marginally better. "I also said his face looked like a doorknob with eyes." I peer into my beer. "Maybe I shouldn't have said that."

"Nah, he asked you out under false pretenses. You get to insult him any way you want, including his dick size."

I scrunch my nose. "I don't want to think about his dick."

"How about his?" Fleur nudges my shoulder, only she's drunk a little more than she should so she ends up leaning into me, like I'm her favorite plushie. "Matt expects you to spend the night."

"Matt's a fool."

We clink our plastic glasses together. "You should sleep with one of his frat brothers. Someone he doesn't like," Fleur proposes. Her gaze sweeps the room and stops on one wearing an untucked pink shirt with small birds—or are those ants? I can't tell from here —printed on the fabric. "How about Allen Moore? I heard he has a massive schlong."

"Where did you hear that?"

There's a beat of silence and then, "I made it up," she admits.

"Fleur!" I exclaim. "You can't lie about that. What would happen if I said yes and then he dropped his pants and all I got was a cocktail weenie instead of the jumbo size I'd been promised?"

"You were engaged to Matt and work with Van Asshole. You're immune to disappointment. Besides, there's a point where there can be too much dick."

As one, we swivel away from Khaki Boy to Ty, who's leaning against the bar, jeans hugging his muscular legs and fine ass, topped off with a T-shirt that stretches across his broad chest.

I sigh. "No. There is no such thing as too much dick."

"You spend too much time with Ty. Learn to lower your expectations. Not everyone has a body like his. Besides, I like a little squishiness. It's nice to hug."

"I'm not comparing anyone to Ty."

"Buuuuuullshit," Fleur says in a sing-song voice.

"What's bullshit?"

The new voice is Leon, Fleur's squishy boyfriend who is as sweet as sweet can be.

"That you're dating Fleur and not me. That's what is bullshit," I announce.

He sits down next to Fleur and pulls her off me, tucking her under his arm. "Sorry, babe. I know I'm a hottie, but I belong to Fleur."

"I saw you first." I make a fake cry and rub my fists under my eyes.

Fleur drunkenly shoves my hand away. "You're being too cute. Stop." She cranes her neck back, almost falling on the floor before Leon catches her. She lists toward me. "Ara's reconnecting with her ex."

"I am not." I stick my tongue out.

Fleur tries to shove it back in my mouth while Leon watches us with bemusement. "Does Ty know this?"

"It's not up to Ty." I jut my chin defiantly. Since when does Ty get to dictate who I'm going to date? "If I want to get back together with Matt, I can." I'd rather poke my eyes out with toothpicks, but still. "Besides, Ty's busy with Business Barbie."

"Ty will probably chop Matt into little pieces if he hears you are even thinking about getting back together with your ex. Any of them. Ty's not a fan of your choices."

I consider this. "That's true. It's his fault I'm single. But it's not like he's making good decisions. Look at that."

I point across the room.

"Yeah," Fleur agrees. "He's with the shark."

"The shark?" Leon echoes.

"She's trying to acquire Ty. Came up to Ara at the coffee house the other day and gave her a business card. Who has cards as a senior?" Fleur is affronted by the cards, but mostly because she didn't think of them first.

"Lots of people," Leon says.

"Really?" I ask. Is this why I'm not getting any job offers? Because I don't have a business card?

"I want a card," Fleur laments. "She's cool, isn't she, Ara? That's why we hate her."

"I set them up," I mumble miserably.

"You did?" Fleur screeches. A bunch of heads turn in our direction, including Ty and Kathleen. She smiles patronizingly over at us.

"Yes." I hang my head even lower.

"Why?"

"I don't know. I panicked, okay? I started having inappropriate feelings and I just...vomited up his number."

"That's pleasant imagery," Leon comments.

"Shush," Fleur says. She bangs her nearly empty cup against my head. "You're dumb."

"I agree."

"If you were going to set him up with someone, why not choose someone less attractive?" Fleur says in frustrated tones.

"Or less confident." Kathleen is no longer watching us so I stare at her profile. Fuck, she is so good-looking. "I think it's because she's tall," I tell Fleur. I straighten my shoulders and try to appear taller than my five feet five inches. "Tall people have confidence. They're born with it. Look at Ty."

We all stare.

"They're really good-looking together," Fleur says in a whisper loud enough to carry across the room.

"I know. They'd have amazing, athletic children."

We watch as Ty's head dips down to hear Kathleen better. The pretty brunette places a hand on his arm. Despite her height, she still has to rise on her tiptoes to whisper in his ear. Whatever she says is funny because Ty throws his head back and roars with laughter. All traces of worry are gone from his handsome face.

Why does seeing him happy make me feel sick?

"Why is *he* so attractive?" I ask, not really to anyone. "I mean, his body is amazing. He's smart. Nice. I even once saw him help an old lady across the street. For real. It's not fair. He should be ugly."

"Guys are never really ugly," Fleur informs us. "They're just different. And they never really age. They just get interesting."

"This world is so unfair," I mumble. Leon wisely keeps his mouth shut.

Kathleen suddenly tips forward and Ty catches her, holding her hip firmly in his hand. My eyes start stinging and I force myself to look away.

"Here's to singlehood," Fleur announces. She raises her cup toward me. Leon reaches up and steadies her shaking hand.

I start to tap my cup against hers and then stop. "You're not even single."

"In the part of my heart that belongs to you, I am," she declares.

I look over her head at her boyfriend, who's watching in amusement. "I knew what I was getting into when I started dating Fleur. I've been hoping that eventually the love you two have for each other would manifest in a sexy threesome but alas..." Leon shrugs.

Fleur shoves an elbow in his gut. "That's disgusting, you perv. My love with Ara is on a higher plane where physicality doesn't matter."

"That's okay. I like our earthy relationship." He grins back at her, his round face looking as sweet as the moon.

"Oh, you're the best."

"I know."

Fleur grabs his face and the two start aggressively making out. I peer sadly into my empty glass.

"I need more to drink," I announce, but my friends are too busy sucking each other's faces off to notice that I'm leaving.

I make my way to the bar, trying to avoid Ty, and in the process, I fail to see my ex slide into my path.

"Thanks for coming. I'm sorry I haven't been able to spend any time with you. House stuff. I'll be glad to be done with it," Matt says, but it doesn't sound genuine. He loves his fraternity. "What do you need?"

"I'm empty." I show him my cup. "Isn't this a sad sight?"

"The saddest," he agrees. "What were you drinking?"

"Keg."

"No way. You're a senior and my guest. I've got some of that Owen Meaney wine you like so much."

"Dad likes it. I'm not a fan of wine."

"I bought a couple of bottles the other day at the Wine Rack downtown. You remember that we went to a tasting party there, right? It was for a fall event, right?" He gestures for me to move down the hall.

I glance toward Ty. He's still engrossed in a conversation with

Kathleen. I should be happy for him. He needs someone to make him laugh. He's a serious guy—different from his happy-go-lucky brother. And if the person that makes him laugh is a gorgeous, smart brunette, then why do I feel the need to rescue him? Besides, I'm the one who hooked them up. *I* made this happen. Go me.

"I also bought this delicious port. I know you don't like port—"

"I don't like wine at all."

"—which is why I bought the other stuff. Maribeth didn't like wine, so now I get to drink whatever I want, whenever I want without her glaring at me for the entire meal."

I give up on interrupting Matt. He's too focused on his own world right now.

"That's one of the best parts about being broken up. Maribeth would be complaining right now about the noise and the smoke."

My gaze flies to his. "You and Maribeth broke up?"

He stops in surprise. "Yeah. Isn't that why you're here? I told you that this morning. Here. Have a seat."

Too dumbfounded to say anything, I do as he says and end up next to a girl who looks vaguely familiar.

"Want a hit?" she asks, holding up a joint.

"Pass."

She takes a drag and then holds it out to Matt.

"You mind?" he says to me.

"Why would I?"

"Maribeth hated it. She said it was low class." He inhales deeply. "Everything was low class to her. My clothes. My car. The ring I gave her. Of course, she doesn't say that shit in front of Grand-mother, but since it's under two carats it's a piece of trash."

Listening to my ex lament about his ex has to be one of the worst party games in all the world. I turn to the stoned girl. "I'm Ara."

"I know," she says, retrieving the joint. "Ty Masters' little friend."

"Little friend?" I look at Matt for help, but he's gone, off complaining to someone else about Maribeth's evil ways.

"You know. The girl who interferes with all his relationships and screws him between girlfriends." She takes another drag. "No judgment from me. You've got a good gig. He's stuck with you longer than anyone. I'm sure he'll eventually marry you and then you'll have all his millions to dry your tears at night. Sure you don't want a hit? You look a little worked up."

"I look a little worked up?" I repeat incredulously. I'm bewildered but not worked up. Hearing that Matt broke up with his girlfriend doesn't upset me. It makes me laugh, if anything, which I won't do because while I'm petty I'm not *that* petty.

"Yeah, like you could use a joint or five. You smoke a few of these and it doesn't matter if your ex is blathering on about some other woman or the man you love is balls deep in another girl's pussy." She bobs her head in a slow rhythm. "The weed's your friend."

The thought of Ty being near another girl's vagina makes me clench my hands into fists. Maybe I am getting worked up. "Thanks anyway, but I'm not in any need of it. And I'm not Ty's anything. We're friends."

"Uh huh."

I throw up my hands and get to my feet. "I give up."

As I'm walking away, I hear her say, "That's the spirit."

Matt's in deep conversation with a frat bother and I'm able to escape without hearing another story about how terrible Maribeth is. I'm not drunk enough for this party, I decide. I make a beeline to the bar.

Behind the counter I spot someone I know. "Joe! Joe!" I yell, climbing halfway up the bar to get his attention. The young fraternity brother finally acknowledges me with a wave.

"What's up, Ara?"

"I'm thirsty. What kind of shots do you have?"

"Jack. Vodka. What do you want?"

"Vodka. And don't put it in a shot glass. Dump what you have left there into a cup and I won't bother you again." I point to the half-full bottle on the back counter.

"The whole thing?" he asks with alarm.

I direct a stern glare in his direction. "Do I need to tell one of your older brothers how you dissed Matt Weitzel's girlfriend?" It's an empty threat, but a girl's gotta do what a girl's gotta do.

"You two are back together?" Joe's eyes grow wide. "I didn't know. I'll get you the drink. Hold on."

He comes back with a glass nearly filled to the brim with vodka. I could go to the hospital if I drank all this, but I merely give Joe a wink of thanks and waddle off to find Fleur and Leon.

Unfortunately, when I arrive Ty is there. His hands are on his hips and he has a mean look on his face. Business Barbie is nowhere to be found. I take a long sip of the vodka and shudder as the cheap liquor slides down my throat.

"Where with Matt did she go? Outside? His room?"

I tap the big guy on his shoulder. "You looking for me?"

"Thank God, Ara. I thought he was going to kill us," Fleur cries, flinging herself into my arms. Vodka sloshes over the rim of the cup and down my arm.

"Where the hell have you been?" Ty growls, filching the cup from my hand.

I grab it back and down some more.

"What is wrong with you tonight?" Again, he tries to take the drink from me.

I fend him off long enough to swallow two more big gulps. By the time he wrestles it away, half of the glass is in my stomach.

"Gimme that back. Get your own cup of vodka. This one's mine."

He tips the cup over and pours the rest of the booze onto the floor. "Oh, look here. Your glass is empty. Now tell me why you wandered off on your own."

"I didn't wander off." I try to frown, but I can't feel much of my face anymore. "I was with..." I trail off, because I don't remember who I was just with. I should remember, but it's all looking real fuzzy at the moment.

Leon appears at my other side. "You got Ara?" he asks.

117

"Of course I have myself," I declare. I throw out my arms to show what a firm grip I have on myself and do a nosedive toward the floor.

Two strong arms catch me. "I've got her."

And those three words, more than the vodka, make me warm all over. So warm that I pass out.

15

Ty

CATCHING HER EASILY, I HAUL ARA INTO MY ARMS. SHE'S A featherweight despite all her bellyaching. Her head lolls against my shoulder. I hitch her up higher and the motion rubs her tits against me.

I grit my teeth. It's hard to remind my body that Ara's a friend and it shouldn't get excited like it does. But, man, it's not easy. In the winter, yoga pants and an oversized sweatshirt is her uniform. In the spring, she ditches the pants for the shortest skirts available. I make sure her legs are together so that no one can see her underwear.

One of the strobe lights catches on the small gold chain that circles her ankle. Her dad got her that in France last summer. Artie is good at buying Ara presents; he's not so good at paying her enough attention. He's too busy plowing through his wives.

I didn't want to come to the party tonight. I have an on-camera interview tomorrow morning with a national news station about the upcoming combine and draft. The last thing I need, with all the bad drama surrounding me, is to look like I went on a bender the night before. But when Leon called and said that the two girls were hell-bent on going to this party, I grabbed a ride with a former teammate.

Of course, the first person I saw was Kathleen. I felt bad for brushing her off so I made nice with her while Ara sat in the corner next to Fleur and drank herself silly. Is she really this cut up over her ex? I thought she was done with him.

"Matt misses Maribeth. They broke up," Ara mumbles, reading my mind.

A chill skitters down my spine. She better not be thinking of getting back together with that jackhole.

"Better her than you." I give a chin nod to a teammate who clears the doorway for me. Ara's head bumps against my shoulder as I thread my way through the crowd. "This is why I told you to stay away from him. He's bad news."

I wait for her retort, but all I get is a gentle snore. Girl has passed the fuck out.

"You know what this is all about?" I ask Leon, who's supporting a drunk Fleur. "Is Ara really upset about Matt?"

That tool doesn't deserve another tear being shed for him and it pisses me off to hear that Ara still has feelings for the dude.

"Nah. I think the two of them really just wanted to get lit and this party was a good excuse. You know Ara would never take Matt back." He pours Fleur into the passenger seat while I set Ara into the backseat.

"I didn't think she'd agree to marry the asshole after dating him all of three months," I point out, getting in beside her.

"True. It's not like Fleur's a big fan of Matt either," Leon assures me. "She wanted to take an ice pick to his dick, remember?"

"I know. Talking her out of that was one of the worst decisions I've made," I grumble.

Leon shuts the door and walks around to the driver's door. He buckles up and then twists to check for traffic.

"It's more like Ara feels bad for Matt and just wanted to lend a friendly ear when he needed to talk. Nothing more," he says.

"She was jealous," Fleur suddenly chirps.

My back stiffens. "Jealous about what?"

"About the girl."

"What girl? You mean Maribeth?" I ask, peering over the car seat.

"Sorry. She's out of it again," Leon says.

Sure enough, Fleur's slumped over her seatbelt.

"I better get these two home before one of them decides the booze in her belly doesn't feel so good."

Leon pulls his Nissan Leaf onto the street. The girls' apartment is only a five-minute drive. Leon's able to rouse Fleur enough to get her up the stairs. I throw Ara over my shoulder and carry her up the three flights and into her room.

"Why'd you get so drunk?" I swipe her hair out of her face and lower her into the bed. She moans something inaudible.

Leon knocks on the door. "Do you need help? Fleur's halfway awake."

"No, I got this."

I tug Ara's sandals off. Her toes are painted with a glittery polish that sparkles even in the dim light. She rolls over onto her stomach, one arm tucked under her body and the other slung over the side of the bed. I toss the comforter on top of her and shove a pillow under her head.

She looks damned uncomfortable, and I stand there for a moment, torn. I scratch behind my ear. I've seen Ara in swimsuits smaller than her underwear. And she's stripped me down to my boxers more than once. After the Championship game, for example. I woke up with nothing but my underwear on and all my clothes were carefully folded on the couch. If I'd undressed in the drunken state I was in post game, the pants would've been kicked under the desk and the shirt would've been hanging from the light.

While I'm considering helping Ara off with her clothes, she scissors her legs wide. The silky comforter slides off the bed, leaving her ass exposed.

I nearly choke on my tongue. Her panties are a thong.

"Fuck." This is wrong. I shouldn't be looking at her in this state. I shouldn't be looking at her ass in any state.

Quickly, I throw a blanket over her legs. She kicks it off again.

"It's too hot," she moans.

My balls tighten again. *Get a grip*, I order myself. "No, it's not," I say.

She flashes me again. Sweat breaks out across my forehead. *Ty. This is your friend. You don't lust after your friends. That's a line you don't cross.*

"Yes, it is." She flips over and starts to wrestle her skirt off.

I dive for the bed, pulling her hands away from her body.

"Get off," she grumbles, her slim body wriggling underneath me.

My dick gets iron hard. I shift the lower half of my frame off the bed so I'm not grinding against her. The irony of the situation hits me. Here I am with a hard-on the size of my truck and a warm, sexy body writhing beneath me, and all I'm trying to do is cover her up.

"Ty," she moans.

It's terrible when she moans. The husky sound goes right to my dick and it becomes impossibly harder.

"What?"

"Are you going to marry Kathleen?"

"Marry who?" What the hell is she talking about now?

"Business Barbie? Are you going to marry her? Have two point five beautiful babies? You are, aren't you? You'd be dumb not to. She's so pretty and smart."

"Kathleen's more interested in managing my money than sleeping with me," I say dryly. The entire dinner the other night was spent talking about stocks, bonds and something called real estate investment trusts. She also advised me to play only until I was thirty so that I wouldn't be too mentally damaged by all my concussions in my retirement. She talked more like an agent than a woman interested in me as a man.

"Don't date her," Ara whispers. "I don't like her."

"Okay."

"You won't?"

"No."

"Why not?" Ara's voice is getting weak and faint. I have to lean in close to hear her. "She's perfect for you."

"Not really."

"She's not perfect if you don't like her. Because any girl I end up with has to be friends with you, too."

"You promise?"

Ara's small hand flops around looking for mine. I grab her fingers and tuck them inside my palm. "I promise."

My response must've been sincere enough for her, because she doesn't say another word for a long time. I start to let her go only to find her hand gripping me tight.

"Stay," she mumbles.

I hesitate.

"Please."

Because I'm weak. Because her voice sounds so pitiful. Because she's my best friend and I can never say no, I lie down beside her.

"Just until you fall asleep. And I'm staying on top of the covers because it's too hot."

"You're always hot," she says. Her words are slurred together. "I love sleeping with you because you keep me warm."

"It's been a long time since we've slept together." Sleeping with Ara is dangerous. I never get any rest because I'm always afraid of what I'm going to do when I fall asleep. Probably dry hump her, which would ruin our friendship. I don't know why I'm lying here now, but I can't seem to summon the strength to move away.

She digs her nose into the side of my neck and throws a leg over my thigh. I reach down and gently nudge her knee away from the family jewels. Into my neck, she says something else, something that sounds like, "I've been cold for so long."

16

Ara

I wake up to voices, plural, in the kitchen. Leon must've stayed over. There are a hundred elves pounding hammers inside my head and another legion of them running around in my stomach. I need some coffee and protein. I roll over slowly.

The room is still dark and I contemplate lying in bed all day. Then I remember that Marissa asked me to stop by the gallery sometime to help re-arrange some of Thompson Moore's pieces. The gallery showing didn't go as well as she'd expected. Unsurprisingly, not many liked his grass work.

Van and I shared a rare moment of *I told you sos*, which neither of us gave voice to. Marissa was too bummed, but she has rallied and is now convinced that she just chose the wrong pieces. Plus, Ty's got his interview today and I should see if he wants to do a dry run before he goes on camera.

Gingerly, I drag myself upright.

My knit miniskirt is bunched up around my waist like a belt and my thong is uncomfortably tight. Holding on to the edge of the dresser, I change clothes with as minimal movement as possible. Dressed in sweatpants and a baggy SU sweatshirt that I stole from Ty, I stumble out into the hallway.

Instead of Leon and Fleur, though, the only person I find in my kitchen is Ty, sitting at our tiny breakfast table, drinking coffee. My mouth starts to water and not just because of the coffee in his cup. He looks delicious this morning in his vintage tee and joggers.

"Tell me there's some for me," I croak.

He jerks his head toward the coffee maker. I drag my hungover ass to the counter and pour my mug to the brim. I don't wait until it cools off before gulping down a healthy swallow. Who cares that it's burning my tongue? I need my caffeine fix.

"Do you know how hard it is to sleep with a chub all night?"

A stream of coffee comes spewing out of my mouth. "What?"

"You heard me." The tone's belligerent.

He's nice enough to wait until I'm on my knees, wiping up the coffee spit, when he lands the next blow. "Want to tell me what happened Bowl night?"

I flush red and then white. "B-b-bowl night?" I stutter.

He gets up on his size fifteens and stalks over to me, planting those big feet next to my knees.

"You talked in your sleep," are his ominous words.

Hangover gone. I'm awake, alert, and panicky as I shoot up to my feet. "Oh gosh, what is that? It's my phone. Be right back."

I sprint to the bedroom, race to the bathroom, and lock the door. Once inside, I turn the shower on full blast and climb inside. Fully clothed. Wet clothes are survivable. Talking about Bowl night with Ty is not.

As expected, he pounds on the door. "You can't hide in there forever."

"You'd be surprised," I mutter, sliding down to sit on my ass. Bowl night was one of the worst and best nights of my life. It was a rollercoaster of emotions. The elation of the win. The giddiness of the after-game celebration. The drinking. Lord, the drinking.

I was drunk. Ty was drunk. Everyone was drunk. It took us a half hour to walk five blocks to the hotel. Nichole hit her head on the handle of her hotel room. Ty couldn't make it to his room. He collapsed on my bed and refused to move. So I lay down next to him.

I don't know who made the first move, but our lips found each other. We went from nothing to tonguing each other as if we were searching for the answers to the universe in each other's mouths. Kissing naturally led to touching, which led to—I fan myself as the images of us rolling around with our hands down each other's pants, up each other's shirts, parade themselves in front of my eyes like a triple-X scene.

A determined pounding on the door makes me jump. "Ara, come out here and talk to me."

The girl in the reflection mocks me. "Scaredy-cat," she says with her eyes.

"Damn right, I'm scared." I wipe the back of my hand across my mouth.

Ty pounds again.

"You're going to break the door," I yell.

"Then come out."

"I'm taking a shower!" Hurriedly I undress so that I'm not actually lying. I'm already going to hell for hiding the post-Bowl night events and pretending nothing happened. "Besides, you have to get to your interview!"

"Dammit," he curses, because I'm right. He would never be late to an interview. He prides himself on being respectful of other people's time. "I'll be back later. Don't even think about hiding from me," he threatens.

Nah. It's a big campus. I can avoid him until graduation.

I sit in the shower for a good thirty minutes until I deem it safe enough to exit. The coast appears clear when I peek out, so I scamper across the hallway and slam the bedroom door shut. What are my options today? I need to avoid being home as well as any of my regular stops like the Commons and the Row House. I can hide in the library. That place is massive and if I'm able to snag one of the study rooms to myself, I can plant my ass there all day and no one will be the wiser.

Unfortunately, my roommate has camped out in the living room. There's no way I can get out of the apartment without talking to Fleur.

"What happened last night?" she demands.

"Last night? What are you talking about?" I ask innocently, adjusting my messenger bag strap.

"When I rolled out of bed, Ty was sitting at our table, looking like he'd swallowed a black cloud."

"He had an interview this morning. Probably stressed about that."

Fleur looks unconvinced. "He's given so many of those, he could do them in his sleep."

"Then it must be the draft."

"You're such a bad liar."

I remain mum.

She sighs and switches tactics. "Where are you going right now?"

"I don't want to tell you, because Ty will ask and this way you'll be able to claim ignorance without lying."

"I'll get it out of you eventually. I'll just wait until the next time you're drunk."

The next time I'm drunk? What did Ty say? That I talked in my sleep while I was drunk. Oh God. Is this a regular occurrence? Am I a chronic sleep drunk talker?

I place a hand on my hip and stare accusingly at my roommate. "How long have I been spilling secrets under the influence?"

"Since forever."

"And you're just now telling me this?" I squawk.

Fleur shrugs dismissively. "Why does it matter? I know everything about you anyway."

Not everything. Not the fact that I had almost-sex with Ty a few weeks ago and I haven't been right since.

"Yes, you do," I say and then sprint out the door before she can ask any more questions that I'm not ready to answer.

I do not get a study room to myself.

"You need to get here before eight to get a study room," the snotty student worker informs me.

"Yeah. Yeah." I haul my tired ass up to the third floor and find the Anthropology section. There are two study carrels open. I throw myself down into a chair and drop my head into my arms. Nothing's gone right for me since I climbed into that bed with Ty. I'd known, from the very first time I met him, that falling in love with him would be my downfall.

For four years, I've managed to hide my secret feelings. But then Bowl night happened. My defenses were down. My inhibitions were non-existent. Every single safety precaution I'd taken in the last four years ended up being as worthless as the trash under my sink.

"Dumb. Dumb. Dumb," I repeat, pounding my head against the desk.

"Shut up, you stupid bitch. Some of us are trying to study," snaps a stern voice two rows down.

I don't even get mad at being called that by some stranger, because I am a stupid bitch. How am I going to face Ty? I can't even lie and say that I thought I was making out with his brother, like I did that first time I met his twin, because his brother is married. Ty would never buy it, anyway. They're both too honorable. Besides, Knox didn't even want to sleep with anyone until he found "The One." And Ty would rather be celibate, too, than cheat.

The phone in my bag buzzes. I pull it out to see Fleur calling. I know if I don't answer, she'll just keep redialing.

In the library. Will call u in ten.

I use the ten minutes in the bathroom, splashing water on my face and giving myself a pep talk. "Don't lie because that'll make it worse. Just don't say anything."

I take out my phone and call my roommate back.

"Do you need something?"

"I was worried about you," she says.

"I'm good." Or rather, I will be. In like a year or so.

"Okay. When you're ready to talk about it, I'm here. In the meantime, you got a certified letter delivered today. I signed for it."

"Oh God. It's from the Whitman House, isn't it?" This time my stomach flutters have nothing to do with Ty and everything to do with the job search.

"Yup. Do you want me to open it or wait until you get home?"

"Open it." I can't wait and she knows it, which is why she called.

"Okay. Hold on."

Fleur tears open the envelope. I hold my breath. There's a long silence. Too long. I already know what it says before she reads it to me.

"Forget it." I sigh.

"I'm sorry. Do you want me to read the letter?"

"Does it say anything other than I was a great candidate in a sea of great candidates and they wish me the very best in my job search?"

"Not really."

"Then, no. Trash it."

"I'm sorry, honey."

I droop against the sink. "Me, too. I had my hopes up." I'd flown to Dallas for a second interview and the hiring manager even took me to dinner before I flew back here. I figured if they were spending money on me, they had to be seriously considering me.

"You still haven't heard from the Philadelphia gallery, right?"

"Right. But that's the last one." I'm running out of places to submit my résumé to. I shouldn't have gone into art. But, hell, it was all I knew. I'd grown up with art and artists.

"You'll find something," she reassures me.

I'm not as confident. "In the meantime, can we kill the guy who interviewed me and use our warehouse supply of nail polish remover to melt the body?" At Fleur's silence, I ask, "Too harsh?"

"No," Fleur replies with a little laugh. "I'm all in. I'll go buy another liter of acetone today."

"You're the best."

"I know."

I start to hang up when she yells my name. "Ara!"

"What?"

"By the way, when you get home, we're talking about what happened last night."

"Oh wow, I'm losing you." I activate the hand drier. "God, terrible reception. Bye!" I hang up while she's screaming that she knows I'm faking it.

Yeah, so I am. I've been faking it for years. I can keep it up for a couple more months.

17

Ara

"Nice of you to show up," Van snarks when I walk through the gallery door that afternoon.

"Leave me alone," I reply sourly. My head still aches and now my heart is aching, too. I don't have the energy to pretend like I care.

"Who pissed in your Cheerios?"

"No one." I push a hank of limp hair out of my face. "Is Marissa here?"

"No," he responds tersely. "She's with Moore going over his inventory."

I can't keep a grimace off my face.

"Oh, is Moore's art too down-market for you? Maybe you should leave if you don't like Marissa's choices."

"You don't like them, either," I mumble and arrow for the coffee maker in the back room.

"What'd you say?" Van seems intent on picking a fight today.

I oblige him. "You don't like them, either," I repeat loudly. "Only you're too far up Marissa's ass to say anything."

"Well, we don't all have famous dads who will get us jobs and pay for everything if our boss fires us for being insubordinate." Van

Asshole puts his nose in the air and sniffs. "No wonder you didn't get that Dallas job."

The coffee sloshes over the rim and onto my hand as I jerk in surprise. "How do you know I didn't get the Dallas job?"

An evil smile spreads across Van Asshole's face. "I might've heard Marissa talking to them last week. She said that you were a nice girl, but didn't have a real eye for art."

"What?" I gape at him. "I have a good eye for art. No. Scratch that. My art eye is fucking phenomenal! Is this because of that stupid Moore guy? Because I said his work didn't belong in her gallery? I can't believe this!" I slam the cup on the counter, ignoring the mess I'm making. I'm too tired, hung over, and upset over the Ty thing to modulate my behavior.

"It's hard to get a job when you aren't banking on Daddy's name, isn't it?"

I'd asked Marissa not to reveal who my dad was to any gallery calling for a reference. I wanted to get the position on my own merit so I wouldn't have to deal with another Van Asshole at my next job. I never expected her to sandbag me, though. "I thought she was happy with my work. I did everything she asked. I came in on Sundays. I ran errands for her. I never complained, no matter how menial the task she asked. I even picked up her dry cleaning a few times when she was too busy to stop."

"Who knows," Van says far too sunnily. He points to the floor. "Better clean that up before Marissa arrives. You know she likes her gallery spotless."

With a sigh, I retrieve some paper towels and set about cleaning up the coffee spill. What had gone wrong with Marissa? Was she really mad about Moore? It wasn't my fault that his showing bombed.

Marissa appears only minutes after I finish tossing the used towels in the trash.

"Good morning, children," she sings. She tosses a giant black felt hat onto the counter and clasps her hands to her breastbone. "I've just come from Thom's studio and he had some marvelous pieces. I think our real problem was in our selection of works. We weren't bold enough last time. Van, if you could go out to the car and retrieve the works, that would be delightful. We can then figure out where we're going to hang them. Ara, you'll need to work up a new buy brochure. Do you think you can do that?"

"Of course," I answer, a bit puzzled she would ask it in that way. I've never told her no. I mean, sure, I might've suggested doing an entire show around grass clippings pasted on canvas was a mistake, but I didn't tell her no.

"Wonderful." But her expression says otherwise. "Van?" She arches an eyebrow.

"Oh, right." He snaps his fingers. "I'll go get the pieces."

"Be careful," she calls after him. "Some of them are very delicate. I don't want any of the ants to fall off."

Ants? I can see the shock in Van's eyes before he turns and leaves.

Marissa hums as she types into her computer. I feel compelled to say something, because if we're hanging the corpses of dead ants on the walls—I shudder.

"So, um, Marissa, these ant paintings—"

"It's genius, isn't it? Thom was telling me that he has this whole natural theme planned out." She draws a line in the air, envisioning Moore's terrible work up on her walls. "It's so immersive. You really feel like you're outdoors, in the fields. It's a respite from this busy, busy world."

"Don't you think it might be a little too..." I search for the right term. "Earthy?"

Her eyes snap to me. She scowls. "Earthy? Simply because you and your father prefer to work with more modern mediums doesn't mean that everyone else's ideas aren't worthy."

Iron and concrete are modern? The Pantheon is made out of concrete.

"I like the classics," I say slowly, trying to figure out where the anger is coming from. "There's nothing quite like oil on canvas. Or watercolors. Monet is one of my favorites. When Dad took me to—"

"Please. I do not need to know any more of Arthur Von de Menthe's opinions." Marissa sticks her nose in the air. "No offense, Ara, but simply because your dad sells a few pieces to art collectors who have more money than sense doesn't make him someone with taste."

My jaw drops open. "What?"

Marissa did not just dis my dad, did she?

"Um, where should I put this?" Van appears in the doorway. For once, the smug, supercilious expression he always wears is gone and in its place is apprehension. He can sense the tension.

"Over on that easel in the front," Marissa directs. "Replace the Schadendorf. I've had that up for ages and no one wants to buy it."

"Because it's priced too high," I say without thinking.

"Only von de Menthes can be five figures?" Marissa mocks.

"He hasn't sold a work that low for a decade," I snap. I won't tolerate smears against my dad. And I can't believe Marissa is going there. Dad helped get her gallery off the ground.

"Money doesn't mean everything, especially in art," Marissa shoots back. "Isn't that right, Van?"

His anxious gaze darts from one angry female face to another, but Van's a survivor and he's picking the woman who's writing his paycheck. His face hardens. "That's right, Marissa. Some people think the size of their wallet means their opinion is worth more."

I've reached my limit with these two. "I don't know where this is coming from," I fume. "My dad has never said anything negative about the art that's sold here. If anything, this place is successful because of him. He sent art here when he didn't have to."

"Oh, so I'm a charity case?" Marissa's face burns with anger. I've never seen the sleek blonde so upset. She snatches an article she printed out on the computer and starts to read. "'The new crop of artists seems to be lost. They aren't speaking from their soul. Instead, they are chasing gimmicks. If they're going to just paste shit on a canvas, I suggest they go back to kindergarten.'" She slaps the article back on the counter. "Your dad has never said anything negative about my art? What's this then?"

"He could be talking about anything," I retort. I don't follow my dad's career online. It's too hard. Most of the time people are saying shit about him. It's the same with Ty. I don't read the comments unless the noise level is so loud I can't avoid it.

"He said this right before poor Thom's showing. If it hadn't been for your father, Thom would've been written up in glowing terms. This is your fault!" She points an angry finger toward me.

"How is it my fault?" I sputter. "Dad didn't even name Thompson Moore. Moore didn't invent multimedia art."

"He's clearly talking about my gallery!" she screeches. "Thom says that your father is jealous that I've moved on and is taking it out on me. This is completely unfair and if he doesn't stop, I'm going to sue!"

I'll take a lot of abuse—have taken a lot of abuse here—but there comes a point in a girl's life she has to draw the line. Calmly, I go collect my bag.

"Where are you going?" Marissa demands.

"I quit," I say simply.

"You can't quit!" she shouts. "We have art to hang!"

I ignore her and keep walking. When I reach Van, I stop. "You're right. It is nice to have a dad who'll support me even if I don't have a job."

"You'll never get a good recommendation from me if you step out of those doors," Marissa warns.

I look over my shoulder. "I don't think I've gotten a good recommendation from you while I worked here."

The silence that meets my statement confirms what I started to suspect. Part of the reason I haven't gotten any jobs is because Marissa's been badmouthing me. I've given this woman two years of my life and this is how I'm repaid?

I let the door fall shut behind me. In my car, I pull out my phone and search for the article Marissa quoted from. It's in the

icICK
Art & Style section from two weeks ago, which would be right before Moore's showing.

It's not a feature about Dad, but rather a piece on avant garde art and whether it's actually art or just out there. Out there, is my opinion and I know that Dad shares it, too. Halfway down, there's the quote from him regarding how new artists seem to be going for shock value. I sigh. This is so unlike Dad. He doesn't speak up about other artists, feeling that there's a professional courtesy he owes, particularly to new ones.

I open the phone app and give him a call.

"Hello, Ara. What is my dear daughter calling me for this delightful Sunday?"

"How's New York?"

"Boring without my darling girl. Stephen says I'm not allowed to come to the city again unless I bring you. Oh, and I found you the perfect dress for their wedding. It's a..." He pauses to rifle through his shopping bags. "Prabal Gurung. Am I pronouncing that right?"

"I don't really know. Um, Dad. How long ago did the reporter from A&S call you for that quote in the paper a couple of weeks ago?"

There're a few guilty moments of silence before he clears his throat. "Marissa saw that, did she?"

I throw my head back against the headrest. "Yes, she saw it and she's furious."

"I'm sorry, but it is the truth. Moore's work is terrible. He shouldn't be allowed to have a gallery showing let alone have actual buyers take his work into their homes. Still, she shouldn't have taken it out on you."

"You weren't here." And I was a convenient target. "What on earth made you reference Moore's work, though? He's nothing compared to you."

"I didn't like the way Marissa was treating you. Having you make copies. Fetching her dry cleaning. And not listening to your opinions! You have one of the best eyes for new talent out there. One of the reasons Stephen was so miffed I came to the city

138

without you is because he's evaluating a couple new artists and wanted your opinion. You really should come work for him after you graduate."

"Dad, no." We've had this discussion a bazillion times. "I'm weeks away from graduating from college. I can't live my life as Arthur Von de Menthe's daughter. The whole mess with Marissa was because they all know that you're my father." And because he slept with her and then never called again, but it's all the same. "I got the job instead of Van Riley and now I'm out of a job because Marissa was angry at you."

"I'm sorry," he says in a small voice that makes me feel like a jerk.

"No. Forget it. It's her that should be sorry. But, Dad, seriously. I need to make it in this world by myself. If I want to be taken seriously, I can't have it known that I'm your daughter. My whole career will be tied to yours, which means my successes won't be my own and neither will my failures."

"I just wanted to help you, but if you want me to back off, I will."

Tears prick my eyes at his soft concession. "Thank you. I love you, Daddy."

"I love you, too. I can still buy this dress for you, right? I don't think it's returnable."

I laugh, because I'm not one to turn down pretty clothes and we both know it. "Yeah, bring it home."

"Take care of yourself."

"I will."

After we say our goodbyes, I lay my head on the steering wheel and contemplate my options. I have one résumé out in a gallery in Philadelphia and that's it. There just aren't a lot of jobs for art curators without a master's degree. I'd hoped that I could work at a small gallery, prove my chops, and then work my way up by networking. But it seems like I might be destined to go back to school. I don't really want to do that. I'm so tired of classes and papers and tests.

The picture of a little bunny and an angry farmer pop into my head. I promptly shove it aside. That's a fun project. A hobby, really. If my dad hated Moore's work, he'd be even more derisive of my doodles.

Art curator is what I'm meant for. Not artist.

In my lap the phone beeps. I pick it up without thinking.

Ty: I'm sure you're thinking this campus is big enough that you can graduate without seeing me again, but you'd be wrong. You might as well come home and face the music.

I blanch at Ty's text. On a scale of one to ten, this day falls under the *never should've gotten out of bed* category.

18

Ty

"I can't believe she's avoiding me," I growl.

"Who?" Remy asks, his eyes glued to the television. He's eating a bowl of bran cereal and watching a Twitch stream of FIFA, trying to pick up tips on how to beat me. It's not going to happen.

"Ara."

"What'd you do?"

"Why is it my fault?"

"Playing the odds. When Nichole's mad, ninety-nine percent of the time it's because I did something."

I rub a hand over my jaw and eye Remy speculatively. He and Nichole were with us on Bowl night. We'd all walked home from the bar together. I wonder how much he knows.

I test the waters. "Ara's avoiding me because we hooked up on Bowl night."

"Yeah? What about it?" He doesn't even flinch.

Seriously? Fucker has known all along and never said a word? Suddenly Nichole's vague implications as well as Bryant's come to mind. What had Bryant said? That I wasn't ready for a girl I already knew? She must've been talking about Ara.

"How many people knew we hooked up?"

"I dunno. A few."

"You, Nichole, Bryant."

"Ace, Travarius, Wyatt." He reels off half the starters. "We came up after the bar closed to see if you were hosting an after party. Nichole had an extra key, opened it, and then shut it. She said you two were busy"—he waggles his eyebrows so I know exactly the type of busy he's talking about—"and we were to leave you alone."

"What the hell? How did I not know this?"

My shouted disbelief causes Remy to drop his spoon into the bowl. "You didn't remember, fam?"

I glower at him. "No. I didn't remember."

"I'm sorry. Had I known she was taking advantage of you, I would've stepped in." He grins like an asshole.

I shake a fist in his direction. "Why haven't you said anything since?"

He shrugs and turns back to his laptop. "You didn't say anything. Ara didn't say anything. I figured the two of you decided that it was a mistake and wanted to move on from it. Then I really thought you were over it when you took Rhyann back. Nichole was so mad, remember? We had a big fight over it."

"This is fucked up." At one point there, Nichole wasn't even talking to me. Before I can probe further, my alarm goes off, reminding me I have that interview. "Shit. I have to get ready, but when I'm back, we're talking about what everyone but me knows."

I grab my glasses and keys and motor over to the training facility. Ace meets me at the door of the conference room.

"Got everything you need?"

"You knew about Ara and me hooking up at the Bowl game?"

Ace's eyebrows shoot up. "You wanna talk about that now?"

Frustrated, I reach up to run a hand over my hair but stop just in time. Can't be looking like trash on national television. I send Ace a dark look from behind my glasses. "No. But we're talking afterwards."

"Fine." He opens the door. "You know where to find me. Remember the media training?"

"This isn't my first interview," I snap.

Ace wisely doesn't respond. Inside the room, the network's remote camera team is setting up. They hustle me into a chair. Ace hands me the mic, which I clip onto my tie. Bryant comes over and brushes something on my face. I try to force my mouth into a smile, but it apparently doesn't work because Bryant hisses, "Try not to look like you swallowed a rock this morning. You're supposed to be happy, thrilled, pleased."

"Thank you, Ms. Thesaurus. I also like to be informed, included, and enlightened."

She scrunches her nose. "I gave you that media training handbook."

"Forget it."

Everyone in the room is busy. Someone adjusts the lights. Another person tests the audio. A cameraman wearing a polo with the network logo signals for my attention.

"Remember to look into the camera," instructs the cameraman.

I nod. As I said to Ace, this isn't the first on-camera, remote interview I've done. Ace and I did a handful right after the Championship win.

I watch the red light above the camera and wait for it to blink on. Before it does, the reporter's familiar voice fills the room.

"Hey, Ty, how is everything going there?"

"Great." I wish I could see him. It'd be a lot easier, but then I'd be looking at him and not the camera.

"Weather good?"

"It's very nice. Thanks." Everything is feeling uncomfortable. The chair's too hard. The tie's too tight. Under the table, I rub my hands over my khaki pants and mentally prep for all the questions about how I compare to my brother.

"I wondered if you'd had a chance to take a look at any social media today. I know you don't post or have an official account on any of the platforms, but you probably have a secret one where you can read what's going on."

I do, but I'm not about to admit that to this guy. "Well, I've been focused on getting ready for the combine and draft as well as finishing out my degree, so I don't have a lot of extra time to go on social media."

Media Training Rule Number 1: Never lie. You can refuse to answer, but you should never lie.

"That's too bad. I hate to spring this on you, but I'd be failing as a reporter if I didn't ask these questions. I hope you don't hate me too much. Hey, can we adjust the volume? I'm getting some reverb." He pulls the earpiece away from his head.

As the techs do the necessary adjustments, I try to calm my racing heart. If this is over the Rhyann thing, I'm not sure how I'm going to convince this dude that it's a bunch of bullshit. I'd like to just outright ask where this interview is going, but Media Training Rule Number 2 is never volunteer an answer to a question that's not being asked.

I force myself to wait.

The reporter flashes me an apologetic smile and sticks his earpiece back in. "We ready?"

"Ready," intones the cameraman on my end.

"Three, two, one," counts a disembodied voice. "Go."

"We're here with Ty Masters of the National Championship-winning Southern University Renegades. How does the off-season feel, Ty?"

Easy softball question. I trot out a practiced response. "I'm still in Championship mode, sir. The combine is coming up, followed by the draft, and then, if God wills it, camp. I have a lot to prove, so I'm not viewing this period as the off-season but another time to prepare."

Ace gives me a thumbs up. Bryant places her fingers at the corner of her mouth and mimes a smile.

"Owners around the league will be happy to hear that. How do you feel your draft prospects are?"

"I'm not worried about that. I can only control my performance. I'm concentrating on eating right, working out, and getting game ready." I force my lips upward and hope I'm actually smiling and not grimacing.

"Still, you have to be concerned about the negative press you're getting on social media. Some scouts have expressed concern that you're not surrounding yourself with the most positive influences. How do you respond to that?"

Media Training Rule Number 3: Keep your answers brief.

"I'd say that I'm devoted to the game."

The reporter smiles tightly. "Of course, your personal life may not be an appropriate topic, but what about your agent?"

"My agent?" I blurt out. Ace grimaces and so does Bryant. I've violated Rule Number 4: Don't reveal ignorance.

"You don't know?" The reporter's tone contains a note of surprise; we both know that his surprise is feigned.

"Like I said, I'm busy preparing for the draft."

Ace nods, confirming that I'd given the right answer. Meanwhile, Bryant is furiously tapping on her screen. I can tell right away when she finds what the reporter is asking about because her face grows taut with worry. I rub my hands again.

"So you're not concerned that Dana Mullen's alleged gambling crimes are going to be harmful to your draft prospects?"

I feel sweat breaking out across my forehead and wonder if these high-def cameras can pick that up. How ironic that now I'm wishing this guy would ask me something about my brother. Anything.

I inhale and say, "I'm not familiar with what you're talking about, but you can be sure I'll check it out after the interview is over."

"And if Mr. Mullen is indicted on fraud charges, what will you do?"

He's trying to back me into a corner and it's not a good feeling. It makes me want to come out swinging. I bite down on my tongue before I say something rash and stupid. If Ara were here, she'd tell me to keep my mouth shut. But I can't. I have to say something.

"As I just said, I'm not familiar with the charges or the crime. This is the first I've heard of it, so I'm not going to comment or do anything without looking into the matter myself."

"But after you investigate, what then?"

I smile again, this time with some teeth. "It feels like you're trying to get me to give you a headline. My job is to play football. That's what I'm good at and what I'm concentrating on. I'm sure that law enforcement wouldn't want some college kid making comments about their investigations."

I glance over the cameraman's shoulder to Ace and Bryant, both of whom are wearing anxious expressions. I can't tell if I gave the right answer or not, but the reporter moves on. I answer the rest of the questions stiffly and by rote. It's one of the worst interviews I've given and I think we're all relieved when it wraps up a few minutes later.

When the red light turns off, I rip off the mic and push to my feet. I want to snatch the phone out of Bryant's hands and find out what the fresh fuck is going on, but I force myself to shake hands with everyone first.

"Thanks," I say. I sign a few autographs, field a few sympathetic smiles, and then give a swift head jerk for Bryant and Ace to follow me. I don't have to ask for the phone. Bryant hands it over and gives me a quick rundown while I scan the article she has up on the screen.

"Dana Mullen was arrested early this morning by the FBI for fraud and embezzlement. It all came out because his former partner is suing him for money. Apparently, he's also been betting on college games and stuff like that," she says grimly.

"What're you going to do?" Ace asks, equally grim.

I toss the phone back to Bryant and give Ace an incredulous look. "I'm firing his ass. That's what I'm going to do."

"And then what?"

Then I hope everything dies down, but this mess following so closely on the heels of the Rhyann drama makes me realize that I've got to get my house in order. If I don't, my dreams of going in the first round, let alone the top five, are going to be in the shitter.

First up—Ara.

19

Ara

Fleur attacks me the minute I step inside the door.

"I want to know everything. I want it to be so detailed we're both squirming with discomfort."

"I don't think so." I drop my bag and make my way to the kitchen. Fleur is right behind me.

"Yes. It's your punishment for hiding things from me. We're best friends. We know everything about each other. Our cycles are even in sync! I'd take a tampon out of your body if it was necessary to save your life."

"Ewww. That's gross. Leave it in."

Fleur crosses her arms. "I won't. I love you too much. Besides, I can bleach my hands after. I'm going to be an elementary teacher, for crying out loud. You think removing a tampon is going to be the worst thing I do? Do you know how much snot I've already wiped away?"

I shudder. "I'm so glad that is not my job." Then I remember the bribe I'd brought, and lift up the bag. "Look at this. Cronuts from the Row House."

Fleur's attention is immediately diverted. She grabs for the bag.

"Oh my God. I thought I smelled heaven walking up the stairs. Don't think I'm letting you off the hook, though."

"I wasn't imagining that would happen for a second." Praying, yes. Imagining? No. While she collects the plates, I pour two glasses of milk and join her at the table.

"I'm going to have a holy moment with this pastry and then we're going to talk about Ty. In the meantime, feel free to vent about the Dallas job. I take it you didn't bring up your dad."

"You guessed correctly." When I first started going out on interviews, the hiring managers would fall all over themselves when I arrived. It was almost like I was the interviewer and they were the newly minted college grad. But then the conversation soon turned from, "where do you see yourself in five years?" to, "do you think you could get your dad to show here?"

After several months of those types of interviews, I abandoned New York and started looking into smaller markets in hopes that people wouldn't recognize me as Arthur von de Menthe's daughter. But now that I'm not surfing in his wake, the path to employment is very choppy. It doesn't help that Marissa has been secretly poisoning the well.

"Oh, and my boss is still mad that Dad won't sleep with her anymore, so she decided to give me a bad reference."

"What?" This news is shocking enough for Fleur to set down her pastry. "That bitch. I'm going for another bottle of acetone."

"Forget it. I quit. It's not like I wanted to continue working for someone who thought crushed ant corpses on the wall made for art."

"Ew."

"It's the latest evolution of Thompson Moore, agrarian lover."

"Ew again."

I take a big bite of the cronut and the buttery goodness goes a long way to soothing my wounded feelings. I eat half of it and then reach for the milk. Fleur snatches it from me.

"Nuh uh. Not until you spill your guts."

I swallow my pastry and then lick my lips. Suddenly my mouth feels very dry.

"How much did you hear last night?" I ask glumly. I'm disappointed at myself about my drunk babbling. It's so inconvenient.

"Not much. Just Ty yelling something about the two of you doing dirty things to each other and how he couldn't believe you didn't tell him. Him? I can't believe you didn't tell *me*!"

Dry? My mouth is like the Sahara now. All dust, no moisture.

"And because I'm an angel of a best friend, I remained silent *all day long* today and didn't push you to talk about it *at all*—"

I snicker. "Seriously? You've been pushing all day!"

"—but I'm officially through with taking the high road."

I snort this time.

"I'm coming down to your level and withholding precious sustenance until you start talking," she finishes.

"I don't think milk counts as sustenance, does it? Like, isn't sustenance more like food?"

"Are you kidding me with your semantics argument right now? Because I can dump this milk over your head." She holds up the glass threateningly.

I throw my hands up and pretend to cower. "Okay. I'll tell you everything!"

With a satisfied nod, she hands me the glass. "Thank you. You may proceed."

I drink half the glass with gusto before scowling at Fleur. "Where'd you learn your interrogation techniques? They don't teach that in the School of Education."

"You'd be surprised. Kindergarteners are wily. You have to be on top of your game to maintain control."

"Those poor kids. Are they going to have any fun?"

"With me?" She flips her hair. "They're going to have so much fun that the rest of their lives will be a big disappointment. Are you stalling?"

"Yes."

"Stop."

I heave a huge sigh. I'm not going to get out of this. "Ty and I were both really drunk after the Championship. I don't know exactly what happened, but we didn't have sex."

"Are you sure?"

My cheeks start to get hot. "We did some stuff," I admit. "But not that. He got up to find a condom and I..."

I remember the scene vividly. He'd been kissing my stomach, pulling my panties down. His breath was hot, his grip secure. *"Condom,"* I remember gasping. He groaned and then pressed another kiss right above my hipbone before rising to his knees. The hard-on tented his boxer briefs and he took a minute to adjust himself before climbing off the bed. I about passed out at the sight of him touching himself. I have no idea why that was such a turn on. Under the cotton, I could see the muscles of his ass flex as he walked away.

"You what?"

I give myself a shake. "I came to my senses. He was in the bathroom and I had this lucid moment of clarity so I pretended I was passed out when he returned."

"What'd he do?" Fleur asks, wide-eyed.

"He cursed. Shook my shoulder and then sighed. I played like a dead person until he fell asleep. He was out of it after about five minutes."

"And you think he didn't remember?"

"No. The next morning, he asked me what time he'd gotten in and where I slept. I told him he got in around three and that I slept on the sofa. His whole response was, 'hope I didn't snore too loud.' To which I said, 'dunno, I was mostly asleep the whole time.' Then he said that he was sorry for everything that happened the night before. I told him it was nothing and we've never spoken of it again."

Fleur knits her brows. "That's not a definitive finding on his recollection."

"He was technically dating Rhyann at the time. Ty's not the kind of guy to cheat on someone."

"He didn't cheat on Rhyann," Fleur says with an impatient shake of her head. "She broke up with him before Christmas, remember?"

"But they got back together."

"Did they really, though? I mean, I don't remember him spending time with her after the Championship. He spent every night hanging out with you."

"He could've gone home afterwards and banged her." In fact, I'd endured many a sleepless night wondering exactly about that. Ty had said that he hadn't slept with her and I don't know that he's ever lied to me before.

"Doubtful. The whole reason that you both got a shower at the Row House was because Ty kept ignoring her. If he was dicking her on the regular there's no way she'd break up with him."

Just thinking about Ty touching Rhyann the way he touched me makes me want to upchuck the cronut. I'm going to believe it when he said he never slept with her—just so I can eat the rest of my pastry in peace. "Can we move past the Rhyann thing?"

"Yes. We should. Let's return to why you're avoiding Ty. Your best friend Ty. How long do you think you can actually keep that up?"

I drop my head to my arms. "I don't know."

"Ara." Fleur puts a lot of scorn into my name. Deservedly so.

"I mean it. I don't know. I woke up this morning and the first thing he said was 'what happened Bowl night?' And I panicked and ran off."

"And have been avoiding him ever since," she concludes.

"That's accurate."

"You can't avoid him forever."

"There are only about ten weeks left of school. I think you underestimate how crafty I am."

She pats me soothingly. "Just sit down and talk it out. Once you clear the air, everything will be fine."

"What's 'fine' under your definition?"

"How do you want it to be defined?" she hedges.

"I don't know."

"There's an easy way to resolve this."

I perk up in interest. "How?"

"You admit that you can tell him and his brother apart and then he realizes that it's destiny for you two to be together and everyone is happy ever after."

I shake my head vigorously. "No. That's a no go. No relationship that's built on a party trick can last."

"It's not a party trick. It means something. Like, how many people can tell that it's him wearing his brother's uniform on the cover of that *Sports Illustrated* magazine?"

"Um, everyone should." Those two idiots played a twin switch for their *SI* cover shoot. Ty wore his brother's uniform and Knox wore Ty's. They laughed themselves silly over it. "Even if you couldn't tell them apart, it's obvious because Ty is not going to hang a life-sized poster of himself in his room."

"That's not obvious, Ara," my roommate insists. "Not telling them apart is normal. The weird thing is that these two played a trick during an *SI* shoot of all things."

I shift uncomfortably under her gaze. "Okay, fine. It's stupid that they play these games."

"Didn't you say they did it to Ellie more than once?"

"Yes," I mumble.

She puts a hand to her ear. "What's that?"

"Yes. Yes. They did it to Ellie, too, but it doesn't matter because she can tell them apart."

"Like you can. You can even tell them apart by their voices."

"It's easier when you can't see their faces." If you've spent any time with either of them, you'd know that Ty has a deeper, sexier voice. Knox, for instance, doesn't make my body clench up when he says my name. Whereas Ty says it and I have to suck on an ice cube until I cool down.

"Whatever. The point is that he's your soulmate. You've been in love with him since your freshman year."

"But we've been friends for that same time, too," I point out.

"Friends last longer than lovers. You never see Lucas anymore and you dated him the entire spring semester, freshman year. But you and me"—I wave my finger between us—"we're closer than ever."

"Ara," she starts.

I put my hand on her knee. "Fleur, life's okay right now. Yes, I don't have a job. But I believe there's one out there for me. My dad just sold another piece for enough money to run a small country for an entire year. My best friend got a job offer in the best school district in this state and my other best friend just won his National Championship, is healthy, and about to get drafted into the NFL. I'm not going to mess up all these great things because sometimes my heart beats too fast when Ty's around. Once you break that friendship seal, our world changes. No more Ty, Leon, Fleur, and Ara. Our group will break up, too."

Fleur looks unconvinced, but she takes a bite of her cronut and doesn't argue with me. We eat in silence for a few minutes until she says, "I'm not the one you have to convince."

"Who is, then? Ty?"

"Nope. You. Until you can convince yourself that you don't love him, all your excuses are meaningless. You'll still be hurting yourself every day. Plus, you're doing your best friend a big disservice."

"How so?"

"Because you're not giving him a chance. You've pigeonholed him, stuck him in a slot in your life, and haven't given him the opportunity to show you that he's more than what you've assumed he is. And, if you really love him as a friend, that's pretty sad."

20

Ara

TY: *WHERE ARE YOU?*

Ty: Call me.

I set my phone on my desk and stare into the mirror. I don't like the timid, uncertain person I see.

Fleur's right. I can't avoid Ty forever. The whole point of brushing all these inconvenient feelings under a rug is so our idyllic friendship can continue, but if I ignore Ty, then what's the point?

I find my spine, pick up the phone, and text him back.

Me: Home. Hungry?

Ty: I could eat. I'll bring something over.

A public place means that I'm less likely to do stupid things.

Me: Or we could meet at the Row House.

Ty: I'll bring something over.

I get the sense that I could suggest a dozen other places and the response would remain the same. I wonder how he convinced Rhyann to meet with him at the Row House. She probably wasn't as stubborn as he is. And, apparently, I'm not either because I give in.

Me: Ok. I'll order something for you.

He doesn't bother to respond. I go to the kitchen and pull out a couple menus.

My roommate hops up from the sofa to peer over my shoulder. "Are we ordering in?"

"Ty's coming over," I reply glumly.

She tsks. "The end of the world is not happening."

"You sure about that?" It feels like the end of something. "This has all the makings of a disaster. Like *Sharknado* except with no sharks, just pieces of Ara flying around in a big cyclonic cloud."

"If it doesn't work out because Ty turns out to be an ass, you'll always have me."

"Are you saying you'll leave Leon for me?"

She taps a finger against her chin, pretending to consider it. "We can have a poly relationship. Leon would probably love that."

"It's nice to have a backup plan."

"I'm going to go over to his place to explain this new situation." She slings her purse over her shoulder.

I grab the strap and pull her back. "Right now? What's the rush?"

"Well, if there is a Sharknado, I don't want to get hit by the debris." With that, she tugs out of my grip and slips out the door.

Traitor.

I pick up the phone and call in my order.

"Chicken breast. Plain. Cooked with chicken broth, if possible. With a side of steamed veggies. For me, I'll take a bacon cheese-burger with extra fries. And a milkshake." I tack on the drink for good measure. Who knows what kind of medicating I'll need to do after this talk.

"You should skip the first order and just serve the cardboard that the hamburger comes in," snarks the order taker.

I ignore him. "There's a buzzer on the door. Apartment four-one-three."

"Got it. Be around fifteen minutes."

I thank the guy, get my cash out, and then sit down to wait. A minute later, I stand. After a few seconds, I start pacing. As each second ticks by, my nerves become increasingly frayed. The firm knock on the door makes me jump two feet straight into the air.

"Who is it?" My heart beats loudly. The delivery guy is supposed to call from the entry.

"Ty," he announces.

I'm not ready. Too bad I already revealed I'm home or I could go into the bedroom and hide again. Slowly, I force my feet toward the door.

He knocks again.

"I'm coming," I say. Irritated, I whip it open. "I heard you the first time."

His arched eyebrow speaks volumes. He pushes inside and takes a quick look around. "Where's Fleur?"

"Leon's."

He nods. "Good. Come on then." He motions for me to step away from the door.

I cling to the handle. "I don't want to."

"I know you don't, otherwise you wouldn't have kept your mouth shut for the last three weeks, but we're going to have this out anyway."

"What if I don't want to?"

He places his hands on his hips.

It's inappropriate, but I can't help noticing how perfect his frame is. His proportions are amazing. The leg to torso ratio is flawless. He has the ideal inverted triangle from his shoulders to his waist. His good looks make me angry and hungry at the same time. *Hangry.*

"Ara."

"Sorry." I shut the door and go into the kitchen, where I busy myself with the glasses and plates. "Do you want water or milk? I ordered a milkshake, but I know you're on a diet. I think I have skim milk if that's what you want. I guess water's the best, right? I ordered you a chicken breast—"

"Ara," he says.

I stop midpour. "You want something else?"

"Yes, for you to stop being so nervous." He pulls the glass out of my hand and sets it on the counter. "Come over here and sit down." He leads me over to the sofa and sits next to me.

We've sat on this sofa together a million times, but it's never felt this small. I fidget, trying to figure out the best way to explain my silence and still keep our relationship on the same, even course it was before.

"Why are you so nervous?" He hasn't let go of my hand. In fact, he's tracing small circles on the back of it, and I can feel the tingles he's creating all the way up to my arm.

I jerk out of his grip. "Why are you randomly touching me?" I accuse, hiding my hands away underneath my armpits.

"We're friends, Ara. Friends touch each other." There's a trace of humor in his voice and I swear he moves closer.

I slide away. "Yes, we are *friends*." I emphasize the *F* word. "Which is why I don't know why we're even having this talk."

"What kind of talk is this?"

"How's Kathleen?" I try desperately to buy some time.

"Ara."

The way he says my name—softly and without a hint of irritation—makes me feel small and foolish.

I clear my throat. He waits. I clear it again. My throat feels scratchy when I start to explain. "You're a very important person in my life. Other than my dad, you know me the best. Your friendship means the world to me. I don't want that to change."

"And?"

"And..." I scratch my bare toe against the carpet. "And that's why I think we should just forget what happened. It's why I tried to forget what happened."

"What if I don't want to forget? What then?"

Because I'm too much of a coward to look him in the eye, I stare at his hands. I break out in a light sweat thinking about how his fingers counted every ridge on my spine, how his palms smoothed a path up my legs, how he spread my thighs to make room for his hard, heavy body.

Ugh. I have to stop thinking that way. Angry with myself, I blurt out, "We got drunk and then horny and because we were the only two people in the room, we took our horniness out on each other. End of story."

"So you're saying every time you're drunk and horny, you're making out with someone? Because I've been drunk and horny around my teammates plenty of times and have successfully avoided climbing into bed with any of them."

I throw up my hands. "What do you want me to say?"

"I want you to be honest." The softness is turning hard and grim.

"Where's your honesty?" I shoot back. "Why do I feel like I'm the one on trial here? I wasn't the only one in that bed."

He reaches out and grabs my chin, forcing me to look at him.

"I thought I'd give you the chance to address it first, but fine, my honesty is that the night at the Hyatt is one of the hottest experiences I've ever had."

I stare at him in shock. "You didn't even remember it until last night."

"No, I remembered it." His beautiful lips press into a flat line. "I thought I'd dreamt it, because you don't like me that way, remember? You've always said we were the best of friends, so yeah, I'd have flashes of what we did, get hard, and tell myself to shut up about it because we were friends and you didn't want that. But now that I've figured out it wasn't a dream and that it all happened, I don't think I can go back."

I slap a hand over his mouth. "Don't say anything more. Just don't," I plead. "I want you in my life as my friend, Ty. That's always been the case. Girlfriends and boyfriends come and go, but we can be friends forever. That's better than anything. If you say what I think you're going to say, you'll break the friendship seal. Can't we just forget about what happened? Pretend it didn't happen and go forward?"

Above my fingers, his eyes glint dangerously at me. I drop my hand and move to the very end of the sofa.

He's quiet for a moment and then, "Is that what you really want?"

It hurts to nod, but I do. A light flickers out in his eyes and guilt and sadness wash over me in a wave.

To my surprise, Ty gets to his feet. His lips curl into an awkward smile. "If that's what you want, then that's what we'll do. Just like our freshman year. I'll see you around."

Those words sound so final. He walks out without a glance behind him, but he doesn't slam the door. He opens it and quietly slips out. I think if he'd had shown some emotion—some anger or frustration—I might have run after him.

But the total lack of emotion tells me that I was right. We should push that night at the Hyatt into the very back of our memory bank and never take it out again.

Being right doesn't stop the tears from forming, though. I blink rapidly to keep them from spilling over.

Then the door flies open, crashing against the wall with a bang. Ty appears in the open doorway. In two strides, he's at the sofa and in another move, he has me in his arms. His mouth latches onto mine. Big hands slide under my ass and position me directly over his very, very hard shaft. I can't prevent a moan from escaping.

"Fuck the friendship seal," he growls.

21

Ty

I keep my mouth over hers as I hoof it to her bedroom. My dick rubs against her with every step. This is torture. The best kind, but still excruciating, barely survivable torture.

Inside Ara's bedroom, I lower her onto the bed. Or, more accurately, I toss her onto the bed and follow her down, kissing her again until she's breathless.

Her small hands curl around my neck and her mouth opens beneath mine. I taste her lips, her tongue, the inner recesses of her mouth. I swallow her moans—the tiny, whispering things that rise from her throat whenever I press hard against her sex.

I want to kiss her everywhere. The curve of her cheek. The fluttering pulse at the base of her neck. The strong thighs. The pert tits. The sweet pussy.

I keep kissing her, not giving her time to spout off more excuses, not giving her time to bring up some stupid friendship code, not allowing her to say no.

Hold up. I force my lips off of hers. My heart's racing and my dick is so hard it might break off, but not giving her an out, not allowing her to say no isn't right. I want her with me the whole way. Nothing more than her full agreement is going to be enough for me or we'll be right back where we started—her protesting and me wanting.

"You with me, Ara?"

She stares numbly up at me. Her lips are wet, plump, and cherry red. I bite the inside of my cheek to keep from attacking her mouth again.

"Ara," I repeat, my voice unintentionally harsh.

The sharp tone wakes her up, though.

"I'm with you."

I drag a shaky hand over my mouth, almost weak with relief. "All right. All right."

Those are the only two words I can form. I slide off the bed and kneel on the ground. She sits up uncertainly. Her dark hair falls over one shoulder. I brush it aside.

The sweatshirt she has on is mine. I pull the fabric down far enough to expose her golden skin. "You're wearing my clothes."

"Is that a crime?" Her voice is as scratchy as my own.

"Yep. Thievery." I press my lips against the apple of her shoulder. I lay small kisses along her collarbone, stopping when I reach the hollow of her throat. "I'll let it go if you return my stuff."

"What happens if I don't?" she says.

I rub a hand over the side of her ass. "Then you get punished."

She shudders beneath my grip. I nearly come in my jeans. My fingers tighten around her hip and pull her to the edge of the bed. "Is that what you need? A good spanking? Because I can do that for you. I can do anything you want," I whisper darkly.

"You're a lot of talk right now," she gasps out.

"Is that right?" I grab the neck of the sweatshirt and rip it in two. She falls silent and I take the moment to drink in her bare tits. I have a brief flashback of this scene and curse myself for being so drunk that I can't remember exactly what she looked like the first time.

I know now and I won't forget.

She's perfectly shaped. Her tits are round and perky topped with pert, pointed nipples. I don't need a second invitation. I dive in, mouthing one and pinching the other between a thumb and forefinger.

Ara moans a sweet sound of encouragement. I lavish her breasts with attention until she's writhing under me. Everything in me screams for release, but I have so many places on her body that I want to explore. Somehow I find my self-control.

I let go of her tits and move south. She makes a protesting sound.

"No, baby, I'm not leaving you," I soothe. "I'm visiting new places."

"Ty," she whines, tugging at my hair. "I want to kiss you."

"Patience, sweet thing. Patience." It's as much advice to me as it is to her.

I peel off her thin, stretchy pants and her equally thin, barely there panties. Her body heaves with want, and I clench my muscles tight in response.

"Look at how pretty you are," I whisper, dragging my fingers down a bare patch of skin to delve between her legs. Her arousal slicks my fingers. I ease two fingers inside her tight channel. "There you are. So good."

"Sooo good," she echoes.

"Just like I remember."

Her breath catches at my words. I wonder how much she recalls. The vague memories of that night have screwed with my mind for weeks. Touching her like this brings everything into sharp focus. Her sounds, her feel, her scents all come flooding back, filling in those black and white memories with vivid, bright color.

I fuck her with my fingers, long and deep thrusts. My cock aches and twitches, wanting desperately to feel the hot, wet clutch of her body. But I want to make her come with just my hand. I want to feel her nerves quiver with excitement. I want the flood of her release to cover my palm.

I want to taste her. I spread her thighs and muscle my shoulders between her legs. Her pussy is pretty, pink, and flushed, all primed and ready for me.

I lay my tongue flat, not rushing. Not this time. This memory will be etched in the part of my brain that remembers the first quarterback I sacked, the first touchdown I scored, the first championship I won.

I let the flavor of her seep onto my tongue.

Her fingers dig into my scalp and hold me tight against her. Yeah, she's with me. One hundred percent with me.

She tastes like heaven. I simultaneously want to stay down here, drinking at the well of her desire, and pound into her until my aching dick falls off.

She takes the decision out of my hands. A quick jerk on my hair has me looking up.

"I want that." She points between my legs. "Inside me. Now."

I swipe the back of my hand across my mouth. She doesn't like the hesitation.

"Now," she repeats.

I have my clothes off in a nanosecond. Dick in hand, I ready myself for the first plunge when I realize I'm going in raw. I roll off, cursing. "Fuck. Condom," I explain.

"Hurry," she begs. Her fingers slip inside herself and my head nearly blows off.

I dive for my jeans and fumble around for the condom. I haven't felt this inept since my first day of camp at SU when I realized that every single guy on my team was better than the best guy I played against in high school.

I roll the condom on and crawl over her body.

The first slide inside her has my eyes rolling into the back of my head. She convulses and I nearly come.

"Fuck, hold on," I gasp. I press a hand on her pelvis. "Don't move." She squirms under my grip. I bite my tongue. "Shit. Shit. Shit."

This is scary good.

I inhale a shallow, shaky breath. I can't get any more oxygen in my lungs. I can barely function. I'm reduced to one motion and one motion only. Sliding in and out of Ara's body.

Her skin is smooth and supple and soft. Different from me in every way. I rough her up with my teeth, the hair on my legs, the calluses on my palms. She shivers, writhes, shudders with each movement.

We find a rhythm, hot and hard. I don't know if it's because we've been friends for so long, but we're in perfect sync, moving together as if we've done this a thousand times before.

Her thighs tighten around my hips. I can feel myself coming apart, splintering into tiny shards as she groans and stiffens beneath me. She cries out, tips her neck back and freezes. The tight clutch of her grows even firmer and I can't hold out any longer. I shout out my release, shooting so hard into the rubber that I fear I'm breaking it. I come down off the mountain slowly, blind and shaking from the power of my orgasm.

Holy holy *holy* Christ. Is this what I've been missing for four years?

I collapse, angling my body slightly to the left so I don't crush her. She's still mostly squashed beneath me. I wish I had the energy to move, but I don't.

"Push me off," I mumble into the mattress. "Because I can't move."

"I don't want to," she replies. I feel the light weight of a blanket being thrown over my back.

I turn my head to see a sliver of skin behind a curtain of hair. I manage to summon up the energy to sweep it aside, exposing her small ear and the curve of her cheek. Both spots beg for me to come and explore.

I get up, take care of the condom, and climb back into bed with her.

"How can you move?" she asks. Her arms are flung above her head.

"How can I not?" I counter. "I think I missed this spot the first time." I taste the tender space behind her ear. "And this one." I flick my tongue against the underside of her jawline.

She trembles lightly. My dick stirs in response. I sweep a hand

167

down her side, pausing to cradle her breast and then moving lower to mark the indent at her waist and still lower to feel the jut of her hipbones. "And all of these."

A bold hand curls around my cock. "What about me? I didn't get a chance at this."

I pause in my exploration. "You didn't?"

"Not this time or last time." She flips me over onto my back. "I think it's my turn now."

I fold my arms behind my head and pretend to be at ease, despite every muscle in my body quivering in anticipation. "Do your worst, baby."

An evil smile crosses her face. "You're in trouble now, boy."

She moves backward, ass up, elbows down until her face is level with my crotch. I sweep the blanket off so I can look at her body. Her ass sways as she gets into position.

I don't know that I'm going to survive this.

"Tell my family I loved them," I say as her mouth descends. "I had a good life."

She laughs. Small puffs of air breeze across my stiff shaft.

"Don't laugh. It's never good to laugh when you're this close to a man's cock."

"I don't see you deflating at all," she teases.

I form a joke about footballs, but it never makes it past my lips because Ara takes me in her mouth. The minute her tongue touches my cock, I'm dead.

She brings me to life with another lick and then kills me with the next. The deadly process repeats itself until I'm a babbling, mindless idiot who can't say anything more than, "yes, please, faster, there. Oh, fuck, yes."

I manage to gain some semblance of control and tap her on the side of her head when I'm about to come. She doubles down, opening her throat to swallow me whole. *God must love me*, I think as I empty myself into her mouth. It's the only explanation for why I'm here in Ara's bed with her hot mouth covering my cock.

"Thank you," I manage to mumble before passing out.

Somewhere in the middle of the night, I wake up, blankets over me, Ara's sweet form tucked by my side. I ease out from under her body and tiptoe out of the room.

"Are you leaving her?" a sharp voice says from the kitchen.

I pivot toward the sound, blinking owl-like at the bright light. I make out a hazy blob. "Fleur?"

"Yeah, it's me." The blob comes closer.

Belatedly, I realize I'm buck-ass naked. I hastily move a hand in front of my crotch. "I'm using the john."

"Oh." She stops about five feet away. "Oh," she says again and slaps a hand over her eyes. "Holy shit. You're naked."

"Yup." And I have to piss. "I'm not leaving her." What do these two take me for? Ara kept quiet about the night at the Hyatt because she was afraid I'd freak out on her, and now Fleur thinks I'm abandoning Ara in the middle of the night. "Why would you think that? I'm her friend. I care about her."

"It's not enough to care about her," Fleur informs me. Her mouth flattens into a disapproving line beneath her hand.

"What's that supposed to mean?"

"You figure it out." She whips around and leaves me in the hall-way, bare-assed and confused.

What am I to figure out? Ara's my best friend. We just had the greatest sex of my life. And I care about her as a person. This seems like a no-brainer to me. How is caring not enough? Fleur's cryptic response reminds me of Bryant's earlier mystical statement about figuring shit out.

I shake myself and go to the bathroom. Women. They should just come out and say what they mean.

I wash my hands and let myself back in the bedroom. A little moonlight creeps in between the open curtains, making Ara look mysterious and beautiful.

I care about her a helluva lot. Maybe Fleur means that I need to show Ara how *much* I care. I'm not great with words. I'm not artistic like Ara, but I do have one skill. I understand my body intimately and I can push myself to physical limits that others can't reach. So I'll show Ara how much I care, expressing myself in the best way I know how. With my body.

I walk over to the bed and pull the blanket down. She won't need it. I'll keep her warm. I run my hands down her arms.

She stirs, her legs parting.

"Ty," she breathes.

"Yes, baby?"

"Make love to me."

My heart seizes. I dip my head low to her stomach. "Absolutely."

22

Ty

I wake up early. Lately, I've been getting used to sleeping in until ten or later. I know I'll have to break myself of that habit when pro camp starts this summer, but for now, I'll enjoy the luxury of letting the roosters crow without an audience.

Ara's dead to the world. She's on her stomach, her face buried in my biceps, and her hands tucked somewhere under her body, like she's afraid she's going to molest me in the middle of the night if she doesn't hold herself in.

This girl. What am I going to do with her?

I stroke my free hand down her back but she doesn't stir. Poor thing. All worn out.

With a broad grin, I lever myself out of the bed, pull my jeans on, and go make us some coffee. Ara's kind of crabby without some morning caffeine.

Thankfully, Fleur's absent. Her late-night cryptic messages don't make any more sense this morning. I scoop the coffee grounds into the filter and grab the filtered water from the fridge.

I feel good about last night, but I know Ara will be filled with regret. Or, if not regret, then worry. My plan to overcome her concern is a bull rush. I ply her with coffee and then have sex with her until she passes out.

Once that's accomplished, I can leave for my afternoon workout and film review session. And then...the disastrous interview pops into my head.

Shit. I can't believe I actually forgot about Dana facing those embezzlement charges. Good sex will do that to you, I guess. But first thing I've got to do today is call Dana, fire him, do some damage control, and figure out who else I can hire at this late stage.

"Damn." I strike a fist against the counter. I don't need this drama in my life. It's tempting to leave now, but if I do, doubts are going to creep into Ara's head.

I exhale heavily and order my priorities. I take this one step at a time. I go in and make sure Ara's memory isn't going to malfunction on her this time and that she's not going to disappear. Then I go straighten out everything else. Might as well start the day off right.

When the coffee is done, I pour two mugs and return to Ara's room. She's in the same comatose position as when I left her. I lean a hip against the desk and survey the wreckage. The sheets are pulled away from the corners. Our clothes are a mess on the floor. My jeans are tangled up with her yoga pants. Her lacy purple panties are lying across the toe of one of my boots.

Seeing our things muddled together seems right, like when I decided I'd go to Southern U instead of Western State, which is what everyone in my family wanted me to do.

I wanted to make my own way without Knox, and I knew when I came here I'd made the right decision, just as I know that I made the right decision ignoring the whole friendship spiel from Ara.

I'd wanted her from the first time I saw her, but I let her convince me that we'd be better as friends. I don't buy that anymore, but she's stubborn as a mule, so moving her off her set path isn't going to be an easy task. But I've fought harder battles.

I lightly stroke the bottom of one bare foot sticking out from underneath the comforter.

Ara shoots upright. Her eyes widen when they meet mine.

"Oh my God," she yelps.

I grin. "Nope, just me."

She whips the comforter over her head. "What are you doing?"

"Bringing you coffee." I shove her mug underneath the comforter.

She grabs it and tries to slink down into an inconspicuous mound.

"I figured it would be like this." Which is why I couldn't leave.

"You're supposed to creep out in the middle of the night," she grumbles.

"I missed that during orientation period. It must've been the topic discussed while I had my head between your legs. I couldn't hear much other than, 'yes, Ty' and 'more, Ty.'"

"Inappropriate!" Still hiding her face, she sticks a hand out. "Yellow card!"

I swallow my laughter with the remainder of my coffee. "You have about a minute to brush your teeth, use the bathroom, drink your coffee, do whatever before I'm throwing you on the bed for..." I pause to count. "Round four."

She remains silent, as if by not moving I'll forget she's there.

"It's about fifty seconds now."

She bursts into motion, running to the bathroom. I pluck her half-empty mug off the nightstand and drop it off in the kitchen sink on the way to pour myself another mug.

After ten minutes, two more cups of coffee, and a bagel, I stomp to the bathroom. Hand ready to knock, I get distracted by my phone. The ringtone signals my brother's on the phone. I drop my hand with a sigh and go answer my brother's call.

"Yo."

"Impatient much, bro?"

"Yes, actually." I glance toward the bathroom across the hall. The shower is still running. She's got to run out of hot water soon. "What's up?"

"I'm here."

173

"Define here." But I know even before he answers.

"I'm standing in your living room. Remy's girlfriend is making me breakfast. I came in on the red-eye. I guess you never made it home last night." The unstated question is clear. Who are you currently doing?

"I'll be home in ten." I hang up because I'm not sure how I want to answer that question.

I gather up the rest of my clothes, shoot a frustrated glance toward the still-closed bathroom door. Knox is here to see how he can help clean up. And while I love him, I'd rather he kept his nose out of my business for now—both personal and football.

I'm not going to hide that Ara and I are together, but I know if I admit this to Knox, he'll want to run the twin test. He believes in that. He stayed a virgin because he believed he'd meet the *one*. I thought this was crazy, but apparently it was true. He met the one last year and married her within months of their first encounter. They seem happy, but I'm not convinced that the twin test is the determinative factor as to whether I'm going to be happy with a woman. I'm sure Ara's the right one for me, but the girl can't tell me from Knox if you put nametags on us. Knox came to visit on his bye week Ara's freshman year. The whole weekend, she kept getting the two of us mixed up, even when I was wearing my glasses.

If Knox figures that out, he'll dismiss Ara as another pretty face. If Ara and I are going to last, my family will need to be on board. My parents will follow Knox's lead. Yeah, now is not the time, when Ara's still grappling with her own feelings. If I throw Knox at her, she'll burrow her head so far down into the sand, I'll need a bulldozer to pull her out.

I knock on the door and yell. "I have to head home for a bit, but I'll be back. Don't run too far. You wore me out last night and I don't have much energy."

I wait for a response but get nothing. I get dressed and then jot her a quick note.

I'll be back around noon. Will bring you a burger. Keep my side of the bed warm. Ty.

I cap the pen and stare down at the note, feeling unsure of myself. Then I crumple the note up and toss it in the trash. I'll call her later when I've got my own house in order.

§

"WHERE'S ARA?" Knox asks after we finish breakfast. "What's she up to these days?"

It's uncanny how he knows things. Our twin sense freaks me out sometimes. My brother is a hundred times more sanguine about it.

"Still looking for a job." I gather the plates and carry them to the sink. "Thanks for lunch, Nichole. You're the best."

"I know," she replies smugly. And then throws a glare in Remy's direction. He doesn't notice. His head's bent over his phone.

I clear my throat at the same time that Knox tries to surreptitiously kick Remy under the table. Remy jerks to attention and looks around bewildered.

"I'm still single," I tell Nichole as I finish putting the dishes in the dishwasher. "Any time you want to dump that mess and climb aboard this fine train, let me know."

"Is it buy one, get one free?" Nichole asks cheekily. "Because I'd take you if you were a package deal."

Knox twists in his chair and shoots Nichole a grin. "You'd have to fight Ellie for me, and I can tell you from personal experience that she might look weak but she packs a lot of power."

Remy perks up. "Is there going to be a girl fight? Because I'm all for that."

Nichole throws a dish towel across the room at Remy's head. When that falls short, she picks up a loaf of bread, walks over and starts beating him over the head with it. "You're supposed to fight for me, you ass!" Bam. Bam. Bam. "You're not supposed to push me into the cage!" Bam. Bam.

"It's not like it's going to happen," he cries, hand over his head to stop the bread assault. "Knox is married and Ty's got Ara—" He grimaces. "I bet I wasn't supposed to say that."

175

"Ara?" Knox arches a knowing eyebrow.

I toss the fallen towel onto the counter. "Nichole, feel free to beat him on the head a few times for me, too."

"Got it."

Knox gets up and follows me out of the room. We hear Remy bleat a few "sorries" in between cries for mercy.

"Ara and you, huh?" my brother says as we climb the stairs to my room.

"Ara and me."

"When'd that happen?"

"Last night."

"I thought you two were just friends."

I push open the bedroom door and gesture for him to go in first. He does, throwing himself on my bed. I settle onto my chair and await the inquisition.

"We are friends."

"But friends who fuck."

"Friends who have enjoyed each other, yes."

"She can't tell us apart, you know."

"I know."

"You're serious about her, though. I can tell."

"Yup."

He falls silent. I know what he's thinking and I don't have to be his twin to read the disappointment on his face.

"We should run the test again."

"I think not. You're just going to have to accept her."

"You know she's not the one, right?" Knox says. "I mean, I like Ara and all. She's a cool chick, but since she can't tell the two of us apart it's not going to work. Remember at the Bowl game how she found me at the bar thinking I was you and told me how I was going to be a 'top draft pick, baby!'" He mimics her voice, badly.

"Yeah, I remember. I was in your hotel suite running another test on your wife." I stare at the ceiling. So Ara gets it wrong from time to time. Does it really matter?

"And she passed."

The smugness in his voice makes me want to punch him. In a brotherly manner, of course. The thing is that I need Knox to buy in, otherwise he's going to be looking suspiciously at her from now until the end of time. That's not going to work for any of us.

"Knox, we're two different people. Okay? It doesn't matter to me that Ara can't tell us apart. She's not going to climb into your bed, if that's what you're worried about. The thing from high school bothers you way more than it does me." In fact, I think that's what made him decide he was going to be a virgin until he found the *one*.

"How can it not bother you?" He props himself up on his elbows. "The girl who proclaimed she loved you to the entire senior class took her clothes off and got into bed with me. When I told her it was me, she said she didn't care!" He shakes his head. "That's why you have to find someone like Ellie."

"No offense, bro, but Ellie's not my type. And what happened with my high school girlfriend isn't going to happen with Ara. Ara would care that she was coming on to the wrong brother. She's not going to shrug it off. She'd haul off and punch you in the face if you tried that shit with her."

His pinched expression says he wants to argue, but I stare him down and eventually he lets himself fall back on the bed. I grab a football off the floor and toss it to him. He catches it without looking.

"Did you come down here because you thought I wasn't happy? Because I am happy," I tell him. "Last night, I was real happy." I pause, reliving the memory of Ara leaning down, her hair curtaining my face, her hands pressed into the middle of my chest as she ground down on my cock. "This morning, too. I was happy this morning." We didn't have sex like I wanted and she was still in denial, but she'll come around.

We were so hot together, it's surprising her bed isn't just a pile of ashes. I can't wait until tonight. I've got a lot of positions I want to try out with her. My tongue tingles in anticipation of tasting her again.

"And you're happy now," Knox observes.

"Yup." I don't bother to hide it. Knox is going to have to get used to Ara, the girl who can't tell us apart. She's going to be with me for a long time.

"Then what about the agent thing?" The ball comes with the question.

"I'm firing Dana."

"Firing?" Judgment is obvious in his tone. Dana should be past tense in my life.

"I was a little busy last night," I remind him and whip the ball back.

"Do you have a list of agents you're considering? My guy still wants to sign you. He says he has a couple of sweet endorsement deals lined up. The companies like the twin angle. They think it's fresh." He tosses me a folder instead of the ball.

Inside, I find a contract of endorsement. "How many other rookies are doing this?" I ask, peering over the top of the paper.

This time it's Knox avoiding my eyes. "None."

"Then I'll pass."

"Come on. This isn't a gift. This is because you just won the Championship. You won all the awards for defense this past season. You're slated to go in the top five."

"If this drink company wanted me because of all that, they would've contacted me."

"Maybe they heard about Dana and didn't want to go through him," Knox points out.

I bristle. "I get endorsement requests, interview requests, fan mail, marriage proposals, and hate letters sent here to the football office every day."

"Does it really matter how the deal came about?"

I set the folder on the desk. "Yeah, it does."

"You're putting the emphasis on the wrong factor. If you had a decent agent like mine, you'd be getting these deals by yourself. I've been playing for a year and I know—"

"That's enough," I say tersely. I'm not going down this path with

Knox. I don't get to see Knox much these days and I don't want to spend our time together squabbling. I change the subject. "How's Ellie? You enjoying your off-season?"

Knox is pissed. He makes a face at me and we stare at each other until he gives in.

"Ellie's awesome," he finally capitulates. "The off-season is awesome. We spent a couple of days up at the shore."

"Still no Wi-Fi there, huh?" Knox bought Mom and Dad a house on the water up in Maine. The place is so remote that there's no decent internet access.

"Nope. Aren't you the lucky one," he deadpans.

I am lucky. The lack of internet coverage means my parents haven't seen the debacle that's gone down. Otherwise, I would've been dealing with my mom, my dad and Knox.

"I wondered why I didn't get any panicked calls after the Dana thing broke."

"They are blissfully ignorant about Dana and your ex. Ellie and I kept them that way."

"I appreciate that." I stand up. "Want to play some FIFA?"

Knox jumps to his feet. "I guess you're in the mood to be defeated."

All feelings of animosity are gone. We can't stay mad at each other long.

I lead the way down to the game room. "Baby brother, you are going to go home disappointed."

He shoves me in the back. I throw an elbow and catch his gut. All's well with my brother. Things are okay with Ara. I just need to fix the agent thing.

No big deal.

23

Ara

"I DON'T WANT TO TALK ABOUT IT," I INFORM AN OPEN-mouthed, overly curious Fleur when she bursts in the door mere minutes after Ty steps out. She must have been lying in wait.

"But—"

"No. I can't. I'm still half convinced I'm dreaming all of this and would prefer to stick my head in the sand for at least a few more hours. Please let me have this," I beg.

Fleur doesn't reply, so I press my hands together and make the most pitiful face I can. It works.

"Fine, but prepare for a full-fledged interrogation later."

I salute her and then quickly leave, grabbing my backpack on the way out. Once outside, though, I'm at a loss for what to do. Anywhere on campus, I might run into Ty. Another time, I'd be able to hide out at the gallery, but since I quit that job, I've got nothing but time on my hands.

I guess I could sketch. I find an empty bench near the Science II building and pull out my notebook. I haven't done much since the last time Ty looked at it.

The bunny is hiding in the bushes while the farmer searches.

"Poor bunny," I croon as I sketch the outline of the fence in the next panel. "I know just how you feel. Trapped and helpless."

After several minutes of drawing, I have everything done in the scene. The bunny's face is peeking out from under a lettuce leaf. The farmer's shadow is shading the bunny's face. A net is held at the ready. It doesn't look right. With the fence to the one side and a rock on the other, there's nowhere for the bunny to go but forward.

I've drawn myself into a literal corner.

I erase the net in the farmer's hand and replace it with a stick.

"The farmer wants to have you for dinner as punishment for eating all his delicious leaves," I inform the bunny.

The bunny's eyes fill with tears. I erase the stick. I should've drawn some friends for Blinkie. They could distract the farmer. I slap down a few more lines and then take a look at my product.

Oh boy. I've drawn a knight on a horse, and he's wielding a big sword. Even in my doodles, I can't get away from Ty. This is no good. I trade my paper notebook for my electronic one to see if there are any new job openings.

Unsurprisingly, there are not. Gallery assistants are not in high demand, particularly outside of New York City. At this rate, I'm not going to get hired, which means I'll graduate and be unemployed.

Do I regret quitting Marissa's place?

I ponder that for all of two seconds. No. I can't say that I do even if Marissa hates me. I'm not sure why I stayed in the first place other than to give myself some résumé padding. If I wasn't going to put my dad down on there, I had to have something else to show prospective employers.

A girl with an art history degree doesn't have a ton of options. Is it too soon to send a follow-up email to the Philly gallery? They said they would call me, but it's been a month since my interview. I open my email tab and as I'm composing a polite but hopefully encouraging email, my phone rings.

I pick it up without thinking.

"Hello?" a familiar male voice says.

"Oh, is this Knox?" I wonder why Ty's brother is calling me.

"How did you know?"

"I can tell," I say absently, tapping my fingers against the tablet's screen. Should I type, *I'm anxious to hear back*? No. 'Anxious' sounds bad. How about 'excited.' Yeah, that sounds better.

"You...can...tell? Does Ty know this?" Accusation hangs heavy in Knox's voice.

And that's when I realize what I've done.

Pulse racing, I scramble for an explanation. "Um, does Ty know what?" I laugh, high and anxious. "That I can tell when it's you who calls? Of course I can tell it's you. Your name shows up on my phone. Doesn't your phone work that way?"

He hesitates, and then, to my relief, buys in. "Oh, yeah, right."

I swipe a metaphorical hand across my forehead in relief. "What can I do for you?"

"Can we meet at the Bean Factory?"

I stare at my unfinished email. "Sure. Are you here on campus?"

"Yes. I was—am, I mean. I'm visiting Ty."

"Are we getting together? Ty didn't mention it."

"Ah, yeah, well, he doesn't know yet."

"Is this a surprise party? Because your birthday isn't until June."

"Nope. I just want to see your pretty face is all."

Uh-huh. I don't believe that for a second.

❧

KNOX STANDS up as I enter the café. All eyes swerve to his frame and then to mine. I'm used to the phenomenon—I've been friends with Ty for four years. It's the same for him. He commands attention and it's hard to look away from him.

I give Knox a finger wave, grab a cup of coffee, and join him.

"Thanks for meeting me." He gives me a half hug and gestures for me to take a seat.

"Sure, but why are we keeping it a secret from Ty? Are we throwing him a pre-draft party? I don't think he'd really enjoy that.

He's still on his no-fun food diet, and who wants a party with wheat germ shots and chickpea crackers?"

Knox looks interested. "Chickpea crackers?"

These athletes. I hold up a hand. "It was a rhetorical question for which I will provide the answer. No person with actual taste buds wants a party like that. Besides, you know Ty doesn't like surprise things."

"It's not a surprise party." He cocks his head. "How do you know I'm not Ty? We got the same haircut recently."

"I know. He told me that you both got it cut like a couple days apart." I shake my head. "You twins are weird."

"But you do know it's me." He doesn't elaborate. It's like he's testing me, which is annoying.

"I know it's you because you asked me to meet you here. Plus, you're not wearing glasses." I say it slowly so he can comprehend it better.

"Ty's glasses are mostly for show. He hardly ever wears them. Like right now, I could be Ty not wearing glasses to see if you guess wrong."

How mad would Ty be if I slapped his brother? I corral my violent tendencies and try to use words to explain this. "I know you two like your little games such as when you wore the wrong uniform for the *SI* cover shoot or when you played the trick on poor Ellie, trying to make her think she was going to marry the wrong twin. You're lucky she has a good sense of humor."

Knox examines me. "She's the only one who can tell us apart all of the time. Even my mom has problems, but not Ellie. She could get it right blindfolded. Mom always said you had to marry the girl who could tell you apart." His words take on a speculative tone.

Time to nip this in the bud. "Good thing you wifed her up then, isn't it?" I mimic his folded hands and lean toward him. "What's this all about? I've got people to see and places to go, so can we get to the actual point?"

It looks like he wants to say one thing but then wisely changes his mind. "Ty's mad at me."

I sip my coffee. "I know."

"Then you know why, too?"

"Sure. You were probably telling him all about how you know best because you've been in the league for a year. You are also likely trying to sell him on the idea that now that he's punted Dana to the curb, you guys can be repped by the same agent and marketed as a pair, which is essentially a suggestion that he doesn't have any economic value individually." At least that's my guess.

Knox scowls and confirms everything. "That's not what I said at all. I told him that we could leverage the fact that we're twins into endorsements that wouldn't be available if he was just a rookie."

"He might get number one."

"And he might get three. Or five. Or ten. This is a deal that isn't contingent on his draft placement."

"You're right. It's a deal that is contingent on his twinness, something he isn't responsible for and didn't work hard all his life to achieve."

Knox makes a frustrated sound. "I want what's best for him, too."

"Don't we all? If this deal is right for both of you, Ty will come around, but insulting him or treating him like he's somehow inferior to you isn't the way to do it."

"I'm not treating him like that," Knox protests.

"I think you once said 'I've played on Sundays and you haven't.' Right?"

Knox pales.

I forge forward. "You're right that he's not inferior. He could have declared last year just like you. And just like you, he would have been drafted in the top five. But he wanted to win the Championship and risked his entire NFL career for that. If he'd been injured, if he'd had some other bad luck, that could've been it for him. He stayed for his team so that they'd win. For some of his teammates, that National Championship was the last time they'd lace on those pads. It was a sacrifice for him. He's not your inferior in any way, so don't treat him like he is. He doesn't deserve anything but praise and admiration."

Knox could tattle on me. He could tell Ty that I was rude to him. That I was disrespectful. But at this point I don't care. Ty would never, ever say anything bad to his brother, but Knox needs to be told. I'm fine with being the one to take the bad guy role.

"I'm a dick." He sighs and performs the patented Masters neck rub, an action I know well. Ty does it, too, when he's frustrated or trying to gather patience. That and the hair move.

Both are sexy as fuck when Ty does it. I'm unmoved by Knox. How can anyone get these two mixed up?

"So what should I do?" Knox asks finally.

"Lay off," I say bluntly. "He's smart. He'll make the right decisions. He just wants to do it in his own time so he knows that they're his decisions. You two are twins and all, but he's still his own person."

Knox's eyes start glowing in a freaky way. "Yes, he is."

His voice lowers a register and he gives me a strange, non-sexual but still invasive once-over. I resist the urge to squirm.

"Does he know?" Knox asks slowly.

"Know what?"

"That you can tell us apart."

Dammit. "Are we back to that again?" I exhale a big put-upon sigh.

He smirks at me. "Yup, we're back to that again."

"I see now you're the slow one in the family. I've told you before that you were obviously not Ty because of how you act. He's not going to call me up on your phone and ask me to meet at the Bean Factory. We locals call it the coffeehouse. And he's not going to ask me silly questions like this."

"If you say so."

"I do." I get to my feet, because I can't sit with Knox another minute without giving myself away. "It was good we had this chat."

"I'm glad to have spent some quality time with you, Ara." He smirks again.

Definitely not Ty. He's not a smirker. I start to walk away when a large hand clamps around my wrist.

I look down. "Yes?"

"If you won't tell him, I will. Ty deserves to know."

"Tell him what?" I bluster.

"He deserves to know you can tell us apart."

I grow angry. What is with everyone and their cousin trying to interfere with my friendship with Ty? It's like they want to separate us.

"I want Ty to like me for who I am, not because of some mystical voodoo crap he doesn't even believe in," I retort.

Instead of being offended by my angry tone, Knox smiles and releases me. "So you do like him." He winks. "I knew it."

"You're a smug bastard."

"Love you too, sis."

"I'm not your sis."

"You will be."

"I have a real urge to smack you, but instead I'll be the bigger person and leave."

"We have Christmas early, just FYI!" he yells after me. "And I like the Supreme brand, if you're wondering what to get me."

Flipping him off isn't very satisfying, but it is all I have at the moment.

24

Ty

I fire Dana that night.

"It's all a bunch of bullshit," he seethes into the phone.

"It doesn't matter if it's true or false." I parrot back his own advice. "It's the optics."

"You're a punk, you know that? You think that you can just play ball and succeed in this business? You're going to be in for a big surprise, buddy. And the way your personal life is a mess, no one is going to want to sign you!" Dana screams into the phone.

"We both know that's a lie. You'd take me back in a heartbeat."

He starts ranting again. I press the end button on my screen and grab a game controller off the coffee table.

"Who's up for a beating?"

Remy stands up. "I think I heard Nichole calling for me."

"Coward," I yell at his retreating back. I turn to my brother. "How about you?"

He gets to his feet. "Let's go for a beer."

I think back to the last time I drank and how I ended up in bed with Ara with very little memory of it.

"How about no."

"One drink in the off-season isn't going to kill you," Knox says.

"I know." But I've set out a regimen and I'm sticking with it. "I'll drink after the draft. How about a movie?" I suggest.

"Done."

We amicably bicker about what to see, but end up agreeing to catch the new Stephen King horror flick, which turns out to be terrifying but awesome and not because of the clowns in the movie. We run into Rhyann on our way out.

In the concession line waiting to get into the late movie, she chats with her male friend—one she's close enough to that he feels comfortable palming her ass in public.

I watch as she rises on her tiptoes and gives the boy a smooch. It turns into a tonguing. I pull Knox to a stop.

"Isn't that the girl who was laying into you on your school app?" Knox says.

"It is indeed." A smile spreads across my face. The Dana thing is shitty and has a lot more potential to affect my career, but wiping this problem off the books will be nice. I snap a pic and then decide to take a video for good measure.

"She accused you of cheating on her," he says in disbelief.

I didn't count the post-Championship game hookup with Ara as cheating. Rhyann had broken up with me months before and didn't come back begging for a second chance until after the game. If anything, I cheated on Ara with Rhyann, although thankfully I didn't sleep with Rhyann.

Never had. Never will. Damn glad about it. "Yup."

"It's a damn shame Mom raised us the way she did," he says with a load of disgruntlement.

"Truth," I yell out. "Rhyann."

The redhead jerks away from her partner's mouth and looks around. When she spots me, her eyes widen. Comically, she releases her friend abruptly, jumping away as if she was caught in bed with her pants down by a priest. She says something to her companion.

"Rhyann," I yell loudly again. "Good to see that you've moved on. I like your new man." I give her the thumbs up and then wave my phone at her so she knows that I have recorded her for posterity's sake.

Even from a distance, I can see her fair cheeks turn red. "Fuck off," she yells.

"I think she's talking to you," Knox says.

"It could be you."

"You're the one who slept with her."

"Nope. Never did."

Knox raises his eyebrows. "Re-virginizing yourself, buddy?"

"I've always been picky. If the girl says she slept with me even if we never did, I'm not going to embarrass her publicly."

"Why should you? That's what you have me for." He cups his hands around his mouth and yells, "Dude, you gotta be careful. Even if you don't sleep with her, she'll pretend like you did and smear you online for saying shit."

The guy's eyes widen. Rhyann's face goes from white to red. "Shut up, you fucker!"

"That was definitely for you." I grab Knox's arm and drag him away.

"Meh. Girl couldn't tell us apart before and I doubt she can now. Unlike some people we know."

"Yes, Ellie's perfect." I steer him toward the car. "I'm glad you found her or you'd still be wondering why God gave you a dick."

"She's not the only perfect one around," he says.

"What's that supposed to mean?"

"Nothing." The smug bastard knows something.

"You can be a real prick, you know that?"

He hums happily. "I do know that."

If he wasn't my brother, I'd want to beat his face in. I settle for an elbow to his chest. He responds with a punch to my gut. We both get in a few more blows before calling a truce.

"So this Ara girl," he says on the ride home.

"Yeah?" I hope he doesn't bring up the whole twin test again.

"If she's who you want, then I'm happy for you. When can I meet her officially and welcome her to the family?"

I cast him a surprised look. This is a much different tune than he sang before. "Not this trip. She's skittish."

"Gotcha." He falls silent and then says, "What's she scared about? Me? The twin test? I don't plan on running it again."

There's an odd note in his voice. I'd label it mischievous, if pressed.

"Nah. You know I don't believe in that shit." I shift in the driver's seat. "She's scared about fucking up the friendship. The outside stuff isn't going to get to her. She's not that kind of person."

"Solid. I can get behind that."

I frown. Knox believes in the power of the test. I asked him once what he would've done if Ellie had failed and his blithe response was, "It would never happen. She's the one."

More power to him. We may be identical on the outside, but we're different in a lot of other aspects. That Ara can't tell us apart doesn't matter. She's my closest friend. I've held her hand through her breakup. She's suffered through mine. She's comforted me when I've lost and celebrated with me when I've won.

She's the first one I think about when I have bad news and good news. I'd rather hang out with her than anyone else.

"Good, because Ara fits me. She's funny, a good listener." Sexy as hell. "You said that the earth moved when you met Ellie. I suppose it did for me, too, but so slowly I didn't realize it until we were on top of each other." Literally.

"If you say she's the one, then she's the one," he says, way too easily, in my opinion.

"If you have something you want to say, get it out," I tell him.

He leans back, folding his arms behind his head. "I got nothing, bro. If she's who you want, then I'm for it."

This isn't like him at all. I feel compelled to offer another, fuller explanation. "I asked her out the first time I saw her," I admit.

Knox perks up. "Really?"

"Yeah. Don't you remember me telling you that I mowed down a girl on my way to class, asked her out and she turned me down?"

"That was Ara?"

"Yeah." Sophomore year, I was running to class with Remy and a couple other teammates. We were tossing a nerf ball between us. Remy threw it long and I ran full out until I ran into an obstacle. A five-and-a-half-foot, long brown-haired obstacle. I was able to catch her before she hit the ground. "Almost crushed her and then skipped class to apologize to her."

"She recognize you?"

"Nah, but even if she had, it wouldn't have meant anything. Her dad's a big-time sculptor. Like his work is in museums and shit. Being around famous people is normal for her."

"So you asked her out and she said no. Cuz why?"

I don't know. "She said she wasn't in the market for a man, but she could use a friend."

"And you two lived happily ever after," he sums up.

"I guess." I pull into the drive and glance at my quiet phone. "The ever after part is up in the air for now."

"Really?"

"Nah. I'll wear her down."

He busts out laughing and I do, too. Knox stays for two more days, during which Ara ignores all of my texts.

I'm not worried. Like I told Knox, I'll wear her down. I didn't become an elite athlete by quitting at the first sign of any resistance.

25

Ara

It's childish to run away, but I figure I'm only twenty-two. I have decades of life left in which I can be responsible and face up to all the drama in my life. For now, though, I'm running home.

I try not to brood for the entire three-hour road trip south to my dad's house. I blare a playlist of my favorite rappers. I try to fall into a podcast on This American Life. Neither of those work so I resort to playing games with the road signs. There are almost no road signs with the letter Q or X. If I ever become rich, I'm going to buy a town and name it Qixing for all the road warriors out there.

You can thank me later.

Unfortunately, there's no distraction strong enough to tear Ty out of my head. Sex with him was...mind-blowing. Yes, literally, every sensible thought I've ever had was turned to ash. He said more and I...I parted my legs.

Well, I did more than that. I dug my nails into his back. I bit his ear. I sucked on his dick, reveled in his deep, throaty groans, and came more times in one twenty-four period than I thought was physically possible.

I woke up wanting him so I did what any smart girl would. I ran to the bathroom. Just when I thought it was safe to emerge, I made that stupid error with Knox. Once Knox tells Ty that I can tell them apart, I'm doomed.

Ty won't ever let up. He *says* he doesn't believe in that "metaphysical" crap as he terms it, but deep down, I know he does. It's why he never has become invested in any other girl. He's waiting for some elusive sign that she's the one. And it's never come because that shit doesn't exist.

I fear for our friendship even more now. I thought about floating the friends with benefits idea to him. Maybe we just needed to fuck our way back to friendship. What guy would refuse that?

But if he finds out I can tell the two apart? He'll never accept friendship only, which leaves me in the position of having no friend at all. Romantic relationships never last. My dad is case example A. His love for women has only ever been temporary. I'm one of the few females in his life he hasn't left and it's because we don't have a romantic relationship. It's filial. The other women in his life who have lasted are friends.

The flame of passion dies out, but the solid coals of friendship burn forever. Ty will get tired of me. Or maybe I'll get tired of him and his dedication to the game. That's what happened to Mom. She didn't want to be second to Dad's art. She left and the two of them haven't spoken more than a handful of times since then.

Dad misses her. Sometimes he'll talk about how grateful he is for all her support. He wouldn't be where he is now if it wasn't for her. But Mom can't get past the neglect. She said he was an emotional vampire, sucking all the energy out of her. That she never had time for herself and her own needs.

I see that. Dad can be very self-absorbed. I love him, but I'm not in love with him. I don't need the constant attention and affirmation that Mom wanted. I've accepted Dad for what he is—a brilliant, flawed man who tries his hardest. His hardest wasn't good enough for her.

If only they had stuck to being friends. Then Dad wouldn't miss her. Mom wouldn't be angry all the time. I wish Ty understood this. He knows my past, or, at least some of it. He knows I don't speak to my mom because it always ends in a fight. He knows my dad is flighty as hell. He knows I value our friendship more than anything.

Why oh why did we have to screw everything up with sex? Stupid sex.

Stupid sex.

Stupid amazing sex.

My body tingles at the mention. Stupid body. My stomach grumbles.

"Fine. I'll feed you food, but shut up about wanting more of naked Ty."

When I finally reach Dad's house, I head straight to the kitchen. Unsurprisingly, the cupboards are bare. He's single now and left to his own devices, he often forgets to do normal people things like buy groceries. Or toilet paper, as I discover a few minutes later.

I wash my hands and root around in the fridge. I'm trying to figure out what to make for lunch when I hear a knock at the front door. I tense. Is it Ty? No. It couldn't be. I didn't even tell Fleur I was coming. It was a spur-of-the-moment thing. I woke up and got in my car to get coffee and the next thing I knew I was fifty miles toward Dad's house.

"Wh-who is it?" I ask, cursing myself at my timidity. "Who is it?" I call more loudly.

"It's Holly...Ara, is that you?"

Oh man. Dad's soon-to-be ex. I take a quick inventory of the kitchen. There's coffee, of course. Some oatmeal raisin cookies which Holly probably baked. God, I hope she baked them. I can't feed her another woman's cookies at a time like this.

"Ara?"

Fuck it. What Dad has will have to do.

"Coming." I hurry over and open the door.

Holly greets me with a tremulous smile. "Ara. You look so beautiful."

I've probably never looked worse, but I don't argue. Holly's eyes are red and puffy. Her whole face looks swollen. Poor woman looks like she spent the whole day, or more, crying her eyes out.

"Is your dad here?" She peers over my shoulder, sounding hopeful.

"No. He's still in New York."

"Oh." Her lower lip trembles.

God, I don't want her to start crying. "I was just about to make myself some lunch. Want something?"

She sniffs and nods. "I don't suppose Arthur has bought any groceries, has he?"

She bustles inside, opening cupboards and doors. Turning around, she gives me a pleased look. "Wait here," she instructs.

I wait and she reappears a minute later with two grocery bags. "Oh, Holly, no."

"He's got to eat. You know he doesn't take care of himself, particularly when he's lost in his work." She brushes aside my further protestations.

Capitulating with a sigh, I help her stow the groceries.

How my dad gets all these women to care about him even after they break up is a total mystery. The only one who doesn't still talk to him is my mom. But she's difficult for anyone to get along with. Since we fight most of the time, we've limited our interaction to once a year. Thank goodness I got that out of the way a few weeks ago.

"How long will he be in New York?" Holly asks as she putters around the kitchen, putting staples in the pantry and fresh foods in the refrigerator.

My stomach growls again, reminding me that I haven't eaten for hours. I grab a banana to appease it.

"I don't know. Maybe a few more days?" I guess. "He's staying with Stephen and Tracy. Apparently those two are getting married. Dad might be working on something as a wedding gift."

"Those two make such a sweet couple," she says. She stops in the middle of stacking yogurt in the fridge. "I wonder if I'll get an invite."

Her voice is so forlorn.

"It's so far away anyway. Why would you want to fly to New York just for a wedding? It'd be boring and stuffy, too, what with all the clients Stephen would have to invite."

Holly sniffles a few times, but manages to hold it together enough to nod. "Yes, it'd be terrible, wouldn't it? I miss all those lovely get-togethers, though. No one calls me anymore," she laments.

"What should we make for lunch?" I ask, desperate for a change of subject. "What'd you bring?"

"I thought I'd make fried chicken."

My stomach leaps for joy. Holly's fried chicken is amazing. Dad might've married her just for that.

"Let me know what I can do to help." I hurry over to the sink and wash my hands.

Holly instructs me on how to make the breading, which is a mixture of cornstarch, baking soda, and salt. We dip the wings and then set them out to dry for an hour.

Holly takes a seat at the table while I pour us a cup of coffee.

"How's school, dear?"

"It's almost over," I tell her. "Which means it's great. I've finished a paper that is due at the end of the year and I've only got two finals—one in comparative art."

"Oh, you won't even need to study for that one."

"No. It's all good."

"And are you going to continue to work for Marissa?"

"No. I've applied for a job in Philadelphia at the Morrison Gallery. She specializes in modern art from coastal artists."

"What happened to the Dallas job? You didn't like the city? The gallery?"

How sweet that she thinks I turned down the job. "They hired someone else."

Holly's mouth falls open. "They hired someone other than Arthur von de Menthe's daughter? Don't they know anything?"

"I never told them I was Artie's daughter, Holly."

"Why?" she cries in surprise. "That would be on the top of every résumé I sent!"

I swallow an impatient sigh and repeat the same line I've said a thousand times. "Because I don't want a job solely because of who my dad is. I want to build my own reputation."

"Oh, Ara. You're so naïve." She throws her hands up. "The real world is all about who you know, not what you know."

"Maybe so," I say lightly. Inside, I'm miffed. Holly was just lamenting missing Stephen's wedding and other art parties because she's no longer with my dad anymore. Doesn't she see that if she had made her own connections instead of relying on Dad's she would still be on the guest list?

"Talk to your dad. He'll get you that Philadelphia job. He could stop there on his way back from New York."

"Maybe." I'm not going to argue with Holly.

I can tell the mention of my dad is already bringing back sad thoughts. Her big eyes are growing wet again. "You know why your dad went to New York? To avoid me. He can't face me."

I shift uncomfortably in my seat. I guess the apple doesn't fall far from the tree.

"I know I shouldn't be saying this to you, but don't fall in love, Ara. It's terrible."

Don't I know it.

With a sigh, I get up and grab the tissue box. Tonight's going to be a long night.

This is my punishment for running away.

Although, if I had stayed, I'd be the one crying.

26

Ty

After driving Knox to the airport, I stop by Ara's apartment.

"Sorry, she's not here," Fleur says apologetically. "And no, I don't know where she is. She said she needed to finish her paper and disappeared."

I scrape a frustrated hand over my face, but hold in my angry words. It's not Fleur's fault that Ara's acting like a scared rabbit.

"She'll come around," Fleur tries to reassure me. "Be patient."

"I leave for the combine in five days," I remind her.

"She'll be back soon. I promise."

I leave then, but when I return the next day, Ara's conveniently gone. The day after is the same and my patience is gone.

"Are you hiding her from me?" I slap my hand against the door.

"No!" Fleur jumps out of my way. "I don't know where she is. She texted me and said she was okay and not to worry."

"Well, I am worried," I seethe. I stalk to Ara's bedroom, but it's the same as when I left to go see Knox. Damn him for coming at such an inconvenient time.

"She'll come around. She just doesn't want to lose you."

JEN FREDERICK

"Funny way she has of showing it. Text me when she comes home," I order as I walk to the front door.

"I can't do that," Fleur protests.

"Why not?"

"Because that would violate the girlfriend code. Not to mention the roommate code."

I stare at Fleur in disbelief.

She crosses her arms defensively. "I'm sorry, but you need to work it out with her directly."

"What the hell do you think I'm trying to do by coming here every morning?" I explode.

"Stop shouting," Fleur cries.

"Sorry." I run a frustrated hand through my hair. I can see I'm not getting anywhere with her. Knox would probably laugh his ass off if he could see me now. "Tell her I stopped by."

"If I feel like it." Fleur steps back and slams the door in my face.

I decide to go to the training facility to work out. Enough pain and I won't be dwelling on the fact that Ara's avoiding me.

Unfortunately, Ace is there wearing a grim expression. I keep my headphones on as a clear sign I don't want to talk. He ignores my silent cues.

"Have you decided what you're going to do?"

I pull off my headphones.

"Be agentless?" I suggest, only half joking.

"Sounds dangerous." He taps a folder against his hand before offering it to me. "Your interview requests are in here."

His sober tone suggests I'm going to see something I don't like in there. "Any good endorsements?" I think back to Knox's offer. "Did I get an offer from another car dealership?"

He doesn't answer. I flip it open and scan the contents.

"This is it, huh?" There are only three. A few weeks ago, I had a couple hundred.

Ace hesitates and then says, "The car dealership decided to go with the lady who won the state fair pie-baking contest."

I'm too surprised to respond. He slaps me on the back. "That

202

endorsement deal was too small for you anyway. There's still some media interested. It might make some sense to do them, even though the outlets are small."

"Ridgewood Elementary School?" I read in disbelief.

Ace grimaces. "Maybe not that one."

I shove the piece of paper back into the folder and slap it shut. "Forget it. The media has moved on. Why stir up shit now?"

My scandal has been superseded by Carlysle Miller, whose hoverboard exploded. That wouldn't have been problematic but for the fact that he was on it, smoking a joint. He's still getting an invite to the draft. At 6' 5", the wide receiver is too fast and too big for teams to overlook, but the shock jock radio personalities are having a field day. A couple of years ago, a player fell from number one to number thirteen due to a weed scandal.

"Feel bad for Miller," Ace says.

"Yup." While I don't wish bad press on anyone, I can't lie that I'm not a little relieved that the focus isn't on me.

"Take this then." He hands me a pink-colored piece of paper. "Bryant made out a list of agents you might want to talk to."

Reluctantly, I tuck paper away.

"Need me to set up some tackling dummies?"

"Nah. I'm just gonna do some lifting." But I don't even get out of the locker room before my parents call.

I knew it was coming, but I was dreading it. I drape my towel around my neck and answer.

"Ty! We just heard the news. Are you okay?" Mom worries.

"Of course. It's no big deal."

"I saw the articles about that Rhyann girl. What is going on?"

Of course Mom is more concerned about the girl than Dana. "It's nothing, Ma. She wasn't happy because I couldn't spend enough time with her and I guess she decided to take it out online. I saw her just the other day with another guy so she's not broken up about it."

"But what about all these things she said? They're all over the Twitters."

I rub a tired hand over my face. "It's nothing. I don't think it matters to anyone anymore." Although, given the rapid decline of interview requests, maybe it has.

"Still. It's not good. Maybe your dad and I should fly out."

"No," I say sharply. Then, because I love my mom and don't want to hurt her feelings, I try for a more moderate tone. "I'm working out and focused on getting ready for the combine. It's less than a week away."

"All right. If you say so. Hold on, though, because your dad wants to chat with you." She hands off the phone and I can hear her tell him to not badger me.

Great.

"What's going on, son?"

"Just some nonsense. Nothing really."

"For being nothing, it's made a lot of press."

Amazing how your parents can still make you feel small and immature even when you're twenty-three.

"I'm sorry."

"It's not me you should be apologizing to. It's your mother. She's been fretting all morning."

And guilty. They make you feel real guilty. "I am sorry. Give her the phone back and I'll tell her that."

"I want to know what you're going to do about Dana. You know I never liked him."

"At the time, he was the best pick for me. He did sign the biggest rookie deals last year."

"Other than your brother's," Dad corrects.

Since I don't have a good response, I remain silent.

"Knox thinks you're giving the Elam model some serious consideration."

I shouldn't be surprised that Knox arrived at that conclusion even though I didn't say a word about it. That damn twinsense again.

"Maybe." A few years ago, Matt Elam was the last pick in the first round and he negotiated his contract all by his little ol' lonesome. "The collective bargaining agreement makes it easy, I suppose," I say. The CBA basically sets what a player gets based on where they are drafted. The only variable is the signing bonus. In the NFL, the signing bonus is the only money that is guaranteed, and for players who will average five years in the pros, that can be very meaningful.

"I'm still figuring it out. There'll be agents at the combine," I tell my dad.

"You should have an agent before then. You need someone whispering in the ears of management on your behalf."

"I'll figure it out, Dad," I insist.

This time it's his turn to grapple with his temper. "You're so damn stubborn."

"Gee, I wonder where I get that."

He snorts and we move on to other things, such as taking a family trip together to Cancún before training camp starts.

After he hangs up, I reluctantly pull the pink slip from my pocket. I'm not one to shy away from conflict. I've always felt it's better to face it head-on so I might as well start calling agents.

I start with the biggest firm. Joe Schwartzenbach's firm handled twenty-three clients in last year's draft. If I went with him, I'd be one of the herd. On the flip side, it's a firm that handles everything from cradle to grave.

I dial him up.

"Joe here," he answers immediately.

"Hi Mr. Schwartzenbach, it's Ty Masters. We met after the Championship game. You might've heard I'm in the market for a new agent."

"I have heard that. Tough luck about the Mullen thing."

"Yeah, I didn't see it coming."

"You're a little disconnected, aren't you?" Joe says, a tinge of skepticism in his voice as if he thinks I might be feigning my ignorance over Dana's deals.

"What do you mean?" I want to know what I'm dealing with.

"I know that you kids are advised to stay off social media, but social media is a big part of an athlete's image. And it's a place where news is broken on an hourly basis."

"Is there some scandal attached to my name I don't know about?" If there was, Remy would've told me. Or Ara. She's got an Instagram account.

"Not so much a scandal but a lot of rumors. Word on the street is that you're a handful. You have big expectations but aren't always willing to put in the extra effort."

"With all due respect, Mr. Schwartzenbach, I have no clue what you're talking about."

"May I be blunt?"

"Go ahead."

"Football isn't played just on the field anymore. It's a big business. The athletes I represent share the same vision as I do. We're a team that's all working toward the same financial goal."

"I work out hard every day. I watch what I eat, what I drink. My combine results are going to look better than anyone else's. No one played better on my side of the ball than me last season." I'm not comfortable bragging about myself, but if I have to, I will.

Schwartzenbach doesn't bite. "Look, kid, my plate is full. Why don't you give Randy Dunne a call? He's a new agent and would be willing to work with you." He rattles off the phone number and barely gives me a chance to say goodbye before severing the connection.

I call the next three agents on the list. They all give me the same variation of Schwartzenbach's refusal. They're looking for a team player. Athletes these days are personalities, not just grunts on the gridiron.

By the end of the fifth agent giving me the same bullshit about how I'm too challenging to work with, I've had enough.

I slam my phone on the bench and stomp into the weight room.

These assholes don't think I'm good enough because I don't want to send out stupid cat pictures or record videos of me doing some stupid stunt in hopes it goes viral?

I have to have a Snapchat and an Instagram account? I have to be a fucking personality?

I pound the weights, envisioning all these assholes in front of me. I'm going to the combine and I'm going to break every damn record there. I'll be faster, stronger, more mentally tough than anyone in the draft pool. And when I sign my own damn multi-million-dollar deal, those agents are going to cry in their bourbon.

At the end, though, my body is tired but my mind is whirling. I need someone to talk to.

I pick up my phone and dial her number. The line clicks.

"Ara?"

"—I can't come to the phone. Text me. I don't listen to voicemails."

Goddammit! I hurl the phone across the room.

If she wanted to be friends so badly, where the fuck is she when I need one?

27

Ara

"It's a good thing you came back. Ty was here a few hours ago and I thought the veins were going to pop out of his neck, he was so mad," Fleur says to me on the phone. "He said you were being a bad friend."

I wince. "Thanks for covering for me."

"You owe me a Lush bath bomb and bottle of red wine. The good stuff, too, not the $2.99 bottles from Trader Joe's."

"Those $2.99 bottles are good," I protest.

Fleur hangs up instead of arguing with me. I can't blame her. I haven't been a good friend to anyone. I ran away, much like my dad does when there's something he doesn't like to face. I thought I was better than that, but apparently not.

Which makes me wonder...was Ty acting irrational or am I the problem? The friendship seal may have been broken, but I'd anticipated that it would be Ty who would drift away. Instead, he's the one knocking at my door and I'm the one hiding.

That's not an image of myself that I particularly like. I guess it's time to face the music.

After some investigation, I find out he's at the training center. Remy meets me there to let me in.

"Are you sure it's okay if I go in?" I ask as Remy waves his student ID over the security pad.

"As long as you don't plan to trash the place, it'll be fine."

"Where is everyone?" Despite it being the afternoon, the hallways look dark and uninviting. I thought that this place was always a hive of activity.

"Coaches are on recruiting trips. Players are partying or studying. Anything but thinking about football."

"Except for a few of you," I point out.

"You stalling, girl?"

"Yes."

Remy slaps me on the back. "Doesn't sound like the Ara I know. Woman up! Show us your ovaries!" he cheers.

"Show us your ovaries?"

"Okay, that was a bad one." He pushes me gently toward the door. "But not as bad as you for standing out here instead of going to see your man."

My mouth falls open. "My man?"

"He's been your man since the first day. Just took the two of you four years to figure it out. Ty's denseness can be blamed on all the on-field hits. I'm still working out what your excuse is, but maybe it's the lack of balls."

"The lack of balls! You—" I stop when I see Remy fold over in laughter. Huffing, I push the big man out of the way. "Your reverse psychology's not going to work on me," I say but grab the door handle anyway. "If I go to jail for breaking and entering, I expect you to come bail me out."

"Sis, I'll be there with you since it's my ID that waved you in." He pats me on the head. "Be good...or don't," he chortles as he walks away.

A reluctant smile curves my lips, but once I'm inside the facility, apprehension sets in. The hallway seems endless; my guilt feels heavy.

I hate how I'm feeling right now. This dread. This nervousness. If the situation was flipped, I would've stomped right down the tile floor and thrown open the locker room door, declaring that he needed to get his head out of his ass ASAP. But I can't do that now because I'm the headass in this scenario. I'm being weird and timid and freaked out because of what? Because his dick was inside me? Because I enjoyed it and want more?

I straighten and quicken my pace.

If this...thing between us turns sour, it's not going to be because of me. I'm going to be his friend no matter what. No amount of dicking is going to change that. In fact, we should just remove dicking from the equation. No friends with benefits. Just friends. That's how I'm going to get rid of all these uncomfortable feelings.

I snap open the doors to the locker room and yell his name.

He appears in front of me, wearing nothing but a pair of loose-fitting athletic shorts.

My next words wither in my throat as I take in his almost-nude glory. God, he's a perfect specimen of a man.

"You are too fucking attractive," I blurt out, almost angry at how hot he is. All my good intentions burn to ash at the sight of his ripped body.

Amused, he rubs his towel against his wet hair. He must've just showered. "You could've spent more time leering at me if you hadn't run out of town like a scared baby."

"Yes, yes, I could have." This is the real truth. I lick my lips.

"What're you gonna do now?" He drapes the towel around his neck.

A rivulet of uncaptured water slides down his chest. I track it with avid eyes.

"Ara?" he prompts.

"Thinking." I have a million ideas battling for supremacy in my head and none of them have a damn thing to do with being friends.

"Still scared?"

I take a deep, shaky breath. "You have no idea."

"Maybe I do." His bright eyes rake down my body in one obvious, lustful glance. "You were gone for nearly a week." He advances. I take a step back. "You didn't answer my texts." I open my mouth to spit out some excuse, but he places a finger against my lips. "You didn't call." Another step. I feel the slick wood of the locker room door against my back. "I was worried." He drags his finger, pulling my lower lip down. I shiver. "And scared. You need to make it up to me."

I slide all the way to my knees because, apparently, in front of Ty Masters, I am a spineless jellyfish. A needy, hungry one.

I run my fingers over the stiff elastic waistband. "How mad were you?"

He widens his stance and braces a hand above my head. "Real mad."

"On a scale of one to volcano?" I tug the shorts down his thighs. How is it possible for thighs to be so hard? I run my knuckles up the outside of his leg. A hand comes down to rest on my head. There's a slight tremble of anticipation in his grip.

His inability to control himself entirely sets me aflame. I thought it was unfair that he affected me so greatly, but knowing I have the same impact on him? Ahhh...my own thighs tighten with want.

I lean forward and lick a line across his taut abs. He shudders and I can't keep in a relieved, delighted laugh.

"I'm waiting," he says. The rough tone implies he's not going to wait much longer.

It's my show, though. I can tell by the way his hand hasn't moved in my hair and the stillness in his frame. He's waiting for me. It's hard, but he's waiting.

I rub my cheek against the length of his cock. It jerks in my light grip. I don't stifle my laugh.

"That's a mean laugh."

"I'm making it up to you," I inform him.

He reaches down and tweaks a nipple. "Don't start what you can't finish, little girl."

I bite my lip, but I can't keep the whimper from escaping. What a horribly indecent thing of him to say! It turns me on so much.

My tongue darts out for a taste. He's silky soft and delicious. A girl could get addicted to this—not just his flavor or feel, but the intoxicating pleasure of knowing that you can control a stallion like Ty with one flick of your tongue.

I curl my tongue around the ruddy head. He groans and mumbles something unintelligible. It's torturous for him but too good to pull away.

We both moan when I take him fully into my mouth. Slowly, I ease my way down his shaft. Too long to take fully into my mouth, I fist my hand around the lower portion and start to move in long, regular strokes.

I revel in the gruff sounds he makes from the back of his throat. Long fingers twine through my hair, pushing it aside so he can get a better glimpse. I suck harder, my cheeks collapsing out as I take long draws down his pipe.

"You look so fucking sexy right now," he says hoarsely. His fingers caress my cheek. A thumb presses into the hollow of my cheek. "You should see yourself."

I look up to find him gazing down at me. His green eyes are nearly black, the pupil so dilated that all I can see is myself. I fill up his gaze.

And even if it isn't true, I find myself believing that I'm his whole world. I coax him with my mouth and fingers toward the precipice, but right when I'm sure he's about to go over, he pulls away.

"What?" I cry. "No."

His cock bobs enticingly in front of me. I scrabble forward, but he lifts me up and plasters his mouth across mine before I can voice another objection.

His mouth is so voracious my head starts to spin. My knees buckle. Ty catches me and carries me into the room, not breaking our contact once.

He sits down on the first seat he can find. His fingers fumble with the zipper of my skirt. I brush his hands aside and simply pull the offending fabric up and scoot closer until I can rub against him like the greedy woman I am.

His mouth slides from my mouth to my throat while his hand slides between us. He twists his fingers around my panties and snaps them with one jerk.

I gasp.

"That hurt?"

Wordlessly, I shake my head no. I stare back into that green gaze. He's wearing the darkest, hungriest expression I've ever seen on a man and it makes me breathless.

"I missed you," he says huskily. He curls his hand around the back of my skull and kisses me again. I feel the press of his lips everywhere. Not just on my mouth but in the pads of my fingers, the soles of my feet. Everywhere.

His tongue licks the roof of my mouth, the insides of my cheek. Two fingers rub over my clit and then slide inside me. I squirm, wet with anticipation.

"You're so fine, Ara," he murmurs against my mouth. "So fucking fine."

The hand that's not busy between my legs runs over my ankle, my calf, teases the back of my knee, and comes to land on my hip.

"Skirts should be illegal with legs like these."

"They're comfortable. It's getting hot out."

"Every time I see you in one of these I want to bend you over, spank your pretty ass, and then fuck you till you scream."

Oh *god*. My insides clench.

He chuckles, deep and low. "You going to come by just me talking about it?"

"Maybe?" I ride his fingers. "But I'd rather you put your dick in me."

"Let's take this off first." He tugs the back of my shirt. I help him remove it.

Nimbly he unclasps my bra. My boobs spill out. He catches one nipple on his tongue. I lean back, allowing him as much access as he wants. Because he's extraordinarily talented, he's able to multitask, keeping one hand inside of me while sucking hard on my nipples, one and then the other.

His free hand produces a condom from God knows where. I take it and despite my shaky fingers, I sheathe him.

I dig my fingers into his shoulders, trying to brace myself for the hugeness of his intrusion. And right when I feel like I've got myself under control, he lifts me up and thrusts me down onto the long, hard length of him.

My head falls back. A choked cry escapes my lips. I can't hold on any longer. I let him take over while he fills me completely. My toes curl. My head spins. The air is thin and in short supply. All I can do is pant out little commands of *more, now, there. There. There!*

The pressure is enormous. It's partly because he's so big and I'm much smaller. But it's more than that. Because it's not merely pressure between my legs. It's in my head. It's in my blood. My body feels like it will burst. This isn't sex. This is communion.

Each thrust feels deeper than the one before. We catch a perfect rhythm of plunge and retreat. His cock is scraping nerve endings that I didn't realize existed. My entire body is reeling from sensation overload.

I shake and shake and shake until I tumble apart, sent to the floor in tiny, miniscule pieces that won't be able to be put back together.

His fingers tighten on my hips. His thrusts grow jagged. His own breath is uneven and gasping.

"Ara. Ara. Ara," he chants.

I feel like a goddess. I raise my arms up and ride him until he comes in a torrential flood inside of me. Sticky, slick with sweat, I collapse in his arms.

Strong hands stroke my back, soothing me while I tremble from the aftershocks.

Did I really think I could run from this? My desire would call me back. Already, I want to tie myself to his ankle, shackle myself to his wrist. Bind him to me so that he wouldn't dream of leaving.

"It's all right," he says. He places his face in my neck. His nose drags along the nerves and veins. "It's going to be all right."

He rises as I cling to him.

"How can you walk?" I mumble.

"Lots of training," he says. But his steps aren't as sure as they could be, as if he was drunk from pleasure, too.

"Here's what we're going to do. We're going to shower. Then I'm going to have dinner and then we're going to your place to have sex again because I want to be horizontal when I pass out."

"What about my dinner?" I protest, running my fingers along his broad shoulders, which flex and bunch under my touch.

"You already had it," he says.

"I did?" And then I realize exactly what he plans to eat.

It's a good thing I'm being carried because I can't walk with *that* image in my head.

28

Ty

"Why are you trading chairs?" Ara asks, coming out of the shower room wrapped in a Southern U towel.

Halfway across the locker room, I pause to take in the gorgeous view. Too bad I don't have my phone on me. It's an image I'd like to take with me—to entertain myself while I'm on the road. I console myself with the fact that I'll have plenty of other opportunities to record her sexy self.

I give myself a mental shake. "You think I'm going to let Townley sit his ass in the same chair I fucked you in?"

"Okay, good call." She gives me a thumbs up.

I cross over to my old locker and pick up my padded chair before switching it with the one that Ara and I just christened. I wipe it down with a couple of towels while Ara gets dressed.

"Oh boy." I look over my shoulder to see her holding up a scrap of fabric. "You ripped my underwear."

I grin. "I feel real bad about that."

"Sure you do." She crumples the fabric into a ball. "I guess I have to free ball it."

"You don't have balls," I point out.

"I'm free vagina-ing it then."

217

I eye her. The skirt she has on is short. No underwear? I blanch. I never thought I'd be the jealous type. Guess it took the right woman. "No. Let me find something." I rummage through my locker and toss her a pair of workout shorts.

She pulls them up, takes a step, and then stops. The shorts fall to her ankles. I swallow a laugh and go tie them up for her.

"Everyone's going to know we did something if I walk around in these," she whines.

"So? We're going to tell them at some point. Why not now?"

"What about Rhyann?"

"What about her?" I grab my ball-cap and give the room a once over. It looks orderly. There don't appear to be any signs of our shenanigans. Not that I would care, but I think Ara might.

"She'll be mad and write ugly things about you again."

"Nah. She's dating someone new. I don't think she has much credibility left." I take Ara's arm and lead her toward the exit.

"But what about—"

"Are you trying to make up problems?" I ask impatiently. "I've got bigger things to worry about."

She stops. "Like what?"

I realize then that I haven't told her about the whole agent mess. I open my mouth but snap it shut when her phone rings.

She raises a finger. "Hold that thought." And then, "Hello, this is Ara Martin." A smile crosses her face. She taps mute. "It's the Philly gallery!" she says in hushed excitement.

"Better find out what they want." I gesture for her to unmute the call.

She does. "Yes, I'm at a place I can talk." Her eyes sparkle in anticipation. She looks so happy. She needed this validation—that she could find a place in the art world without her dad's help. I'm hoping that once she gets this job, she'll start gaining confidence in her own work.

Her children's art is very special. I can imagine reading her books to my children. An image of Ara holding our baby flicks into my head. I don't run in fear of that thought. In fact, it—

The blood drains out of Ara's face.

"No, no, I understand. It's hard, though, because for some jobs I'm overqualified and others, I don't have enough." She nods miserably. "Yes, I'll keep looking. Thank you."

Her hand drops to her side.

"You didn't get the job?" I guess.

She shakes her head. "I think I'm going to have to apply for a secretarial position," she says glumly. She pushes away from the wall and starts walking. "What were you saying earlier?" she asks.

Yeah, I'm not going to bother her with my shit now. "Nothing. What's going on with your dad?'

"He's still in NY."

"You went down to your dad's place by yourself?"

"Holly was there. She was so sad."

I can see where this is all unfolding and realize I need to squelch it immediately. Ara thinking about her dad's past bad relationships is going to make her question ours. She's the most confident about this connection of ours when we're naked.

I speed up and grab her hand. "Let's go."

"Where?"

"Your place."

"Why?"

I don't bother to answer. Instead, I pack her into the car, motor over to her apartment, and then hustle her up the stairs.

"Where's the fire?" she asks.

"Don't tee up the bad puns so easily," I chide. "I'm only human and it's hard not to say, 'in my pants.'"

"But then I'd have to respond that you should go to the health clinic because that's not healthy."

"I'll remember that the next time you tell me that something 'hurts so good.'"

She's punching my arm when her roommate opens the door.

"This is foreplay, Fleur," I announce. "You probably want to go for a walk because it's going to be loud in Ara's bedroom."

"Shut up!" Ara cries in mortification.

Fleur merely grins. "I have noise-canceling headphones."

I pick Ara up and throw her over my shoulder. "Turn the music to at least eight."

Ara beats her tiny fists against my back. "Let me go!"

"Make that ten." I make straight for the bedroom and kick the door shut behind me. I toss her on the bed and reach behind me to grab the back of my T-shirt.

"You've got about sixty seconds before I start tearing your clothes off—in case you want to save your bra or your T-shirt."

It takes me half that to get naked. She's still struggling with the waistband of the borrowed shorts.

I bat her hands away and pull the shorts down her legs.

"The outside world is fucking up, baby," I tell her as I pull her to the edge of the bed. "Let's hide in here for a while."

"You have to leave for the combine tomorrow."

"And I will." I push her back. "But for now, I'm going to enjoy my girlfriend's perfect body."

She bends forward and reaches for my dick. I push her back again.

"What are you doing?" she asks in frustration.

I kneel at the edge of the bed and throw her an impatient look. "What do you think?"

"What about that?" She points to my hard-on that bobs eagerly between my legs.

"That can wait."

"But—"

I slap her ass lightly. "Ara, I want to go down on you. Why are you fighting me on this?"

"But you already went down on me in the shower."

With exaggerated patience, I explain, "And I want to do it again."

At her stunned silence, I ask, "How many guys have you dated? Actually, no, don't answer that. I like going down on you. I like having my mouth on you. I like the way you look. No, scratch that. I love the way you look. The way you taste. The way you smell. If I could I'd spend an entire weekend with my face between your legs. Does that answer your question?"

"Yes, but—"

I hold up a hand. "No buts. Any further comments should be held until after you come."

She doesn't shut up, but it's okay. Her dialogue consists of, "Oh my God," and, "Yes, fuck yes," and, "Ty, please," and "Tyyyyyy."

She does taste like heaven. Sweet, sweet heaven. Her pussy is smooth and soft and slick. I use my fingers to spread her apart and then devour her.

She does fall quiet then. Her thighs close around my ears. The heels of her feet dig into my shoulders. Her fingers pull tightly on my hair.

Her excited response, the flavor of her on my tongue, all of it makes my dick rock hard. Hell, yeah, I could spend an eternity down here.

I suck and bite and lick her until she comes screaming. This girl is good for my ego.

"Any complaints?" I wipe a hand across my mouth.

Wordlessly, she shakes her head.

"Good." I climb onto the bed, sit back on my haunches and palm my aching dick. "You have a couple choices," I tell her while I stroke myself. A hungry expression creeps over her face. I know the answer before I present her options. "You can go to sleep while I jerk myself off. You can watch me. Or, if you want, you can climb on top and ride me."

"Ride," she chokes out.

I spread my arms wide. "Come on, cowgirl."

29

Ara

"FROM THE LOOK ON YOUR FACE, I DON'T NEED TO ASK HOW IT was," Fleur notes as I shut the door behind Ty.

He's off to pack for the combine. He proclaimed he didn't need to pack, but I needed a breather. I think he understood, but he warned me he was coming back to talk after he was done. The message was that I get a little time to get my head together and then he wants to clear the air.

"Yes, watered my crops, cleared my acne, and obliterated the need to study, is that what you wanted to hear?"

"I knew all that already. You two weren't quiet."

I try not to blush. Fleur has been my roommate for four years. She knows everything about me. Why should I be embarrassed that I was a little noisy? My cheeks heat up anyway.

"So?" I shrug, making my way into the kitchen. I need some sustenance. Sex makes you hungry.

"So why'd you kick him out like he was a mistake you dragged home after an all-night bender?" Fleur follows me. "You're acting like you aren't even friends."

I grab some sandwich meat and the mayo. Fleur hands me the

loaf of bread. "I don't know," I admit. "Every time I start thinking about what's going on, I start panicking."

"You need to stop thinking and just enjoy yourself."

I wish I could. "I'm trying, but I keep thinking of the future and it scares me." I point my knife at the bread.

She shakes her head and pushes herself up on the counter. "And your reflexive response is to sabotage the whole thing before it even gets off the ground."

"That's not fair."

She falls silent while I finish making my sandwich.

"You know, I really hated that you kept working at Marissa's. She always introduced you as Artie's daughter, like you didn't have your own identity."

"Um, yes," I say between bites, "and that's exactly how I think I'd feel dating Ty. I'd be Ty's girlfriend, but he wouldn't even be there mentally. Look how he doesn't eat anything but healthy shit. And he hasn't drunk even a drop since the night of the Championship game."

"But that's because the draft is coming up. It's the single biggest event in his life."

"I know, but after that it will be his first NFL game and then his first night game and then his first playoff game."

"Those are all excuses," she barks out. "You're a coward, Ara."

I stop with the sandwich halfway to my mouth. "What? A coward? How can you say that?"

"You're an emotional scaredy-cat. You'd rather hide and play the victim than take control of your life. The thing with Marissa? You allowed that. You could've told her to stop treating you like you were a line on her résumé. And if you end up with Ty, the only way you'll only be *his* girlfriend is if you don't speak up for yourself."

My appetite disappears. I slap the half-eaten sandwich on the counter. "You don't know what it's like. Leon *adores* you. He lives to serve you."

Fleur calmly picks up my sandwich and takes a tiny nibble. "And Ty'd be the same way if you gave him half a chance, but for all your big talk about wanting to create your own place in the sun, you don't do anything about it. Take Blinkie the Rabbit."

"What about him?" I have half a mind to rip my food out of her mouth.

"He sits in your notebook. You won't do an official piece and put it in your portfolio. You're like the literal definition of hiding your light under a bushel. Instead of taking the chance of rejection, you'd rather no one see it at all. You'd be doing everyone a favor if you got your head out of your ass." After throwing those bombs at me, she takes another bite.

Fuming, I grab my sandwich out of her mouth.

"You can make your own damn food."

"I will." She hops off the counter.

"I hope you choke on it." I stomp off to my bedroom.

"I love you, too," she sing-songs to my back.

In my bedroom, I start throwing stuff around. The bed is a wreck. I snap a sheet off the ground.

"Head out of my ass? I'm a coward? She doesn't know what she's talking about," I rant. "I'm the only one with my head on straight here. Ty's blinded by his dick, and Fleur..." I pause. I don't know what Fleur's problem is. "She's PMSing," I conclude.

"I can hear you!" she yells.

Startled, I drop the sheet. Damn, these walls are thin. It's hard to vent when you have to whisper, but I try. Meanwhile I can hear Fleur fucking whistling out in the living room. I huff and puff as I clean the room, muttering about how no one understands me.

Finally, after the room is neatly arranged, I end my childish tantrum and pull out my notebook. I started drawing this two years ago. Every so often, I'd pull it out and doodle in it some more. Only a few people have ever seen it, and only by accident.

I've kept it private because it's not good. It's not that I'm afraid of rejection, but rather I'm realistic. There's nothing wrong with facing your flaws or recognizing that perfect things don't exist in this world.

That doesn't make me lazy or cowardly or afraid. It makes me smart. I flip open the book to the last sketched page. I haven't progressed beyond Blinkie cowering in the corner from Farmer Brown. I trace a finger around his furry face.

Ty's right. No one wants to cheer for the scared rabbit. I grab a pencil off my desk and shade in a couple of front teeth. *There*, I think. Not so helpless. Ty's suggestion of a sword and horse pop into my head. I draw a stick in the rabbit's mouth and a goat behind Farmer Brown. Not exactly the knight in shining armor, but more fitting for a farm. I giggle over the idea of Ty as a goat.

I finger a corner of my notebook. Would it kill me to show my dad? Gauge his opinion? What's the worst thing that he'd say? That it's no good? I already think that. No, I must think it's worth something because if I really, truly believed it was no good then I wouldn't be scared of honest criticism. I think it's decent and am afraid to hear from my dad that it's not.

I am a coward.

I pick up my phone. I'm going to tell him. I'm going to tell Dad about this work. Then I'm going to go to Ty and tell him I love him and see if he runs toward me or away. Because I'm tired of hiding.

Dad picks up on the second ring. I hear road noise. "Hey, Ara, honey. What are you doing right now?"

"Are you driving?"

"I'm just pulling up to your apartment," he admits.

"What?" I jump to my feet. "I thought you were in New York."

"I decided to fly home. Stephen was getting tired of me," he jokes.

"I'm on my way down." I pull on a knit miniskirt and grab an oversized sweatshirt. It's Ty's, of course. I hug it to me. Ty's life and mine are intertwined. I was nuts to think I could separate my feelings for him forever. I wonder if I should text him.

My phone beeps. I raise it and see a text from my dad.

Campus police r behind me. Hurry. I'm not good in enclosed spaces.

I send the eyeroll emoji but abandon the idea of contacting Ty for now. It's better I see him in person. I jam my feet into a pair of flip-flops, stick my phone in my pocket and, at the last minute, grab my notebook.

Dad gives me a peck on the cheek when I climb into the car.

"When did you fly in? I would've met you at the airport."

"I already had my car here," he reminds me. "Besides, this way I get to take you to dinner. You hungry?"

I remember my aborted attempt to eat. "Yeah, I am." He drives over to the Row House. As we climb out of his car, he gestures to the notebook under my arm.

"What's this?"

"Nothing," I say by habit.

He comes around the front of the car and wraps an arm around my shoulders. "You look different."

Oh God. Am I wearing a sex face? I pat myself self-consciously. "Prettier?" I boast, trying to throw him off the scent.

"Stressed." He points to my forehead. "You have wrinkles."

Frantically, I rub my forehead. "Dad. You're supposed to tell me I'm the most beautiful woman in the world."

"You are. Only you're the most beautiful stressed girl in the world. Is this because you were fired?"

My jaw drops and I stop walking. "How did you know? And no, I wasn't fired. I quit."

Instead of responding, he opens the door to the Row House and ushers me inside. Jeanette greets us. Dad orders the evening special and then hustles me into a booth.

When we sit down, he says, "Dear, the art world is tiny. I know that you no longer work for Marissa, although the word is that you were fired. I also know you got turned down for the jobs in Philly and Dallas."

"Damn," I curse softly.

"When were you planning on telling me about this?" He looks distressed.

I feel low. "When I got another job."

"And how is that going?" he asks.

We both know it's going nowhere so I don't bother to lie. "I'm thinking of applying for a secretarial position or maybe volunteer as a docent."

He laces his fingers together on the table. Concern is written all over his features. "Why is it that you don't want my help? Are you ashamed of your dad?"

I rear back in surprise. "No. My God, why would you say that?"

"You go by Martin. You hide that I'm related to you. You don't ask for my help and don't even tell me when you quit your job. What's so terrible about being my daughter?"

It had never occurred to me that I would hurt my dad's feelings by trying to succeed without using his connections.

"You won't even share your art with me."

If I was surprised before, it doesn't even begin to compare to the shock that strikes me at his new revelation.

"How do you know?"

"You left it out during the holidays. I may have sneaked a peek." He leans forward, full of parental earnestness. "Why haven't you showed it to me?"

I drop my guilty, shamed eyes to my hands. "I don't know. I'm...scared."

He makes a hurt sound in the back of his throat. God, Fleur was right. I was a coward. A self-centered one at that.

Stiffening my spine, I push the notebook across the table. Jeanette has brought us steaming piles of roast beef on homemade mashed potatoes. I dig in, surprisingly hungry despite how intently my dad is inspecting every page.

He flips through the book slower than it took to draw some of the pages. Finally, he sets it aside and picks up his fork.

"It's very good."

"You're saying that."

He slams down his fork. I jerk upright in surprise. "You always do that, Ara."

"Do what?"

"Downplay yourself. You are a woman of worth. Your art is good. I don't believe it is studio ready, but it will be with more work. It's obvious you only spend a little time on this instead of immersing yourself completely. You need a few classes perhaps and a lot more practice, but you have talent. You'll go nowhere, though, if you don't start valuing your own work. Now, eat your dinner and we will talk about where you should go from here."

Meekly, I pick up my fork. "Yes, Daddy."

Inwardly, though, I'm grinning wildly. Dad liked my work and I know it's a truthful, unvarnished opinion because he didn't say I should immediately submit it. He recognized that it had flaws and told me to keep working.

It's what he'd say to anyone.

After dinner, the first thing I want to do is tell Ty. I hug my notebook to my chest and race off to find him.

"He's not here," Remy says at the front door of their house.

"Is he working out again?"

"No. He said he was going for a walk. He needed some fresh air or something."

My face falls. Is he having second thoughts? "Okay, will you tell him that I stopped by?"

"Yeah, but Ara..." Remy stops, licks his lips.

"What?" I prompt.

"The combine is a big deal for him. Don't mess with his head too much, okay?"

Chastened, I nod. "I promise. I'll fix it all."

Remy daps my fist and closes the door.

I have really fucked up, I realize. If I lose Ty, it'll be my own damn fault and no one else's.

30

Ty

"Ara stopped by," Remy informs me when I get home. "She looked real sad that she missed you."

"Yeah?" It took me all of five minutes to throw my combine shit together so I went for a short walk to figure out what I needed to do about Ara. Knox kept buzzing me. He can sense I'm upset, but I don't think he has any answers.

The only people who can solve this are her and me. Ara agreed to marry Weasel, not because she loved him, but because the khaki-wearing dude was the exact opposite of her dad. And while I'm not an artist, I do have a singular passion for football.

That scares her to death. Solution: a full frontal assault.

The only thing that will break through for her is committed, direct action. I have to show her I'm as dedicated to making this thing between us work as I am about football. And that we can still have a great friendship that's made better by seriously awesome sex. The last part is in the bag, frankly. It's the first part that'll take effort.

"Yeah. She was almost crying."

"Now you're overselling it." I take the stairs two at a time.

"She was," he yells after me.

It doesn't matter if she was or she wasn't. That she came looking for me is a good sign.

"You got everything packed?" Remy says at the door.

I throw my duffle on the bed. "A month's worth of underwear, socks, extra shoes." I point to the garment bag. "And one suit. What else are you bringing?"

"My agent's got everything covered. He said to just get on the plane and bring my ass to the hotel."

I arch my eyebrows. "Is that normal?"

Remy shrugs. "Don't know, don't care. My guy is still interested in repping you. I told him all that shit being said about you is fake news."

"All the shit? There's more than Rhyann and my agent?" Make that former agent.

Remy suddenly shows interest in the carpet.

"Remy?" I prompt, my tone a bit hard.

"Well, just stuff about you being difficult to coach."

"Oh fuck." My heart sinks. Uncoachable is the kiss of death. I can feel my draft status sliding downhill.

"It's nothing, bro." Remy gives me a weak smile. "Oh shit, is that my phone?" He skips away.

There was no phone call, but I let him go. He doesn't need to get caught up in my drama. Instead, I grab my own phone and call Knox.

"Real talk," I say after he answers. "How much is it going to hurt me to arrive at the combine with no agent?"

My brother takes a moment to consider his reply before answering. "I don't know. I think if you hadn't had the issues with your exes, it'd be okay. The agent's there to smooth things over—be the good angel to the devils that are out there. Most of the agents at the combine are going to be working out the contracts for their existing roster of athletes. Is my guy getting cut or an extended, that sort of thing."

"Remy tells me the word out there is that I'm uncoachable."

"No way," Knox fires back to my relief. "That's bullshit. Where'd he hear that?"

"His agent."

"He's just saying that to build Remy up. That shit," he fumes. I don't know if Knox is talking about Remy or Remy's agent. "Here's what you should do. Kill on the interview portion. It's at night because they want to catch you when you're mentally weak. If you put in a great performance, all the rumors will be brushed aside. After you're done with all the workouts, you can stick around and case out the agents. They are all going to be there, including mine."

It sounded like a decent plan. "Okay. I'll do that."

"Whew. Ty Masters taking advice from his little brother. It's a miracle. Hold on while I write this down."

"Shut up, asshole," I say laughingly. Having a plan takes the weight off my shoulders, but Knox's next words weigh them down again.

"So how are things with you and Ara?"

"They're working themselves out."

"I can come down after the combine. We can run her through another twin test. I'll make it easy on her."

"Seriously, bro, you're hitting me with that now?"

"Just trying to distract you," he teases, but he's only half joking. "Look, let's get it over with. I know it's bugging you."

"It's really not. I don't think about that."

"Come on," he wheedles. "It'll be fun. After it's over, we'll all laugh about it."

"Like you and Ellie do?" Ellie purposely failed the twin test and it hurt Knox bad. I have serious doubts they laugh over this.

"Okay, so maybe we don't laugh about it, but you won't feel good about Ara until you do. I want your draft day to be perfect. Having Ara by your side, getting drafted fourth—"

"First, you mean," I interrupt. Jackass put me one behind him.

"First, fourth, what does it matter? Here's my plan. I'll wear your glasses—"

"No." I bang the phone against the desk a couple of times. "Shit, we're breaking up." I replace the phone at my ear. "I've got this. I promise." The phone beeps. I glance at the screen. It's Ara. "I have to go," I tell my brother. "Trust me. I know what I'm doing."

"Buzz me if you need anything," he says.

I say goodbye and then switch over. Only it's not Ara on the phone. It's Fleur and she's crying.

Alarm jolts me to my feet. "What's wrong?"

"Ara's dad has been in a bad accident. She needs you."

"Where is she?"

"Packing, but she's a mess. Ty, I don't think she should drive down to the hospital. It's three hours away and her eyes are so swollen from crying, she can barely see. I'd drive her but I'm subbing for my teacher tomorrow," Fleur wails.

"I'm on it."

"Oh, God, I didn't mean you. Don't you have to go to the combine?"

My heart pounds. Abandoning the combine is crazy. My reputation is already low. If I don't show up for my interview tomorrow, word will spread and I'll be marked as pariah. I can already see the draft numbers tumbling and my signing bonus growing smaller.

But Ara low key thinks I'm the same as her old man. This is my opportunity to prove that I'm not.

"I can catch up. I'll drive her down and come back. There's a flight at—" I pause and quickly type in an internet search. Results pop up. "There's a flight tomorrow at six that should get me to Indy in time. I'll just be late. There's nothing official until the morning." This isn't exactly true. I have an interview tomorrow evening with the GM of Denver, but I'll text him and ask him if we can do it early the next morning.

"If you're sure."

"I'm sure."

I pause briefly by Remy's room to inform him of what's going on. "Can you take my stuff with you? Just check it through and throw it in my assigned room."

"Man, you can't leave," Remy says, getting to his feet. "I'll get Nichole to drive her down."

"No, it's got to be me." I feel a sense of surety. This is the right decision.

"You've got an interview tomorrow," he balks.

"I'll reschedule."

"Are you nuts? They're not going to reschedule. They're going to write you off as a flake! Uncoachable will be the kindest thing they'll say about you."

"If they're going to do that, then I don't want to be on the team." I wave goodbye and leap down the stairs.

"You're fucking crazy, man. You can't leave," Remy yells after me.

I let the slamming door behind me supply the answer but meet with the same resistance from Ara.

"No, absolutely not," she says when I show up at her bedroom door. She doesn't bother to look up from her suitcase. "Go home."

"Ara." She throws another pair of socks into her case. "Ara." Her head disappears into the closet as she rummages for her black heels. I pull them from underneath her bed and set them on top of the socks. She hunches over.

I go over to her, picking her up. Tears hang onto the end of her eyelashes. Her cheeks are wet. I brush my thumbs over her face and pull her in for a hug.

"You need me."

She sags into me, one sneaker squeezed in her fist. Never very heavy in the first place, she feels lighter than the weights I curl with. Panic sets in. Ara's always strong. She withstood nearly two years of abuse from Van Asshole, but the news about her dad is cutting her off at the knees.

"You have the combine," she mumbles into my chest. "So you're not going."

"Lots of players don't go to the combine and still get drafted."

"Not in the top ten."

"Yeah, even in the top ten." I have no idea if this is true. I wrestle a shoe out of her hand and toss it aside. "I'm coming. End of story."

She picks herself up off the ground. "I really don't want you to come, Ty. I'll feel guilty every time I look at you. You'd resent me for the rest of your life if you missed the combine." She brushes me aside to go into the bathroom.

Fleur appears at the empty doorway, wringing her hands. "You can't let her drive herself."

"I know. It's fine," I say soothingly. "It'll all work out." Although I don't have the first clue how it will. I need to call Denver guy. Fuck, I really wish I had an agent now.

I drag a hand over my mouth. I'm not out of options. I corral my frantic thoughts. First, fix the combine thing. I dial my brother.

"Need a goodnight kiss?" Knox says as he answers.

"I need a favor."

"Oh?" Surprise colors his voice. I never ask for favors, not even from my twin. "I'm on it. What do you need?"

"I need to borrow your agent." Quickly I explain what's going on. "Ara's dad is hurt and I'm driving her down to the hospital."

"Oh, shit. Is he okay?"

"No word yet."

Knox falls silent.

"What? No lecture?"

"From me? No way. I'd do the same thing you're doing." I hear some rustling. "I can handle things from here. You take care of Ara."

"Have your agent call me."

"No need, bro. I'm going to the combine as you."

That solution hadn't occurred to me. My first instinct is to protest. This is my opportunity to set records and show teams what I've got. I've been training for this for the last several weeks, abstaining from all the best foods, not drinking, working out several hours of day. Knox, on the other hand, is in full off-season mode. Before he went to visit the parents, he was cruising the Mediterranean with Ellie.

"How's your conditioning?"

There's a beat of silence. "It's decent."

"I can't be *decent* at the combine."

"It's better than not being there at all."

"Fuck that's true." I drag a hand down my face. "Okay. You're my best option."

"It's a good thing that Ara and Ellie aren't on staff otherwise this would not work."

"Yeah," I huff out a relieved laugh. Then straighten from the wall. "What do you mean, Ara and Ellie."

"Ahhhh..." There's a prolonged bit of silence this time.

"What do you know?"

"So I'm guessing she hasn't told you yet."

"Told me what?"

"Ara's going to pass the twin test, bro."

"What?" I shoot a glance toward the closed bathroom door. "What are you talking about?"

"Last time I was up there, I called Ara. She recognized it was me from my voice."

A tingling sensation shoots down my spine. "There's something called caller ID, bro."

"Nope. When I arrived, I wore a pair of glasses, just like yours and she laughed in my face. Knew immediately it wasn't you."

"Then why the fuck did you say we had to do the twin test?"

"So you'd feel good about her."

"I don't need that to feel good about her. I already love her!"

The bathroom door opens. Ara steps out. She still looks pasty. "I'll be ready in five," I tell her.

She doesn't answer but instead disappears inside her bedroom. I move down the hall and hiss into the phone. "I've got to go."

"I'll do my best at the combine for you," he says.

"Not your best, asshole. Do *the* best."

"Got it! Aren't you glad we're identical twins?" he says. He's far too excited about this. As for me, there's a rock in my gut that says this is a major, major mistake.

Ara re-appears, this time with her suitcase. I reach for it. "Let me help you."

She takes my hand and pulls me over to the sofa.

Behind us, Fleur says, "I'm going to my bedroom and put my headphones on."

Ara pushes me down. "Ty. I heard what you said," she begins.

"About the twin test? Look, I don't care about that shit."

She places a finger over my lips. "No. That you love me." Her lips curve up a tiny amount. They tremble at the corners.

I run a hand over her small head. I want to tuck her against my side and block all the bad stuff from hurting. "I do love you," I say. My voice is hoarse with emotion. "This isn't really the way I thought I'd tell you though. I envisioned more flowers."

"And a horse maybe?"

A chuckle escapes. "A horse and a sword. Maybe even some banging battle armor."

She brushes a hand over my shoulder. "I like the battle armor you wear on the field. It's very hot."

"Yeah?" I arch an eyebrow. This is the first I've heard that seeing me in a football uniform turns her on.

"Yeah." She captures my hand and presses it to her cheek. "I love you, too. I've loved you for a long time but was too scared to tell you. And that fear kept us apart for too long. That fear kept me from showing Dad my drawings. And that fear is going to result in the two of us making a big mistake today."

"Me supporting you isn't a mistake." Her skin feels cold beneath my palm. I draw her closer.

"There are lots of ways to support someone, Ty. In this case, you need to go to the combine because if you don't, I will always, always worry that you resent me for it. Don't put that burden on me."

Her hazel eyes plead for me to understand.

"If you're worried about the combine thing, don't. Knox is going to cover for me."

"Are you kidding me?" She jumps up.

I fall back against the sofa cushions in surprise. "I know you're worried right now—"

"Yes!" she yells, throwing her arms out wide. "I'm sick to death with worry." She grabs my hands. "Please. I love you, Ty. I'm going to love you while you are in Indy and I am with my dad. Do not do the stupid twin switch with your brother. I know you want to get number one. You've trained so hard. You've gone without. You almost dated that shark Kathleen. You signed with an agent you didn't like. All to get to the top. You love Knox, but everything you've done is to beat his record. If you don't go, I will always wonder if you resent me. Don't put that on me. Please. Go to the combine. Blow their socks off. Let me see to my dad."

I've never been able to tell Ara no. "I'm not happy about this."

She kisses my hands. "Thank you, anyway." Her phone beeps. "My Uber is here."

I make a disgusted sound in the back of my throat. She'd already planned to go by herself. Slightly disgruntled, I grab her luggage. "I'm carrying your bag down to the car."

"Good."

"And I get to name our first born."

"Whatever you say, Ty." She pats me on the arm. "But it's going to be Kintyre."

"I hate that name," I yell at her back.

She laughs. I breathe a sigh of relief. It's going to be all right.

31

Ara

I KNOW I MADE THE RIGHT DECISION BY SENDING TY AWAY, BUT I end up crying on and off the entire three-hour road trip. The poor Uber driver keeps asking me if I'm going to give him a bad rating on the app. I promise him that I won't and give an extra-big tip, but I don't think he's going to drive me back to Southern.

Inside, the emergency room I find a mess. Holly is there. So is my mother. They're sitting on opposite ends of the emergency room. Both of them stand when I enter. Pulling up my metaphorical trousers of courage, if there is such a thing, I force myself deeper into the emergency room. I avoid picking either of them to talk to and head straight for the registration desk.

"I'm Ara Martin, Arthur Martin's daughter." I shove my license in her face. "Where can I find him?"

She takes five years to type something into her computer and another decade to read the stupid screen. I'm close to climbing over the desk when she says, "It appears he is still in surgery."

"Can you tell me what's wrong? Where's he hurt? What's the surgery for?"

"Hmmm," is my response.

I'm about to vault over the desk and read the screen myself when Holly appears at my side.

"I can tell you, dear." She draws me away.

Out of the corner of my eye, I see Mom looking angrily over at us. I shrug out of Holly's grasp.

"How'd you get the information?"

"I'm still his wife."

"Right." I feel terrible. "Sorry."

"Don't worry about it. Your dad was tired and he drifted onto the shoulder. His tire got caught and pulled him into the ditch. Because of his speed, the car rolled. He was ejected."

I gasp. "How is he?"

"Good. Asking for you."

"How did it happen?"

"He fell asleep at the wheel, wasn't buckled in. May have been texting."

I wince. My dad is such a child sometimes.

"How bad is it?"

Out of the corner of my eye, I see Mom get to her feet and walk toward us.

"Six stitches in his forehead, a concussion, but miraculously he's okay. They're keeping him for observation." Holly tells me where his room is.

My knees feel watery. "He's a cat."

"He's a fool," Mom says sharply when she reaches us. She hitches her purse higher up on her shoulder and gives me a stiff nod. "Since you're here, I'll be going now. I've already given your dad a piece of my mind."

I give her a sharp look. "God, Mom, really? He's in the hospital."

"He's there because he has poor impulse control and little consideration of others."

How like my mom to be judgmental. I want to chalk it up to fear. Kind of like how my dad yelled at me after I pulled down an easel of his when I was a kid. Later, I figured out it was because he was terrified I'd be hurt, but at the time, I thought he was mad at me.

With Mom, though, no one can live up to her impossible standards. She proves it with her next words.

"Your father said that you don't have your job at the gallery anymore."

"I quit," I admit.

"Just like your dad," she says. "You don't have the persistence to stick with things."

"I stuck with dad longer than you," I shoot back, hurt by her insults.

Her eyes narrow. "That's because you, like your father, are foolish."

I start to argue with her, but realize there's no point. At her age, she's not going to change her opinion about me. I'm my daddy's girl, but Mom was the one who left us—not the other way around.

"I'm okay with that," I say. I summon up a smile for her. "I love Dad, because the part that makes him foolish is also the part that makes him so loveable. I'm okay with imperfect people and imperfect love."

I don't wait for her response. I don't need her approval anymore. Unconsciously, I think I've always longed for it, but it was never going to come because I was my daddy's girl.

He nurtured and loved me when she walked away. She may say she walked away from him, but it was both of us.

I've been trying to be perfect for so long. I guess that is what Fleur was getting at. That I tried to please others, wanting their validation, but settling for whatever was tossed my way. Like the shit job with Marissa or the "just" friends thing with Ty, even though I'd wanted so much more for so long.

And then being stubborn about not accepting help when I needed it because that would just prove my mom's critical estimations right—that I was a weak and foolish child, incapable of really making it on my own.

But being vulnerable isn't a bad thing. It's what makes me human and *real*.

That's why Dad's art is so wonderful—because people are touched by the emotional quality of his work. That's why the post-breakup art of his is magnificent.

"That's a big sigh for such a little girl," I hear from the doorway.

I look up to see that I'm at my dad's room. I push the door wider and walk in. Seeing my powerful dad in a pastel-colored hospital gown with a huge bandage around his head hooked up to what seems like a dozen IV lines nearly sends me to my knees. I curl my hands around the bottom of the bed for support.

"I didn't realize you were in this much need of attention," I joke. "Perhaps you should have just had a local showing. Maybe rented out a stall at the farmer's market and have a buy one get one free sale."

"I thought about the last one, but I don't have enough work to last longer than fifteen minutes." He pushes a button and the back of the bed slowly starts to rise.

I rush over to the side. "Do you think you should be doing that?"

"Yes, I'm allowed to sit up."

I stare at him skeptically until he lowers the bed with a deep exhale of frustration.

"I already have a battery of mean nurses," he whines. "You should be extra kind to me."

"Holly's out there if you need someone to flatter your ego."

He makes a pained face, but I don't think it has anything to do with his physical injuries. "She left me food," he says plaintively. "And I ate it. I don't think we're breaking up."

"It will give you incentive to recover, then," I say. I pull up an uncomfortable hospital chair and sit down. "Speaking of ex-wives, Mom was here."

Again, he makes a face. This time I know it has nothing to do with his injuries. "I know. I had to get more stitches after she laid into me for being a foolish—"

"Child?" I finish for him.

"Yes, that was actually one of the nicer things she said." He shifts uncomfortably on the bed.

"You weren't wearing your seatbelt, Dad," I remind him.

He flushes guiltily. "Yes, yes. I know. This is partly your fault," he says.

"How so?"

"I was telling Stephen about your work. He says he knows the perfect person for you to mentor with. It's an artist in Michigan. She has a background in animation and now does experimental work with celluloid as a canvas. It's very innovative. I think you could learn a lot from her. If you want her help, that is." He peers shyly out from under his lashes, almost as if he's afraid of my response.

My first instinct is to say no.

He must see it, because he looks away. Staring out the window, he says, "You don't want to, do you?"

I swallow the hard lump of pride. "No, but I think I should."

When he turns back to face me, his face is lit up. "Ahh, sweetheart. I'm so glad." He launches into a detailed explanation of the animator's work.

I listen intently, holding his warm hand in mine.

"You won't regret taking this opportunity, Ara. Every artist has help getting discovered, including me," he says. "Don't you remember? It's why I can never be mad at your mother for leaving us. Not when she gave me the gift she did."

I sit back. I'd forgotten, although I'm not sure why. Dad's discovery story is told in countless magazine and newspaper articles. A famous art critic had gotten lost on her way to authenticate a newly discovered Whistler piece. She ended up with a flat tire about a mile down the road. Mom found her, fixed her tire and brought her home.

"I was so embarrassed to show my work, but your mother insisted."

And that was all it took. The art critic fell in love. The Whistler was abandoned, which didn't matter because the artwork turned out to be a fake while Dad was the real fucking deal.

"I don't spend one moment wondering if I could've made it myself. I'm so grateful for all the help. It was destiny, you know."

"Because the Whistler was fake."

"Right," he says. "Because the Whistler was fake."

"How hurt are you?" I suddenly ask because I can't sit here anymore.

There's a pull on my heart and if I don't respond, my heart may just be dragged away without me.

He arches a brow. "Does this have to do with my man, Ty?"

"He's at the combine." I look at my watch. "Or should be. He wanted to come here, but I told him no."

Dad clicks his tongue against the roof of his mouth. "He shouldn't be sent into battle without your full support. Even your mother didn't withhold support while she was with me."

"I know," I wail. "I was stupid."

"Well, go on and fix your problem."

I leap to my feet.

"Wait," he shouts from his bed.

"What?" I hurry back.

He hands me his wallet. "Take my NetJets card. You can fly direct to Indy."

"Oh, bless you." I kiss the wallet and then my dad.

He laughs softly. "I know you really love him."

"Why do you say that?"

"Because you accepted my help without even one word of argument."

§

ON THE PLANE, I call Knox.

"Ara?"

"Yeah, it's me. Where are you?"

"Indy."

"Oh my God. Are you going to pretend to be Ty at the combine? Where is he?"

"Calm down," Knox says. "He's on his way here. I am not taking his place."

My heart rate subsides a bit. "Good, because you wouldn't perform half as well," I retort. Ty did not forgo beer and steak for eight weeks to have his combine stats ruined by his brother who has been loafing since January.

"If you're saying I'm not in game day shape, you might be right," Knox concedes. "How's your dad?"

"He'll be fine."

"That's good." He pauses. "Is there a reason you're calling me, Ara?"

I pull up my Captain Courageous underpants. "Ty needs to be able to focus completely tomorrow, which means you need to run the test. Tonight."

"What test?" Knox asks dumbly.

What test? Is he concussed like my dad? I slap my hand against my forehead. "The stupid twin test you're always going on about!"

"Ohhhh, that test." There's silence and then, "Tonight? There's no flight from Southern U to Indy tonight."

"I'm using my dad's NetJets account. Private plane whenever you want."

"Oh, fancy. When do you get in?"

I hear rustling in the background. He must be getting up. "The screen says thirty-five minutes." The plane is fancy. The people at NetJets explained repeatedly that it was more expensive than Dad usually took, but it was the only plane they had at the airport. Dad had to get on the line to approve it. Let's just say it was a good thing he was already lying down with professional medical experts at the ready when they recited the final cost.

True love is costly, apparently.

"Should we do it at the airport?"

"No. Hotel room. And make it convincing," I order.

"Yes, ma'am."

"By the way, the twin test isn't for Ty, Knox. It's for you. I'm doing it so you will believe that Ty and I belong together. He knows it. And deep down I think you do, too. But I don't mind reassuring you or him." I surprise myself with my own inner confidence. Before when I was just a new freshman I didn't believe that. I didn't have enough confidence in myself. Now, I do. "I want there to be zero distractions for him during the combine."

"Welcome to the family," Knox says smugly.

Despite the horde of athletes, coaches, agents, and press that descended on Indy, the player hotel is surprisingly not full. The desk clerk gives me a suspicious glance as she swipes my credit card. "Just for the record, we are not allowed to give out the private information of any guests that are staying at this hotel. And for the next week, you must know the number and name of the room guest in order to make a room-to-room call."

"Got it." She obviously thinks I'm a stalker. It probably doesn't help that I have no luggage. I left it back home, not wanting to take time to sort shit out. I say thanks, take my key, and while I'm walking to the elevator, text Knox my room number.

When I step off the elevator, he's waiting. He has a pair of reading glasses perched on the end of his nose.

"Took you long enough," he says, pushing away from the wall. Another player pops out of a nearby room, throws a questioning glance in our direction, and then turns and walks the other way.

"You're blocking the path to the ice machine," I tell him.

"You should've asked for a more private room."

"I spent all of my dad's money just to get here. I'm lucky there's still space on the credit card for any room, let alone a more private one." I wave my key card. "Should we go in, or do you want to have reunion sex out here in the hall?"

The player down the hall coughs suddenly. The one in front of me grins. "By all means, let's go inside."

He waves me forward. "I take it your dad must be okay since you're here."

"He's had better days, but he's going to be fine." I cast a look to the right and then the left. No one jumps out of the shadows—not that there are many shadows in this hotel hallway to hide in.

I wave the keycard in front of the security pad and walk into the hotel room. He closes the door behind us. I fiddle with my card, wondering what I should do. Should I wait for the big reveal? Am I supposed to do something? Is there a special code word?

This is stupid, I decide.

Then he starts pulling his shirt up. I fly at him.

"Oh, for crying out loud. I can't take it anymore." I jerk the shirt down. "You look ridiculous. Take those glasses off. Where's Ty?" I fling open the door only to find the mystery player walking by with a now-filled bucket of ice. "Where is he?" I demand.

"I have no idea who you're talking about, but I'm in room four twenty if you're unhappy with the big fella behind you." He squints. "Actually, I take that back. I think I need some sleep because I'm starting to see double."

A big hand flies out from behind me and slams the door shut.

"No soliciting strangers for sex," he chides me. The big fella is clearly happy though. He's wearing a huge smile.

"He invited me," I point out. "There was no solicitation on my end."

Knox takes the glasses off and rubs them with a corner of his shirt. There's a frown on his face. "I think we should do this again. Why don't you leave and come back in."

"Are you for real?" I squawk.

Ty pulls me back before I can attack his brother. "This was good, bro." He takes me by the shoulders and pulls me to face him. "What gave it away? The glasses? His clothes?"

"First, those are your clothes. Your mom bought that shirt for you two Christmases ago. Second, it's obvious." I peek over at Knox, who's dropped into the chair by the window and is avidly watching us. I lower my voice. "Not to be mean, but your brother is not as attractive as you. His eyes are weird."

"His eyes are weird," Ty repeats.

"Yes." I nod vigorously. "They're big and kind of creepy." I shudder lightly.

"Creepy. His eyes."

"Are you going to repeat everything I say?"

Ty hauls me into his chest. "No." The broad expanse of muscle and sinew and tendon shakes beneath my cheek. "Time to go."

Reluctantly, I peel myself away from his embrace. He doesn't release me, though. "Not you," he says. He dips his head at his twin. "You. Time for you to go."

Knox gets to his feet and ambles to the door. "Don't expend too much energy tonight," he teases.

I give him the finger. Ty grabs it and holds my hand in his. "She says goodnight and that she loves you like her very own brother."

"That's the fuck-you gesture," I clarify.

"I'm the only Masters brother who gets to fuck you," Ty says, pulling me away from the door so his brother can exit.

Knox stops, clasps his hands around my head, and pulls my forehead to his lips. He drops a noisy wet kiss right below the hairline. "I've always wanted a sister."

Ty pushes Knox away. "Go get your own girl."

"She's at home," his brother pouts, but he obediently opens the door. Before leaving, though, he sticks his head back in. "Ellie says that I'm the one with the great eyes and that Ty's are too far apart."

"Ellie's clearly blind because why else would she pick you over Ty," I retort.

Knox opens his mouth to reply, but Ty has had enough. He shoves his brother out of the doorway and slams the door shut.

"Do you have something to say to me?"

I think for a minute. "I'm sorry?" I guess.

"About what?"

"Is there more than one thing I have to apologize for?" I ask.

He crosses his arms against his chest. "Many, many things."

"If I'm on my knees, will the forgiveness come faster? How about if I add my tongue? I've been practicing some deep throat methods with a cucumber—Wait!" I yelp. My view is suddenly distorted. I'm no longer looking at his face, but rather his ass.

It's a fine ass though. I give it a happy squeeze. In response, my butt gets slapped. I don't mind it though. I wriggle around to let him know he could do it again.

He groans and then bites me through my jeans before tossing me onto the bed.

I watch in avid fascination as his T-shirt comes off, followed by his jeans, socks and shoes. I pause to appreciate his glorious nakedness before getting down to the business of removing my own clothes.

"If I'd known that I'd get such a great reception to the twin test, I would've taken it sooner."

"Liar," he breathes into my neck.

My hands still at my waistband. "Wh-what do you mean by that?" I stutter.

"You did take it before and you intentionally failed it," he reminds me.

He doesn't sound too mad about it. Probably because we have our clothes off. I stroke his muscled abs, appreciating how firm and sculpted they are. It's like touching a piece of art.

A fucking awesome, ripped piece of art.

"I couldn't break the friendship seal, remember?" I tease. More seriously, I say, "But, in truth, you haven't been a good boyfriend. I wanted to be with you forever and being your friend seemed the best way to do that."

He dips his head lower to fan kisses across my collarbone, which feels incredible. Who knew the collarbone was so sensitive?

"I wasn't a good boyfriend because I always wanted to spend time with you. You and football are the only things I really care about." His delicious lips glide over the top curve of my left breast while his nimble fingers cup and mold my right one.

I squirm under him, trying to keep the contact and take my jeans off at the same time. It's not easy. His deft hands help me tug my jeans off. They sweep up my bare legs and end at my hips, where he roughly pulls me against him. I suck in a breath when my wet, sensitive parts make contact with his silky hardness. I forget what we're talking about.

He moves lower.

"I think I'm supposed to be doing the work and you're supposed to be conserving your energy."

He places a kiss on my stomach. "Tomorrow is medical and interviews. I think I have the stamina to make love to my girlfriend tonight and make it through tomorrow with no problems."

His girlfriend. My heart flutters like a fifteen-year-old girl's.

"You liked that, did you?" He flashes a grin. Then his face turns serious. "I can be a good boyfriend," he vows. "Give me a chance."

I run a hand over his hair. It's soft and silky under my palm. "I know," I say quietly. "You need to give me a chance, too. I'm bound to screw up. We're too stubborn sometimes. I think we need to give more."

The wicked grin is back. "I've lots I'm ready to give you." He dips down to press a kiss on one bare thigh and then the other. His hot breath turns my already heated skin molten.

I close my eyes and thank everything in the universe for giving me Ty. And then I put everything I have into showing him how much I love him.

32

Ara

I DECIDE TO WAIT IN THE HOTEL BAR INSTEAD OF THE BALLROOM where they are holding the draft. I'm too nervous. I don't know how those boys handle it, sitting in there with about a thousand cameras pointed in their faces, looking for the slightest reaction that they can blast to the millions that watch. Then there are the hardcore fans in the stands who might boo if you get drafted to their team because they were hoping for some other player.

There's a long introduction by the commissioner who is soundly booed. No love lost between any of the fans and the head of the NFL.

There are awards and a speech. I drink three glasses of Coke. My bladder's going to burst before the first draft pick is announced.

Ty said his interviews went great. He ended up hiring Knox's agent who smoothed over all the bad rumors that had dogged Ty at the combine. Plenty of the interviewers asked about both the ex-agent and Rhyann, along with a host of other dumb questions.

It helped, Ty admitted, to have both a new agent and a new girl-friend. I told him I expected a cut of the signing bonus. He presented me with a pair of diamond earrings so I've shut up about the money. I'm afraid if I tease him again, I'll end up with a Bentley or something.

I tap the glittery earrings and admire them in the mirror behind the bar. They are nice.

On the television screen, I see the general manager of Las Vegas on the podium. As a new expansion team, they get first pick in the draft. They're going to pick a running back, likely Boots Byers from USC. I doodle on my napkin. Ty's projected to go third, like his brother, which puts him in Minnesota. Ty says he wants to go fifteenth because then we could live together in Michigan. Somewhere along the line, he got the impression that I have to live in Michigan in order to be mentored by this artist that Dad hooked me up with.

I've given up explaining to him about planes and Skype and email and figure that he'll get the message when he finds me camped outside his apartment in whatever city he plays in.

"Need another drink?" a deep voice asks me.

I drop the pen on the counter. "What are you doing here?" I ask in shock.

Before he can answer, the bartender hops over. "Knox Masters, right? I'm a big fan." The two shake hands. "What can I get you to drink?"

"He's gearing up for the season," I interject, somewhat afraid of what the big guy next to me is going to say. He's wearing a smile I don't trust. "He'll take a water, hold the lemon."

The bartender's eyes dart to me and then back.

"I'll have a water, hold the lemon," is the laughing response. The boy slides onto the stool next to me.

I wait until the bartender's out of earshot before hissing, "What in the hell are you doing here?"

"And with the number one pick of the draft, the Las Vegas Dragons select Ty Masters from Southern U," blasts the television.

"Oh my God!" I turn to my companion who grins. "You knew all along."

A huge cry of surprise erupts in the bar along with cheers and a couple scattered boos.

"I got the call earlier."

"You didn't tell me?" I punch him in the arm and then shake my bruised hand. It definitely hurt me more than him.

I watch as the camera spans to a familiar face and zooms in. "I hope he trips and falls on his face with those glasses on," I mutter.

"Here's your water," the bartender says. "Pass along my congrats to your brother."

"I will."

"You're going to hell," I say under my breath.

"You have no sense of humor."

"You two find this twin switch stuff way too funny."

Behind the glass, his lips curve up. "Come on. It is kind of humorous, right?"

"I thought you didn't like the twin switches."

"Knox couldn't resist."

"You two are crazy. I can't believe you let him go on stage as you."

"I don't like that shit anyway." He leans over to give me a kiss, which I dodge expertly. I jerk my head to the bartender who is watching us.

Ty sighs and slides a hand up my thigh. "Let's go upstairs."

I take a second to resist and then give in. If he doesn't care to celebrate this event like a normal college football player, then I'm not going to worry about it. Sex sounds good. More than good.

I hop off my stool. He starts to follow. I shake a finger at him. "Can you at least put some effort into pretending you're Knox? Otherwise, everyone's going to talk about how kinky the twins are, swapping girlfriends and wives."

Ty slides back on his stool. "Whoops. Okay. I'll be up in five."

"Thirty minutes."

"Five."

"Twenty-five minutes."

He looks at his watch. "It's gonna be four minutes now."

I run off, his crazy laughter following me.

I manage to get to the room and disrobe before his key is in the lock.

"Nice," he says approvingly as he approaches the bed. His clothes are flying off—shirt rocketing to the left, suit pants on the floor. "This is how you should always greet me. In bed and nude."

He dives under the covers. His hand finds me immediately. Not gonna lie. I'm already wet.

"And ready," he adds. His mouth covers mine. He kisses me tenderly at first. Some little nips at the corners of my mouth. Tiny flicks of his tongue against the seam of my lips. I grab his hair and mash his head to mine. After kissing him breathless, I release him.

"First, congratulations. Second, enough with the teasing."

I push my hips upward to show my eagerness. He laughs then, but his laugh turns to a husky groan when I reach between us to clasp his erection.

"Now," I demand.

He pries my fingers off his dick. "Not yet. I need a little taste." His own hand delves between my legs. I'm already wet and ready. "Nice." He smiles approvingly. "You're such a hot piece, Ara."

Another time, that might be offensive, but when it comes out of his mouth, it's damn hot. Like he owns me, which he does. I'm totally his. I spread my legs wide.

"This hot piece needs some special attention."

"I know. Your little clit is going to be so lonely while I'm traveling," he says, flicking his finger against the swollen bundle of nerves. "How are we going to make this work when I'm playing ball? You gonna Skype sex with me?"

"If you want. I guess that means I can't have a roommate."

"Why would you? I'm buying an apartment and you're living with me." He licks my clit to emphasize his point.

"That sounds like I'm your kept woman."

He hooks his arms under my thighs and palms my ass. Better access for his mouth. I stroke his hair away from his forehead.

"Nah. Think of it as a down payment." His inquisitive tongue dances along my sex. It takes a lot of effort not to push myself onto him, but he wants to play. "When you become a world-famous author/illustrator, you'll be responsible for buying me expensive shit. I'll take a Rolls Royce, please."

"I can't see you driving a Rolls Royce."

He gives me one long lick before saying, "We won't know until you buy me one, will we?"

"Do I get to order you around then?" He kisses me again, this time plunging his tongue inside of me. I bite on my lower lip to keep from crying out.

"Of course. Why don't you start practicing? Like, Ty, baby, put your cock in my pussy. Or lick my clit and tongue me until I pass out."

He switches positions, pushing a finger inside of me. Then another. Sweat breaks out on my forehead. Come on, Ara. Hold out a little while longer. For womankind.

"How about clean my bathroom?" I say between pants.

"I can pay for that." His finger-fucking is slow and steady. I'm dying.

"Why not pay for someone to tongue me?"

The movement stops immediately. "No. Anyone touches you and they die."

"Your NFL career would be over."

"That's a hill I'm willing to die on."

His face is dead serious. *Now's not the time to be teasing him, Ara.*

"I would never," I say, reaching down to cup his jaw. He presses a kiss into my palm.

"I hope you know I would never either."

"I know."

"You do?" He seems surprised, but pleased.

I draw a heart on his face. "We've been friends for the past four years. I know you. If you wanted to sleep with another woman, you'd probably fly here and tell me to my face. You wouldn't cheat on me."

"Some girls can't handle this life."

"Some guys can't either."

He nods and presses another kiss on my palm before rising up and covering me with his body. "Good thing we're a perfect fit."

He glides into me in one strong, sure movement. My breath catches at the back of my throat, but I manage to gasp out, "Yes, perfect."

And then I'm done talking. My mouth is put to better uses such as sucking on his neck, licking the sweat off his perfect skin, and whispering over and over how much I love him.

He shudders, weak at my barest touch. Electricity courses through me as he brings me alive with each thrust of his body.

"I love you, Ara. I'd love you if I were in another body, or another mind, in another time. I'd always know you. I'd always love you." He captures my mouth and I can feel the tenderness pour out of his body into mine.

We fuse together. Our mouths, our bodies, our hearts.

I don't know if it's destiny that made him run into me that first day of school. I don't know if it's fate that has brought us together. It doesn't matter, though. What matters is that we put our vulnerable hearts on the line, and we have been fully rewarded.

NEWSLETTER

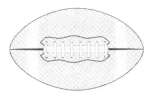

Want to read Wyatt's short story? Sign up for the newsletter and receive a free copy of DELAY OF GAME, another friends-to-lovers romance.

Sign up at **JENFREDERICK.COM**!

#GETSACKED

by Jen Frederick

Available Now

WHAT HE WANTS HE GETS...

Knox Masters is a quarterback's worst nightmare. Warrior. Champion. And...virgin. Knox knows what he wants--and he gets it. All American Football player? Check. NFL pros scouting him? Check. Now, he's set his sight on two things. The national title. And Ellie Campbell. Sure, she's the sister of his fellow teammate, but that's not going to stop him. Especially not when he's convinced Ellie is the one.

...BUT HE'S NEVER MET HER BEFORE.

But Ellie isn't as sure. She's trying to start a new life and she's not interested in a relationship...with anyone. Beside it's not just her cardinal rule of never dating her brother's teammates that keeps her away, but Ellie has a dark secret that would jeopardize everything Knox is pursuing.

KNOX HAS NO INTENTION OF LOSING. ELLIE HAS NO INTENTION OF GIVING IN.

#GETJOCKBLOCKED

by Jen Frederick

Available Now

SHE'S ALWAYS PLAYED IT SAFE...

College junior Lucy Washington abides by one rule—avoid risk at all costs. She's cautious in every aspect of her life, from her health, to her mock trial team, to the boring guys she dates. When a brash, gorgeous jock walks into the campus coffeeshop and turns his flirt on, Lucy is stunned by the force of attraction. For the first time ever, she's willing to step out of her comfort zone, but can she really trust the guy who's determined to sweep her off her feet?

HE'S ALWAYS PLAYED AROUND...

Entering his last year of college eligibility, linebacker Matthew "Matty" Iverson has the team captaincy in his sights. And it's his for the taking, if he can convince his quarterback Ace Anderson to give up the starting position. Luckily, Matty already has an edge—the hottie he's lusting over just happens to be Ace's childhood best friend. Getting Lucy on his side and in his bed? Hell yeah. Matty is more than confident he can have both, but when he falls hard for Lucy, it's time for a new game plan: convince the woman of his dreams that she's not sleeping with the enemy.

ABOUT THE AUTHOR

Jen Frederick is the USA Today bestselling author of *Unspoken*, part of the Woodlands series, and *Sacked*, part of the Gridiron series. She is also the co-author of the *New York Times* Bestselling series, The Royals. She lives in the Midwest with a husband who keeps track of life's details while she's writing, a daughter who understands when Mom disappears into her office for hours at a time, and a rambunctious dog who does neither.

Drop her a line:
jenfrederick.com
jensfrederick@gmail.com

Made in the USA
Middletown, DE
13 February 2018